"Do You Really Practice Free Love, Tess?" Keith Asked.

Tess met his gaze. "Yes," she said stubbornly.

"I think you're lying."

Her lower lip trembled almost imperceptibly.

He strode over to her and unpinned her hair, so that it fell about her shoulders in shimmering waves and curls, catching the early morning sunlight, smelling of fresh air and woodsmoke and castile soap.

It seemed natural to kiss her, and he did, cautiously at first and then with a hunger that was so intense that it could not be denied.

The onslaught of emotion washing over Tess in the wake of the kiss was devastating, buckling her knees.

"Good Lord," she breathed.

"My sentiments exactly," he replied.

Books by Linda Lael Miller

Angelfire
Banner O'Brien
Corbin's Fancy
Desire and Destiny
Fletcher's Woman
Lauralee
Memory's Embrace
Moonfire
My Darling Melissa
Wanton Angel
Willow

Published by POCKET BOOKS

MEMORY'S EMBRACE

LINDA LAEL MILLER

POCKET BOOKS

New York   London   Toronto   Sydney   Tokyo   Singapore

An *Original* Publication of POCKET BOOKS

POCKET BOOKS, a division of Simon & Schuster Inc.
1230 Avenue of the Americas, New York, NY 10020

ISBN: 0-671-70538-5

First Tapestry Books printing January 1986

First Pocket Books printing May 1990

10 9 8 7 6 5 4 3 2 1

For Pamela Anne Lael
I love you, little sister.

Chapter One

April 5, 1890
Simpkinsville, Oregon

A DENTED ENAMEL DISHPAN SOARED, SPINNING LIKE A discus, high into the slate gray sky. Curious, Tess Bishop wheeled her disabled bicycle to the edge of the road, laid it carefully on its side, and, holding her box camera under one arm, made her way through the brush and into the clearing beyond.

A peddler—the gilt-painted legend on the side of his grim black wagon indicated that his name was Joel Shiloh—dodged the falling dishpan and flung a coffee-pot heavenward in almost the same motion.

"Come down here and fight!" he bellowed, as grounds and coffee splattered upon his disreputable

1

shirt and vest. He was a tall man, probably in his early thirties, and, as Tess watched in amazement, he shook one sun-browned fist at the sky and shouted again. "Come on, damn it! Fight!"

Tess lifted questioning hazel eyes, and saw nothing but clouds. Threatening clouds. Who was this man talking to, anyway? God?

The peddler placed his hands on his hips and tilted his head back so far that Tess thought his dirty bowler hat would surely fall off into the grass. "Well?!" he yelled, resting one booted foot on the stones surrounding his campfire. "What are you waiting for?!"

Tess was just about to scramble back to the road, and her bicycle, when the man suddenly roared an exclamation of mingled pain and rage and dashed, hopping awkwardly as he went, toward the stream that edged the clearing.

"Don't—" she began, in warning, lifting her free hand as though she might stop him in time.

But, of course, she couldn't, for she was too far away. The peddler plunged into the stream at exactly the place Tess had feared he would and disappeared to the brim of his bowler hat.

Tess carefully set down her camera in the grass and then, gripping her calico skirts to keep from stumbling, raced across the verdant clearing, with its sprinkling of wild violets, to the stream bank.

The peddler came up sputtering before Tess could reach him, and, glaring up at the sky, his hat floating beside him, his hair plastered to his face in dripping tendrils, he roared, "That was a dirty, underhanded trick!"

Tess, who had forgotten her first impression of this

man, that he was either drunk or insane, stopped just short of the stream and stared at him. "Who on earth are you talking to?" she demanded.

Joel Shiloh looked at her in exasperation, but if he felt any chagrin at behaving in such a maniacal fashion, he didn't show it. He snatched his hat before it could swirl away on the current, tossed it into the windblown grass, and struggled out of the water to stand, gasping, on the bank.

After a few moments, he sat down in the grass with a disgusted grunt and began tugging and wrenching at one sodden boot. Having no luck, he looked up at Tess, azure eyes flashing in a beard-stubbled and yet strangely aristocratic face, and said, "Help me, will you?"

Tess was never able to say why she didn't turn and flee, as any sensible young woman would have done— after all, the man was clearly mad and it was about to rain and she was still nearly five miles from home. Aunt Derora was going to skin her for sure.

"What?" she asked, befuddled.

"Pull my boot off!" he snapped back, impatiently, and cast another scathing look at the dark, rain-burdened sky.

"You could say *please*," Tess pointed out reasonably.

"Please, then!" he shouted.

"You have a truly nasty temper, Mr. Shiloh," she remarked, but she did grasp his muddy boot—there were holes in the sole—when he extended his foot. Pulling required such effort that she grew red with the strain, and a mischievous light danced in the peddler's eyes as he looked up at her.

"I do, don't I?" he agreed companionably.

Tess tugged with all her might, and when the boot

came off, at last, she went tumbling backward into the grass. She got up quickly, disgruntled and stunned, certain that the peddler would laugh at her.

Instead, his attention was absorbed in peeling off a stocking as wet and shabby as his boot had been; Tess might not have been there at all for all the notice he paid her.

There was an angry burn on the bottom of his foot, which accounted for his strange hopping and the imprudent leap into the creek, and he frowned at the injury and then frowned at the sky. "Thank you very much," he said to the grumbling clouds. "Thank you very, very much!"

At that precise moment the rain began, in a fierce torrent, drenching Tess's hair, which fell free to her waist, and causing her dress to cling.

But dresses were the last thing on Tess Bishop's mind. "My camera!" she shrieked, bounding to her feet and racing across the clearing to snatch up the treasured black box, clutch it to her breast, and cast wildly about for a place of shelter.

She tried to reach the latch on the rear door of Mr. Shiloh's wagon, but it was too high. Muttering, Tess began to leap for the thing, falling short each time.

Mr. Shiloh, oddly calm and resolute now, materialized at her side, deftly worked the catch, and opened the creaky door. Tess thrust her camera inside and then sighed with relief, caring nothing for the fact that she herself was soaked to the skin. She had saved for a long, long time to buy that camera.

"Thank you," she said.

Instead of answering, Joel Shiloh boldly grasped her

4

waist in his hands and lifted her, so that she sat on the floor of the wagon, her feet dangling from the door. Rain thundered on the curved, sturdy roof and further soaked the peddler, who stood for a moment, seemingly oblivious to the downpour, watching Tess with a sort of wonder, as though he had seen her before and thought he should recognize her.

"Come out of the rain," she said practically.

A wry grin twisted the peddler's mouth, and he turned and vaulted up to sit beside her in the doorway of the wagon. "What's your name?" he asked, watching her.

Tess gaped at him, let her eyes slide down his long, muscular legs to his feet. He was wearing one boot, but his injured foot was still bare. "Tess Bishop," she said, after some time. "How is your foot?"

He laughed and ran one hand down his face as if to brush away the rain. The gesture didn't do much good, of course, for his hair was sodden. "Fine, Tess Bishop. My foot is just fine."

"I tried to warn you, you know."

"About what? Burning my foot?"

Tess shook her head and droplets of rain water flew. "About jumping into the stream. It looks shallow there, because the water is so clear, but it's actually over seven feet deep."

Another wry smile. "So I discovered. Does your family know that you're out wandering around in the countryside, Miss Bishop? In the middle of a rainstorm, yet?"

Tess sat up a little straighter. She didn't have a family, really—just Derora, her aunt. And while she was certain to catch the devil, if not pneumonia, she couldn't see where it was any of this man's business. "Does yours?" she countered.

The peddler grinned. "Actually, my family doesn't have any idea where I am."

Tess was intrigued. It was odd, she thought, the way the rain shut out the rest of the world, made it seem as though only she and Mr. Shiloh existed. "But you do have a family?"

His blue eyes were distant, and, even though he wasn't looking directly at Tess, she could see a shadow of pain flicker in their depths. "Yes. I have a family," he said, after a very long and introspective silence.

"You're estranged from them," guessed Tess, shivering.

Powerful, rain-sodden shoulders moved in a shrug. "You could say that."

"Tell me about them."

He looked at her now, keenly, almost suspiciously. "You're probably freezing to death. Let me get you a blanket." With that, he turned and scrambled into the dark depths of the wagon, returning in a few moments with a heavy woolen wrap, which he draped around both of them.

Again, Tess experienced that sensation of sweet isolation; they were creatures of the mist, she imagined, living in a special universe hidden away behind a thundering waterfall. "Thank you," she said, snuggling into the warmth of the blanket. But, suddenly, a giggle erupted from deep within her.

"What is it?" asked Joel Shiloh, arching one butternut eyebrow.

6

"My aunt would kill me," she confessed, "if she knew I was sitting here in a wagon, wrapped in a blanket—"

"With a man," finished Mr. Shiloh, grinning again.

"Tell me about your family," Tess insisted, blushing a little.

"I have two older brothers, a younger sister, and a mother. My father died several years ago, in an accident."

He had told her what she wanted to know, and yet he hadn't told her anything, really. "Why are you estranged from them?"

The beard-stubbled jawline hardened just a little. "Why are you five miles from town in a rainstorm?" he countered, and his voice was brisk now.

Tess was injured by his tone, but she squared her shoulders and lifted her chin. "I'm a grown woman," she pointed out.

He was smirking at her. Smirking! Tess clasped her hands together in her lap, beneath the folds of the blanket, to keep from slapping him right across the face.

"Well, I am!" she declared.

"Sixteen if you're a day," he teased.

"I am eighteen!" defended Tess, furiously.

The peddler put one hand to his chest and drew in a dramatic breath. "As old as that!"

Tess had learned to bear many things during her tumultuous life, but mockery was not among them. "I suppose you're so very old and wise?" she taunted, chin out, color aching in her cheeks.

He said nothing for a long time; he just sat there,

swinging his feet, looking amused. When he did speak, he shocked Tess to the marrow of her bones. "Take your clothes off," he suggested affably.

"I beg your pardon?" whispered Tess, every muscle in her body poised to leap from the bed of that wagon and take desperate flight.

"You shouldn't be sitting there in that wet dress," he said rationally. "I'll get you something else to wear and you can—"

"I have no intention of disrobing!"

He bit his lower lip—probably to keep from laughing —and although Tess was annoyed and still ready to run for her life and her virtue, she did not move. Could not move.

"Do you imagine that I plan to accost you?" Joel Shiloh asked, finally.

"You could. After all, you're not sane."

He gave a startling shout of laughter and then looked at her with those ice-blue eyes. They seemed to caress her, as well as laugh at her, but there was no threat in them and no vestige of madness. "You are referring to that shouting match I was having with God," he said.

"With God?" echoed Tess.

He nodded and the rain eased at the same moment. "I'm going to build another fire under those trees over there," he said, with a smile in his voice. "You'll find dry clothes in the drawers built in under my bunk. Change into them while I make some coffee."

Tess's face felt like it throbbed with color. "You threw the coffeepot at God, remember?" she reminded him, in acid tones, to hide her alarm and the strange, tingling wonder that came hand in hand with it.

Joel Shiloh chuckled, unwrapped himself from the

blanket, and leaped nimbly to the ground. "Fortunately," he said, with a sweeping spread of his arms, "he threw it back."

Tess couldn't help smiling, but she made no move to follow his orders and change her clothes. No, she just sat there, watching him through the drizzling rain as he built the promised fire and gathered up the coffeepot and its lid.

When he finally looked in her direction, there was an expression of good-natured sternness on his face. "Under the bunk!" he shouted.

Tess stiffened and looked back over one shoulder. "It's too dark in there—I wouldn't be able to find anything," she retorted, in lame tones.

He was striding, long-legged and effortlessly masculine, toward her. Even wearing just one boot, he managed to look authoritative.

Tess found herself huddling deep in the blankets, the side of the wagon's door frame digging into her back. A chill shook her and her teeth began to chatter. "Stay away from me," she whispered.

Joel Shiloh laughed and sprang past her into the wagon. "Your virtue is safe with me, Miss Bishop," he said, rummaging around in the darkness behind her. "I prefer grown women."

"Grown—" Tess choked out, in aborted protest. A sulphur match was struck, its scent acrid in the moist air, and then the light of a kerosene lantern flickered, revealing an unmade bunk, stacks of wooden crates, and Tess's camera.

"Women," he finished for her. "You, of course, are only a girl." He wrenched open one of two drawers beneath the quilt-tangled bunk and plucked out a shirt and a pair of trousers. Trousers! "Now, put these things on or I'll do it for you."

"I am not a girl!" argued Tess, as the garments were literally flung into her lap. Why was it so important to impress him with the fact that she was old enough to support herself, and did; that she was not a child as he obviously thought?

Glacier-blue eyes swept her; it was as though he could see through the blanket to her small but well-shaped breasts, the slender waist and smoothly rounded hips of which she was circumspectly proud. "I could have sworn you were," he replied, and then he was gone, leaping out of the wagon, gasping at the insult to his burned foot, and limping back to the struggling fire he had built in the limited shelter of the trees.

Tess looked down at the trousers and shirt and knew that she was going to have to obey his edict, however improper it was. She was cold to the bone and it was still raining, and the walk back to Simpkinsville and her aunt's boardinghouse would be a long one. The chances were that she would come down with a bad cold, or even pneumonia, if she didn't remove her wet clothes and warm herself a while beside the peddler's fire.

Drat him anyway, she thought, as she got awkwardly to her feet and made her way into the privacy of the wagon, wrenching the door shut behind her with a clatter that elicited another shout of amusement from the direction of the fire.

Glumly, muttering to herself all the while, Tess Bishop removed her calico dress and the muslin drawers and camisole beneath it. Then, teeth clattering like a telegraph key sending an emergency message, she pulled on the trousers and the shirt. They were much too large, of course—the shirt hung well down her thighs and the trousers had to be gripped tightly at the waist or they would have fallen off.

Grateful that she could at least wear her own shoes and stockings, Tess moved toward the wagon door. She would stand by that fire, all right. She would wear those outrageous clothes. And she would let Mr. Joel Shiloh know, in no uncertain terms, what she thought of his orders and his condescending manner. He had his nerve being so patronizing, a man who carried on arguments with and even threw things at God!

She was just reaching for the catch on the door when a well-worn Bible caught her eye. It lay open in the twisted bedding on the bunk, and, for a reason Tess could not have explained, she took it up. The print was smudged here and there, and passages were under-scored. Why would a man with so obvious an animosity toward heaven make such thorough use of the Scrip-tures?

Frowning, Tess turned the book and read the name embossed in gold on the front cover. Keith Corbin. Keith Corbin?

She set the Bible carefully back in its place, open to the same passage, and bit her lower lip as she once again worked the catch on the wagon door. Why would the peddler carry a book with another man's name embossed on its cover?

The name—Keith Corbin, not Joel Shiloh—was fa-miliar, too. Where had she heard it?

Tess was startled to find Mr. Shiloh standing just outside the wagon door, and a guilty flush moved up her face. Did he know that she had been snooping?

His bright blue eyes moved over her with a look of mingled amusement and appreciation, and then he extended his hands to lift her down from the bed of the wagon. His fingers lingered, it seemed to her, at her waist, but the time was so brief that she might have imagined it.

"The fire is going and the coffee is ready. Be careful—the cups are metal and they get hot."

Having made this announcement, he moved past her to climb into the wagon and shut the door. Tess didn't move until she heard a drawer open and close and realized that he was changing clothes, too. Her face hot again, she bolted toward the inviting fire.

There, she warmed her hands and ran outspread fingers through her thick hair, trying to dry it. She noticed for the first time that a mule was grazing near the wagon, its long ears down. As if to acknowledge Tess's instant surge of sympathy, it gave her a mournful look and brayed.

"Poor thing," she muttered, starting toward it, but the reappearance of Joel Shiloh stopped her, distracted her so completely that she forgot all about the mule. He rounded the wagon at a bound, wearing clean, dry clothes, grooming his hair with the fingers of both hands as he moved.

Tess found herself wondering distractedly whether his hair was brown, like her own, or blond, or some color in between the two. Because it was still wet, it was impossible to tell, though she could see that it was slightly too long.

He joined her at the fire and, after tossing her one look of good-tempered reprimand, crouched to take the coffeepot carefully by its wooden handle and fill the two mugs he had set out. He held one out to Tess, without rising.

She took the coffee, letting go of her borrowed trousers in the process, and very nearly disgraced herself. "Why do you leave your poor mule out in the rain?" she asked, while grappling to catch the waistband without dropping the cup.

Joel Shiloh took a leisurely and ponderous draught of his coffee, and Tess had the distinct feeling that he was hiding another smile. Finally, he answered. "Last time I put him inside the wagon, he complained that the bunk was too narrow for the both of us."

Tess lowered her head to hide the grin that had come, unbidden, to her lips.

Mr. Shiloh sighed philosophically and went on sipping his coffee.

"Why were you throwing dishpans and coffeepots at God, Mr.—Mr. Shiloh?"

Her hesitation over his name brought Joel's eyes slicing, sharply, to Tess's face. He rose slowly to his feet, both booted now, his coffee mug cupped in both hands. "I don't think that's any of your business, Miss Bishop," he said coldly.

Tess was as stricken as if he'd slapped her; she felt the color drain from her face. "I'm sorry—I—I guess you're right—"

He looked exasperated, distracted. And quite miserable. "Finish your coffee," he snapped, "and I'll hitch up the wagon and take you home."

"No!"

He stared at her, that butternut eyebrow arched again. "No?" he repeated.

Tess regrouped, realizing that she had protested too

quickly and too earnestly. "I mean, I have my bicycle and it really isn't that far—I can make my own way home."

"Nonsense," he said, and unaccountably he flung his coffee into the fire, where it sizzled and snapped. "Simpkinsville is five miles from here, and you've got that camera to carry. Besides, it might rain again."

Tess felt her shoulders slump a little. If it weren't for the flat tire on her bicycle, she could get home just fine, rain or no rain, camera or no camera. But pushing the contraption all that way in another downpour was a disheartening prospect to say the least. "Derora will murder me," she muttered.

"Who, pray tell, is Derora?" He was being deliberately caustic, and Tess was hurt.

"She is my aunt—although it's none of your business," she pointed out stiffly.

"Touché," he said, with a gruff laugh, lifting his empty mug in a corresponding gesture. "Now, tell me why your aunt would 'murder' you, as you put it?"

"Derora Beauchamp is a very difficult woman," Tess answered, with miserable dignity, "and she doesn't like me very much as it is. Her opinion is bound to plummet when I appear in the company of a bedraggled peddler, wearing these clothes!"

Joel Shiloh smiled and shook his head at the prospect. "Bedraggled, is it?"

"You do need a shave," Tess allowed, defensively. "Perhaps a haircut and a bath—"

He pretended to wield a pencil, making a note in the palm of his hand, the coffee mug wriggling as he "wrote." "Shave. Haircut. Bath," he listed aloud.

Tess laughed in spite of all her contradictory feelings.

"You really are strange. You argue with God. You have one name on your wagon and another on your—"

The taut alertness in his face was alarming. Gone was the look of humorous indulgence that had curved his lips, the mirth that had danced in his blue eyes. "Another on my what?" he prompted, in a frightening rasp.

Tess retreated a step, wishing that she hadn't stopped at this peddler's camp at all. How much safer it would have been to push her bicycle the rest of the way to town, even in the rain! "I just meant—well—"

"You meant what?"

Tess swallowed the aching lump that had gathered in her throat. "I—I saw the Bible," she confessed. "I didn't mean to pry—"

"Oh," he said, and he turned away quickly, ran one hand through his hair. Now that it was drying, Tess could see that it was a color somewhere between honey and ripe wheat. "That belonged to a friend of mine."

"Y-You don't need to explain."

"I know," he answered. And then he turned back to face her again and the smile was in his eyes. "Where is this bicycle of yours? I'll put it in the wagon while you're finishing your coffee."

"I really—"

He waved away her protest and started off toward the road. Moments later he returned, wheeling the bicycle along.

"Really, Mr. Shiloh—"

He opened the wagon's rear door and lifted the bicycle inside. Tess wondered if he ever listened when people tried to dissuade him.

With deft, practiced motions, Mr. Shiloh went on to

harness the beleaguered mule. Coming back to the fire, he kicked dirt over the flames, took up the coffeepot and the mug he had used, and gestured grandly, like a footman about to help a queen into her carriage.

Exasperated, Tess flung what remained of her own coffee out of the cup and proceeded, scrambling up into the high seat of the wagon before he could contrive to help her.

"If you would like," Joel offered, settling into the seat beside her, putting the coffeepot and mugs beneath it, taking up the reins, and releasing the brake lever with one foot, "I'll explain to your aunt."

"That would only make matters worse!" pouted Tess.

"I'm sorry," he replied, and he seemed to be sincere. "I've made a hell of a first impression on you, haven't I?"

He had. And Tess hoped that it would be the last impression he made, as well. "No matter," she said coldly. "You'll be moving on, as peddlers do."

"Perhaps I'll stay," he said.

Tess looked at him in horror and then decided that she didn't care whether he stayed or not. Her chores at the boardinghouse would keep her so busy that she wouldn't encounter him again, anyway. "As you wish," she said.

They drove in silence for a long time, the mule laboring diligently along the muddy logging road that led to the small Oregon town where Tess had spent the last five years of her life. The beast's breath made a misty fog around its muzzle, and at least one of its burdens pitied it.

When the Columbia River, with its log booms and its

steamboats, came into sight, Tess forgot the mule and its master and dreamed. She would leave Simpkinsville one of these days, just up and leave. She would go to Astoria or to Portland or even to Seattle. She would get herself a real job. . . .

The peddler's voice broke gently into her thoughts, scattering them like so much silvery flotsam. "What are you thinking about?"

Tess smiled at him. And even though they were very close to Simpkinsville now, close to the boardinghouse, close to Derora, she felt warm and good. "Steamboats," she answered, raising her voice so she could be heard above the shrieking screech of the saws in the mill they were passing now. "Steamboats and all the places they go."

Joel Shiloh's mouth quirked, and he nodded slightly. He understood and Tess liked him for that.

Chapter Two

SIMPKINSVILLE WAS NO BETTER AND NO WORSE THAN ANY of the other lumber towns the peddler had seen in more than a year of wandering. It was a small but noisy community, nestled close to the Columbia River and flanked by mountains thick with blue-green timber. He thought of Puget Sound and then of Wenatchee, another town on that sometimes turbulent waterway, and felt a pang of homesickness.

Tess directed him onto a side street within walking distance of the cacophonous sawmill. She was a pretty thing, with her wild cascades of rich brown hair, her impertinent nose, her wide, hazel-green eyes.

And she knew that he was not Joel Shiloh. Keith was

sure she had seen through his hasty, awkward lie about the Bible and the name printed on its battered leather cover. Damn.

He was about to turn to her and tell her who he was when she pointed out her aunt's boardinghouse. Keith had never seen anything quite like it; it was part house and part passenger train, and the sight of it pushed every thought of confession out of his mind.

The center of the structure was an ordinary wooden building, square and unremarkable, weathered by the fierce Oregon winters and the hot sun of at least two dozen summers, but branching out from it in four directions were railroad cars, apparently serving as wings.

Tess glanced quickly at his face, and her lower lip jutted just a little, telling him that she was sensitive about the oddness of her home. "I live here," she said, quite unnecessarily.

Keith squinted at the place, still unable to believe what he was seeing. "How—"

Tess tensed, and her stirrings had an unsettling effect on Keith Corbin. It had been too long, he guessed, since he'd had a woman.

But he had no intention of having this one. She was innocent, sweet, and entirely too young, and even though he'd left the straight and narrow path long ago, he still had a conscience. Sometimes to his regret.

"My uncle bought the cars from the railroad, when the spur into Simpkinsville was built," Tess explained stiffly. "He was going to have a freight line of his own."

Keith drew back on the reins, and the mule, sometimes recalcitrant, came to an obedient stop. "Your uncle? You didn't mention—"

"He left my aunt two years ago, Mr. Shiloh. He ran away with another woman." She sat still in the seat, a challenge flashing in her eyes. Probably, given the nature of small towns, she had taken considerable guff about what her uncle had done. "My aunt and I needed a way to make a living, so we had the cars brought here and we attached them to the house, so that we could take in boarders."

"I see," said Keith, softly. Watching her, his throat suddenly felt thick, and his stomach began doing strange things. He wondered if he was coming down with something.

Tess was scrambling out of the wagon seat, an awkward undertaking, since she was wearing trousers that were about to fall off. "Thank you very much for all your help," she said, standing ramrod straight and holding her borrowed trousers up with one hand.

Keith swallowed a laugh. God, but she was beautiful, even if she was a child, even if she was wearing his clothes instead of her own. "Don't you want your things?" he asked, and before she could answer, he set the brake lever and jumped to the ground. The burn on his right foot stung so fiercely that he winced. That's what you get for standing in fires when you have holes in your boots, he thought, as he rounded the wagon and opened the door at the rear.

Tess was waiting on the rickety wooden sidewalk—weeds were growing through the cracks—and casting nervous looks toward her aunt's boardinghouse as he wrestled the bicycle out of the wagon and then reached for the camera.

She wheeled the bicycle a few feet away and let it rest against a picket fence in no better repair than the sidewalk and came back for the camera. Her eyes were alight with mingled caution and fondness as she reached for the cumbersome box, and Keith wished incomprehensibly that she would look at him that way.

"Will you take my picture someday, Tess Bishop?" he found himself asking.

She colored richly, averted her eyes for a moment, and then looked at him with a sort of tender defiance. "Yes, but only if you shave," she said importantly.

It was then that he saw the sign swinging from the roof of the boardinghouse's narrow porch. "Lecture Tonight," it read.

Keith rubbed his beard-stubbled chin thoughtfully. This place was getting more and more intriguing by the moment. Besides, he did need a bath and a shave, and the prospect of sleeping in a real bed had distinct appeal, after all the nights he'd spent in his wagon. "Does your aunt have any rooms to rent?" he asked.

Tess stiffened and her cheeks flared, yet again, with an appealing rose color. "No—I—"

Before she could finish, the front door opened and a woman almost as tall as Keith himself came sweeping down the walkway, looking at once interested and annoyed.

"Tess Bishop, where have you—" Dark eyes swept Keith's frame, stopped at his face.

This would have to be Derora, Tess's aunt. Keith was taken aback, once again, for he'd expected a scarecrow or a fat curmudgeon. This woman, a few years older than himself and flawlessly beautiful, was certainly neither.

She smiled. "Derora Beauchamp," she said, extending one elegant hand. Her morning gown was made of some fluttery pink fabric, and Keith's desire for a proper bath and a bed was redoubled by her touch.

"This is Mr. Joel Shiloh," Tess announced, from somewhere in the shimmering fog. Then, disparagingly, she added, "He's a peddler."

Derora Beauchamp smiled, revealing a set of perfect, pearl-like teeth. "A road-weary traveler," she said. "Ours is the finest roominghouse in town, Mr. Shiloh. Won't you avail yourself of the comforts we offer?"

"Ours is the *only* roominghouse in town," put in the hoyden at Keith's side, grudgingly.

The warmth of Mrs. Beauchamp's hand, resting in Keith's, made sweet shivers run up and down his weary spine and dissipate in the aching muscles of his back. Too long. It had been too long.

He managed to nod and sensed rather than saw the scathing look Tess flung in his direction. Little Tess. He smiled and rumpled her wind- and rain-tangled hair and allowed Derora Beauchamp to lead him down the primrose path.

Tess Bishop simmered as she watched her aunt usher that crazy peddler into the house. She'd make tea, Derora would. She'd offer him the best chair in the parlor and perhaps even a cigar.

Stopping before the sign proclaiming tonight's lecture, she glared up at it. Free love. How fitting that the topic was free love!

But it won't be free, Mr. Joel Shiloh, she thought, with bitter satisfaction. It won't be free.

Not wanting to face either Derora or her aunt's prospective conquest, Tess walked around the house, with its railroad-car wings, and slunk up the kitchen steps, holding the trousers in place with one hand and cradling her camera against her middle with the other.

Juniper, the black woman who, with Tess's help, cooked for the boarders, came to the screened door, with its tears and rusty places, and looked out, rolling her great round eyes so that only the whites showed. "Tess Bishop, you little scamp, what you doin' wearin' them clothes? Where you been?"

Tess returned the thin woman's stare with a baleful one of her own. "Just open the door, Juniper," she pleaded tartly. "I'll explain later."

"You sure as the devil will," retorted the ascerbic Juniper, but she did open the door. "Lord ha' mercy, will you look at this chile—hair flyin' like a Jezebel's—wearin' pants—"

"Oh, hush!" hissed Tess, embarrassed and curious beyond bearing about what might be taking place in Derora's overdecorated parlor. What did she care if her aunt seduced that maniac, anyway? It would serve him right.

But she did care. Oh, she did. Tears brimmed in Tess's eyes as she remembered the way Joel Shiloh had looked at her aunt. He'd forgotten that Tess was even there, except to reach out and ruffle her hair, as though she were a gawky child.

"You get to your room and put on somethin' decent!" ordered Juniper, turning to an enormous bowl of batter and stirring furiously. "I swear I ain't never seen such a chile—"

"I'm not a child!" Tess shouted, and then she hurried across the kitchen, through the small dining room, and up the stairs to the second floor. As fast as she moved, she couldn't help hearing Derora's sensual, throaty laughter and the masculine timbre of Joel's.

In her small room, she put her camera carefully onto the bureau top and began tearing Joel Shiloh's clothes off her body as though they were on fire. Damn him, damn Derora. Damn the whole world!

The idea dawned, glowing and ignoble, as she was putting on her best satin camisole. The lecture! Of course! Tess Bishop was no child, and by George, she'd prove it. She would attend that lecture and she would listen as she had never listened before. And then she would adopt the philosophy of free love. Who could call her a child then?

The water was gloriously hot, and Keith Corbin sank into it with a sigh of contentment, a cigar clenched between his teeth, his burned foot propped comfortably on the edge of the tub. This, indeed, was the life. All he needed now was a drink and a woman, and if he'd read the promises in Derora Beauchamp's gypsy eyes correctly, he wouldn't have to wait long for either.

He shifted in the metal tub so that the water covered his aching shoulders and, with his teeth, tilted his cigar at a jaunty upright angle. "I knew a girl in Till-amachuck," he sang around it, under his breath. "She couldn't dance but she could—"

Just then, the door of Derora Beauchamp's well-equipped bathroom swung open. The little devil, thought Keith, with a grin.

His cigar fell into the bathwater when Tess peered around the corner. "Oh, sorry," she said, and she turned the color of watermelon pulp.

Keith slid downward until the water covered his head, his strangled curses bubbling to the top. When he surfaced the door was closed, and Tess, of course, was gone. He fished his ruined cigar out and flung it against the wall.

Maybe he wouldn't take his pleasure with Derora after all, if Tess was going to be peeping around doors all the time. Hell, he'd find a brothel, a place where a man could buy a drink and be assured of some privacy.

"Make up the bed in the west wing," Derora said coldly, her eyes never quite meeting Tess's. She took a chocolate from the box beside her chair and nibbled at it with her elegant teeth.

The west wing. Tess would have laughed if she'd dared; since when did a converted passenger car qualify as a wing? "Yes, ma'am," she said sweetly. "The front part of the car?"

Derora flung her a scathing look. "Certainly not. The room at the rear."

Tess bit her lower lip. Her stomach was still quivering from her scandalous encounter with Joel Shiloh, only minutes before, in the upstairs bathroom. She hoped the crimson blush had faded from her face. "Mr. Wilcox is in that room," she pointed out.

"That sweaty millworker," said Derora dismissively. "Yes. Well, just move his things. I want Mr. Shiloh to have the room at the back."

That way, Tess reasoned bitterly, Mr. Wilcox wouldn't walk through and see his landlady cavorting with the new tenant. "But—"

"Tess, just obey me. For once, just do as I tell you. And don't think I'm going to let that little matter of

25

your coming home in a man's clothes pass unchallenged, either."

"I'm—"

"If you tell me that you're eighteen, Tess, I swear by all that's holy that I'll snatch you baldheaded. A young lady does not comport herself in that manner, no matter what her age."

"I was caught in the rain, that's all. And my bicycle wheel was bent. Mr. Shiloh merely—"

Derora's gaze was on the ceiling now, and her lush lips curved into an anticipatory smile. She took another chocolate and ate it in a fashion that Tess found oddly indelicate. "Mr. Shiloh presented no danger to you, I'm sure. It would be my guess that he takes little note of bounding schoolgirls with their hair tumbling down their backs."

"Schoolgirls!" Tess protested. "I'm not—"

"Tess, really." Derora, who prized her figure, put the lid back on the candy box, not even looking at her niece. "Just go and do as I told you, please. And after that, I'd like you to help Juniper with tonight's refreshments. We're expecting a number of women to attend the lecture."

Tess sighed. She wondered what her aunt would say if she knew that her dear niece planned to attend, also. "Has Mrs. Hollinghouse-Stone arrived yet?" she asked, poised in the fringed parlor doorway.

"She has," replied Derora crisply, smoothing her sateen skirts. "That tiresome sheriff is forcing her to apply for a permit to address us. Can you believe it? And in a country where free speech is so prized."

Simpkinsville, for all its brothels and saloons, had a conservative quarter. A certain segment of its popula-

MEMORY'S EMBRACE

tion didn't take kindly to some of the lectures that took place in Mrs. Derora Beauchamp's front parlor. They hadn't minded the spiritualist, though, or the round, earnest little man who had demonstrated the dying art of phrenology. Tess grinned, patting her hair, which she had carefully pinned atop her head in order to look more grown up.

She supposed free love was quite a different kettle of fish from summoning the dear departed—to her great disappointment, none of that elusive group had shown up—or determining someone's most intimate nature by feeling the bumps on their head.

Yes, indeed, she thought, as she made her way into the "west wing," there was an interesting night ahead.

Mr. Wilcox had few belongings, fortunately, just a Bible and a shaving kit and a "bindle," the bedroll carried by all itinerant timber workers. Tess moved all these things into the front part of the car, which had been partitioned off from the rear, hoping that he wouldn't mind too much. Though Derora had been quite correct in referring to Arthur Wilcox as a "sweaty millworker," he was still a very nice man, quiet and polite. He'd paid Tess two dollars to take his likeness with her camera and then mailed the sepia-tinted result back East, to a girl he hoped to marry.

Tess smiled, stripping the sheets from his bed, remembering the shy, delighted way he'd posed. It was a shame to put him out like this, and all for a drummer who didn't have any more sense than to stand in campfires and leap into creeks when he didn't know how deep they were. Her smile faded and she worked with hasty, angry motions, putting fresh linen onto the bed that would be Joel Shiloh's.

That done, she dusted swiftly. She'd been very late getting back, thanks to that broken bicycle wheel and the rainstorm, and Juniper would be working herself into a state in the kitchen, trying to get dinner and prepare refreshments for the lecture guests as well.

In the hallway, still lined with windows although the train seats had, of course, been removed, she encountered Joel. He smelled of soap and cigar smoke, and his clothes were clean, his hair neatly brushed. He had even shaved.

Tess meant to scurry past him but instead she stopped cold, her stomach and heart waltzing with each other, forcing the breath from her lungs as they twirled, entwined.

"Are you planning to attend tonight's lecture?" she heard herself ask, with a dignity she wouldn't have thought she could manage.

His wonderful, arrogant mouth lifted at one side, in a half-grin. "To hear of the wonders of free love? Not hardly."

"Mrs. Hollinghouse-Stone is a fine speaker," Tess said, in lofty reply. "She was here last month. She spoke about suffrage—"

That wry, partial grin lingered, spreading to his eyes. "A subject dear to my mother's heart," he said quietly. "Not to mention those of my renegade sisters-in-law."

Tess wanted to ask about his mother and his sisters-in-law, about his entire family, but she didn't dare. She'd already learned that the topic was off limits. Besides, her throat was so tight that she couldn't have gotten a word past it anyway.

"Do you believe women should vote, Miss Bishop?"

he teased, his voice deep and quiet, his powerful body awakening, by its very nearness, something that had slept secretly within Tess.

She stepped back. "Yes," she managed to reply.

"And free love? Do you practice that?"

Tess's heart spun out of its dance with her stomach and careened off her windpipe. "Of course," she lied, in a very shaky voice. How was she going to get past Joel Shiloh, in this dratted, narrow hallway, without touching him?

He looked surprised and more than a little angry; in fact, some of the color drained away from beneath his tan. "You're not serious?" he breathed.

Tess drew a deep breath. In for a penny, in for a pound, she thought. She tried to remember what her aunt had said, at dinner the night before, about the philosophy in question. "Oh, yes," she said, feeling worldly. "How can there be wars if everyone—if everyone—"

He folded his arms, arched one dark-gold eyebrow, and waited.

"If everyone loves each other," she finished, with breathless triumph.

"Love takes many different forms," Joel pointed out, and he looked very displeased. "Are we talking about the same expression of that worthy emotion, Miss Bishop?"

Tess wanted to die, but she couldn't back out now or she would look the fool. She would again be a child in this man's eyes, and she couldn't bear that. She squared her shoulders and lifted her chin. "I believe we are, Mr. Shiloh."

"In that case, I ought to take you across my knee," came the infuriating response. And he made no move to step out of the way, so that she could pass.

"I invite you to try, Mr. Shiloh," she replied, with cold politeness. "If you do, I promise to bite off part of your thigh while you're at it."

He threw back his head and shouted with laughter, and Tess jumped, startled.

"P-Please," she said, when her racing heartbeat had settled to a pace that allowed her to speak. "Let me by. I must help Juniper with supper and the refreshments—"

He stepped aside then, his broad chest still shaking with amusement, but when she tried to squeeze by him, he suddenly shifted his weight, trapping her against the windows of the converted railroad car. Her breasts were crushed against him, and suddenly it seemed that her insides were melting down to form a throbbing pool in the depths of her femininity.

"Mr. Shiloh—" she whispered, half in protest and half in pleasure. So this was what it was like, the weight of a man's body! What a frightening, delightful pressure it was.

His hands rose to cup her face and tilt it upward and her hair, hastily pinned, fell about her shoulders in gleaming brown cascades. His mouth came tentatively to her own, tasting and nibbling and then, with breathtaking swiftness, devouring.

Tess responded as instinct commanded, letting his lips mold hers, parting them for the tender and then fierce conquering of his tongue. She had been kissed once before, behind the bandstand at the Independence Day picnic, but it certainly hadn't been anything like this. . . .

As suddenly as he had taken her, Joel Shiloh thrust her away. His jawline was tight with annoyance, and the brisk swat of his left hand stung Tess's pride more than her derriere.

She glared up at him for a moment, insulted and hurt, and then stooped to gather up her hairpins, which lay on the floor of the passageway.

Tess was so angry that tears burned in her eyes, making it next to impossible to find her hair pins. And he was just standing there, so tall and imperious, too self-important to help her.

Her bottom still stung where he had swatted her. The nerve . . . the gall of him. . . .

Before she realized what she was doing, Tess lunged forward and sank her teeth into his left thigh. He howled in surprise and pain, and Tess let him go, scrambled to her feet, and ran down the passageway as fast as she could go.

He caught her easily, and she thought her heart would stop beating when his hand closed over her shoulder, tight as a vice, and swung her around. It did not occur to her to scream.

"You little—" he began, his azure eyes flashing with some dangerous emotion.

"I told you I would bite you and I did!" Tess blurted out, in a hissing rush. "I am not a child and I will not be treated as one!"

Though he was struggling against it, a grin was tugging at one corner of his mouth. "No," he said hoarsely. "You are not a child."

Tess smoothed her skirts and her dignity. "Then you're sorry for striking me," she assumed.

"I didn't say that."

Tess was maddened. "Why, you—"

"I can't believe you seriously expect an apology," he broke in, in an evil undertone, "when you bit me like that."

"I bit you after you struck me!"

"A minor point, Miss Bishop. Now get out of here before I lose my temper!"

More than happy to comply, Tess turned and swept away in high dudgeon, chin up, shoulders back.

In the kitchen, Juniper was prattling as usual, but Tess barely heard her. All she could think about was that drummer and the way he'd pressed his body to hers, the way he'd kissed her. And the way he'd thrust her away, as if in disgust, and then swatted her! What reason had he had for doing that?

Peeling carrots with swift strokes of a paring knife, Tess blushed to remember the way she had bitten him. The way he'd howled.

"Stop that right now afore you cut yourself!" snapped Juniper, grasping Tess's hand and staying the motion of the paring knife. "What's the matter with you, girl?"

Unaccountable tears sprang up in Tess's eyes and flowed down her face, dropping off into the fragrant curls of carrot peelings. She had bitten that man, *bitten* him. Like an animal. "I don't know, Juniper," she wailed. "I don't know!"

For all of the older woman's complaining, Juniper loved Tess, and she lifted a practiced hand to the young woman's forehead to check for fever.

"You's a little warm," she fretted.

Tess was warm, all right, but not because of any fever. Thanks to that scandalous scene with Joel Shiloh, in the passageway, she felt like a candle left too close to a stove.

"I'm all right, Juniper," she insisted, sniffling a little and trying to brush away her tears with an anxious motion of one hand. "Honestly, I am."

Juniper was not easily convinced. "It ain't that time, is it? If it's your misery, girl, you just get yourself off to bed and—"

It was a misery, all right, but not the kind that Juniper was suggesting. "It isn't that," Tess declared, taking up the carrot she had been slashing at and peeling it in a way meant to suggest that she was competent to handle a knife.

Reluctantly, Juniper let the subject drop and went back to her own work, which was considerable.

At dinner, Mr. Wilcox was in attendance, along with Miss Shaeffer, the schoolteacher, and Mr. Johnston, the bookkeeper at the mill. Mrs. Hollinghouse-Stone, a reed-thin woman with a wart jutting out of her one long eyebrow and a wig that had seen better days, sat in the place of honor, beside Derora. Mr. Joel Shiloh was nowhere in sight, which was just as well, as far as Tess was concerned.

Maybe he'd thought better of taking a room in Simpkinsville, maybe he'd gotten back in his wagon and driven away, never to be seen—or bitten—again.

Tess pushed her boiled carrots around her plate with the prongs of her fork, miserable in a way that was completely new to her. Lord knew, she'd known misery when her mother had drifted into quiet madness, misery when her letters to her father had gone unanswered, misery when she had realized that Derora Beauchamp, her mother's only sister, would tolerate her but never love her. But this was something different, this feeling she had now, had had since meeting Joel Shiloh that morning. It was a sweet, piercing sort of anguish and she knew instinctively that the malady was going to get considerably worse before it got better.

If it ever got better.

Chapter Three

ALONE IN HIS RENTED ROOM, KEITH TOOK THE CHAIN FROM around his neck and caught the gold band suspended from it between his thumb and index finger. Inscribed inside were the ironic words, "Forever and ever. Amelie."

He let the ring and chain sink into his palm, closed his fingers, and sat down on the edge of his bed. How short forever could be. How very, very short.

Sounds from the main part of the house indicated that the lecture was about to begin; buggies and wagons had been pulling up out front for over half an hour. Keith smiled and shook his head and rubbed the sore place on his thigh, where Tess had bitten him.

His smile faded. The bite was something he could live with; in a way, he'd deserved it. But the idea of Tess Bishop practicing free love was another matter. Good Lord, she couldn't be serious, could she? She couldn't actually believe that the problems of the world would be solved by so fatuous and simple-minded a concept?

She could. She was only eighteen years old, younger than his starry-eyed sister, Melissa. She was naive, gullible, a succulent fruit ripe for the plucking.

A tremendous rage surged through Keith, sent him rocketing to his feet. His head felt bloodless and light and his stomach churned—to think, just to think, of Tess giving herself to every Tom, Dick, and Harry, and all for the sake of some crack-brained philosophy!

Slowly, after drawing a deep, steadying breath, he sat down again. She claimed that she was already a practicing free lover. If so, why hadn't anything happened in his camp that morning?

He imagined taking her into the shadowy privacy of his peddler's wagon, imagined baring those lush and shapely breasts, imagined having her on that narrow cot. Now, in retrospect, Keith realized that, despite his blithe observations that she was too young for such things, he would have possessed Tess in every sense of the word if she'd given him the slightest encouragement.

Reminding himself that Tess was younger than his sister did no good at all, not now. At eighteen, she was a woman, not a girl. And he wanted her more than he had ever wanted anyone, including his bride.

Tentatively, he touched the ring Amelie had slipped onto his finger only moments before her death. The whole scene came back to him, the outdoor wedding in a Wenatchee churchyard, the presence of his family and friends, the nightmarish explosion and the horrors that had followed.

Amelie had been killed instantly. Even now, after all the time that had passed, Keith could hardly bear to remember the screams of injured people and the shrieks of horses, the hot, acrid smell of dynamite, the still, tulle-and-lace-clad form lying on the ground.

Keith's eyes were damp now, and he brushed the moisture away with a motion of one arm. He wouldn't think about the wedding. He wouldn't think about Amelie. And he wouldn't think about making love to Tess Bishop, either. She wasn't like the women he'd used in recent months.

She wasn't. She couldn't be. That talk about free love was just that, talk. Talk designed to convince him that she wasn't a child.

Keith shrugged into a dark suit jacket, freshly brushed by a solicitous Derora Beauchamp, took out his wallet, and counted the bills inside. If the patent medicine business didn't pick up soon, he was going to have to find himself a job. Lord knew, he couldn't risk wiring the bank in Port Hastings again. His brothers might be onto that tactic by now, and tracing him to Simpkinsville would be easy if they were.

He sighed and tucked the wallet back into his inside pocket. Life would be so much simpler if Adam and Jeff could be counted on to leave him alone until he'd worked things out, but he knew they couldn't. The private detectives that had been dogging him for the last year were proof of that.

With a grin, Keith took his bowler hat, also freshly

brushed, from the top of the bureau. He put it onto his head with a flourish. Time enough to think about his brothers and their hired goons later. Right now, he needed a drink and a woman. Or maybe several drinks and several women.

He opened the door at the rear of the converted car and went out, unaware that he'd left Amelie's wedding ring behind for the first time since that tragic day in Wenatchee.

Tess was careful to sit at the back of the parlor, in a shadowy corner, lest Derora see her and order her away before she could hear Mrs. Hollinghouse-Stone's lecture. That wasn't likely to happen, it was true, because there were far more people in attendance than anyone could have dared hope, many of them strangers.

"Did you hear?" whispered Emma Hamilton, Tess's friend, as she sank into a chair nearby.

"Hear what?" Tess countered, craning her neck to see if Joel Shiloh—if indeed that was his name—was anywhere in the crowd.

Emma was about to burst, her pink cheeks glowing with excitement, her red curls bobbing. "I can't believe you don't know! Tess, there's a showboat at anchor—a real showboat—in our own river! See that man over there—the tall one with the chestnut hair? He's an actor!"

Tess looked at the man in question and observed to herself that he wasn't half as handsome as Joel Shiloh. There was something too studied about his smile, and his features were too even, too perfect, to be at all interesting. Still, he was an actor, a rare enough bird in Simpkinsville, Oregon, and, as such, he was a curiosity. "Does my aunt know?" she asked.

Emma giggled behind one glove as Derora zeroed in on the gentleman. "She must. Look at her fuss over him!"

Tess experienced an odd sense of relief. Perhaps a friendship would bloom, however brief, and distract Derora from Joel Shiloh. After all, wasn't an actor more interesting than a peddler?

"Isn't he wonderful?" marveled Emma. "I could perish!"

"Do you know his name?" asked Tess, without much interest. There was still a chance that Joel would come in and see her with a free love lecture program in her hands, and she didn't want to miss his reaction.

"Roderick Waltam. Roderick!" Emma fairly crooned the name. "It's so much more romantic than everyday names like Joe or Bill, isn't it?"

Before Tess had to respond to this inanity, Mrs. Hollinghouse-Stone took her place at the podium Derora kept for just such occasions and cleared her throat. An immediate silence fell. All eyes were on the unprepossessing woman in her dramatic, flowing white robe.

"Mercy," observed Emma, in a stage whisper. "She only has one eyebrow!"

Tess bit down hard on her lower lip because she couldn't afford to giggle and attract her aunt's attention. "Hush!" she hissed, when she dared.

For all her physical shortcomings, Lavinia Hollinghouse-Stone was a convincing speaker, and she touted free love with authority and flair, just as she had touted suffrage a month before. She paced and she gestured, she raised and lowered her voice at all the most effective times. At one point, she even wept for all the human suffering that could be avoided if only physical intimacy was not so foolishly suppressed!

"I'm going out and love somebody," Emma confided, with conviction, when the speech was over and the tentative applause had subsided. "Preferably Roderick Waltam!"

Tess had been greatly impressed by the lecture, but not swayed from her own beliefs. "Emma Hamilton, don't you dare!" she rasped, blushing to the roots of her hair.

It was later, at the refreshment table set up in the dining room, that Roderick Waltam approached Tess, beaming down at her in a way that seemed rehearsed.

"Hello," he said. His eyes were brown, like his hair, and he was clean-shaven except for muttonchop sideburns. Tess noticed that his blue velvet jacket, however well fitted, was frayed at the collar and cuffs.

"Punch?" Tess offered politely, her hand on the ladle.

Mr. Waltam nodded; he had taken a plate and was loading it with teacakes and cookies and the tiny, elegant sandwiches Juniper had worked so hard to make. Apparently, the acting profession was not a lucrative one. "Thank you," he said, and his voice was as commanding, in its masculine way, as that of a politician or a schoolmaster. "What is your name?"

Tess was ladling punch into one of Derora's crystal cups, and, before she could answer, she spotted Joel

Shiloh. He carried his bowler hat in one hand, and he was wearing a suit entirely too perfectly tailored for a peddler.

"Discussing your pet theory?" he asked, with acid politeness.

Some of the punch slopped over to stain the linen tablecloth, and Tess's face flamed.

"Now, see here—" began Mr. Waltam, lamely, glancing from Tess to Joel and then back again.

Joel gave the poor man a look fit to skewer steel and the actor retreated, careful to take his plate and his glass of punch with him.

"That was very rude!" hissed Tess, glaring. Only moments before, she'd been wishing that Joel would appear, actually wishing! How could she have been so stupid?

He was drunk. How he had managed that in such a short time Tess did not know, but he had. His eyes had a glazed look, and the smell of whiskey wafted across the watercress sandwiches and the teacakes and the punchbowl to assault her nostrils.

"If you really must explore the mysteries of free love," he began, causing several feathered-and-beaded heads to turn, "I would like to volunteer as your guide."

Tess was mortified. Was there no end to the shame and embarrassment this man could cause her? "I would sooner mate with a monkey," she replied, and the wife of Banker Flemming fanned herself and rolled her eyes back, about to swoon.

Joel scanned the room for Roderick Waltam, found him, and swung his condemning gaze back to Tess's berry-red face. "So I see," he answered. "Does the organ grinder know he's loose?"

Tess had not often been relieved to see her aunt, but at that moment she could have kissed the woman for sweeping imperiously up to the refreshment table and demanding, "Is there a problem, Mr. Shiloh?"

Not "Is there a problem, Tess?" Oh, no. The implication was that Mr. Shiloh was the offended party. Tess sighed.

"Absolutely not," said the peddler, swaying a little and smiling stupidly down into Derora's upturned face.

Derora's responding smile was dazzling. Sweetly forgiving. She hooked her arm through Joel's and ushered him away from the table, chattering about Mrs. Hollinghouse-Stone's theories and then proceeding to introduce him to every respectable matron in the place.

Exasperated, Tess forced herself to brace up and even to smile as she served punch to guest after guest. The men were eagerly polite, the women venomous.

It was very late when the occasion ended; Mrs. Hollinghouse-Stone retired to her room in the "east wing," and that prompted the departure of her audience. As Tess helped Juniper clear away the mess, she told herself that she was glad Joel Shiloh had disappeared again. Glad! The sot, he was probably passed out in a drunken stupor.

Which was better than his spending the night in Derora's room, she had to admit. Mr. Waltam had been chosen for that honor, anyway; he'd tried to be subtle about the whole thing, but as Tess washed glasses and dessert plates at the kitchen sink, she saw him climb the wrought iron steps of the car that pointed due south.

The moment she realized that it was Sunday morning, Tess Bishop's eyes flew open and she bounded out of bed, raced across the hallway to the bathroom, and made short work of her morning ablutions. If she hurried, she could get out of the house before it was time to leave for church.

Because Juniper would already be in the kitchen, preparing breakfast, Tess made her escape through the front door. The morning was gloriously clear, washed with rain and tinted gold by a spring sun. Lilacs, in white and purple, spilled their luscious perfume into the dewy air.

For all her problems and all the curious feelings that had kept her up half the night, Tess had to hold back a shout of pure joy.

"Good morning," greeted a familiar masculine voice, from the vicinity of the fence.

Tess squinted, saw Mr. Waltam between the pickets. Wearing no coat or vest, but only a lacy white shirt, he was kneeling on the sidewalk, his hands busy with the bent wheel of her bicycle.

"Good morning," she answered, feeling alarmed but drawn to the actor nonetheless. "What are you doing?"

He gave a great wrench at the tire, using both his hands, and then stood up, looking pleased. His fingers were stained with grease, and there was a splotch of the stuff on his elegant shirt, too. "Fixing your tire. It is your bicycle, isn't it?"

Tess nodded, amazed. Roderick Waltam certainly

didn't look like the mechanical sort, but apparently he was. The wheel was straight again, she could ride whenever she wanted. "Thank you."

"Not so fast," he said, in a teasing voice, using a handkerchief to wipe his long-fingered, callous-free hands clean. Or, at least, nearly clean. "There is a price for my services."

"And what would that be?" demanded a second masculine voice, from behind Tess.

She whirled, startled, to see Joel standing behind her, his arms folded across his chest, his bowler hat at a cocky angle on his head. Gone was the fashionable suit he'd worn the night before; today he was clad in ordinary trousers, a vest, and a patched shirt.

"A ride on her bicycle," answered Roderick Waltam evenly, holding Joel's gaze as he had not been able to do the night before. Perhaps a night of abandon had made him brave.

Speechless, sensing that the two men were discussing something completely unrelated to a common bicycle but having no clue as to what it was, Tess turned her eyes back to Joel. A muscle leaped in his jaw and stilled again, as though forced into submission.

The fresh air was suddenly charged; each man took a step nearer the other. God knew what would have happened if Derora hadn't appeared at that very moment, wearing a lavender satin dressing gown, on the front porch.

"Tess, dear!" she sang out sweetly. "Church!"

Church. Tess shook her head. Although Derora was anything but religious, whenever she entertained a gentleman guest of a Saturday night, she invariably attended services the next morning. The curious thing was that the special smile on her face and the light in her eyes showed no inclination whatsoever toward penance.

"I'm not going to church," Tess summoned up the courage to say. "I have a headache."

Derora opened her mouth to protest, but Roderick stayed her by striding toward the porch. "I'd be honored to accompany you," he said adoringly, and Derora forgot all about Tess and her duties as an aunt. She and Roderick disappeared into the house, gazing into each other's eyes as they went.

"I'd be honored to accompany you!" mimicked Joel Shiloh furiously.

Tess stiffened. Incredibly enough, she'd forgotten his presence for a moment. Bad planning, for now she was alone with him. "Are you jealous, Mr. Shiloh?" she asked acidly. "If so, I would suggest that you go to church with Mr. Waltam and my aunt."

He made no response, except for a rude noise that came from low in his throat.

Tess went to her bicycle and grasped the handlebars, ready to go for a Sunday morning ride along the river road. With any luck, she wouldn't encounter another deluded peddler in her travels.

Joel stopped her with startling ease. "Will you take my picture?"

"What?" She stared at him, wide-eyed. Confused. And wanting more than anything to take Joel Shiloh's photograph. When he moved on, as peddlers invariably did, she would have the likeness to remember him by.

But why should she want to remember, for heaven's sake?

45

"Please?" he prompted, in a disturbingly gruff and humble tone.

"All right," Tess answered shyly, and then she hurried into the house and up the stairs to her room. Her camera was on the bureau, where she had left it, and the counter indicated that there were still three plates inside.

In the hallway, she was waylaid by a frowning Juniper. "Ain't you goin' to hear the preachin', girl?"

It was almost ten minutes before Tess managed to escape Juniper and rush down the stairs with her camera. On the porch, she stopped cold, for Joel's wagon was in the road, hitched and ready to roll. The peddler was bent over, checking the harness.

Somehow, Tess got to the gate; she didn't remember walking there. Clutching her camera close, she asked, "You're leaving?" How was it that she could feel such despair when his going away was what she wanted most?

He straightened, fixed his hat in place with one hand, lifted his eyes so that he was looking past Tess, to the roof or the skies or maybe the mountains. "Yes and no," he answered.

"What do you mean, 'yes and no'?" Tess demanded. "You're either leaving or you're not!"

"I'm going back to my campsite, by the stream," he replied patiently. "That will be better for all concerned, I think."

Tess managed to shrug. "Whatever you say."

"Are you still going to take my picture?"

"If you want me to," she said. Let him think she didn't care, one way or the other.

"I want you to," came the gentle answer, and then

46

Joel Shiloh took up a pose beside his peddler's wagon, his gilt-scripted name clearly in view, his hat at a jaunty angle, his lips curved in an almost imperceptible smile.

Tess took careful aim, glad that she could look down through the little window in the top of her camera instead of directly into Joel Shiloh's knowing blue eyes. She took a picture, removed the photographic plate, and took another, just to be on the safe side.

"Now let me take your picture," Joel said, striding toward her and helping himself to the camera.

Tess's throat was constricted, and her eyes were burning a little. She tucked the two plates she'd used into the pocket of her skirt. "Why?" she asked lamely, full of despair because he was going away.

He laughed and plopped his silly bowler hat onto her head, spoiling her carefully upswept and very adult hairdo. "Why not?" he countered.

Tess went to stand beside the wagon, as he had, posing as he had. He laughed again and took the picture, then surrendered the camera to its owner and reclaimed his hat.

They stood still on the sidewalk for some moments, Sunday coming alive, in all its blue-gold April glory, all around them. In the distance, church bells chimed, and the sound broke the spell, causing Joel Shiloh to stiffen and look patently restless.

"That actor—" he began, but his words fell away. He let out a long breath. "I'll be where I was yesterday," he finally said. "If you need me, I'll be there."

Tess could only nod. There would only be five miles between them, not five hundred. Why did she feel so bereft and broken? She should be happy to be rid of Joel Shiloh, troublesome character that he was.

To her surprise and, if his expression could be
believed, to his own, Joel bent and kissed her forehead.
And then he was gone, bolting up into the wagon seat,
driving off. His voice floated back to her on the April
breeze, singing a bawdy song.

Half laughing and half crying, Tess went inside the
house, climbed the stairs to her room, and closed the
door. She put her camera in its place on the bureau, sat
down on her bed, and covered her face with both
hands.

At noon, she went downstairs to join Derora, Mr.
Waltam, and the other boarders for lunch. All except
Mr. Wilcox had been to church and were respectably
circumspect. Tess was grateful for that, because the last
thing she wanted to do was make conversation.

Among other things, Derora Beauchamp prided
herself on her modern, forthright opinions and her
knowledge of current affairs. For this reason, she took
weekly newspapers from Seattle, Portland, and San
Francisco, reserving Sunday afternoon for the pleasant
task of reading each tabloid from beginning to end.

Today, however, she was somewhat distracted.
Roderick had gone back to the ship, to rest up, he said,
for tonight's performance.

Settling back into the rumpled satin pillows, Derora
allowed herself a contented smile. After last night, she
could believe that the dear lad needed a rest. She
needed one herself.

But good habits are nothing if they are not studiously
maintained, she reflected, opening the first newspaper
that came to hand, *The Seattle Times*, with a determined flip of the pages.

The advertisement was there, as always. Until now, Derora had always skimmed it to see if any changes had been made and then gone on.

But this time the thing took up a half-page—they had to be rich, those Corbins—and a sketch was included. Derora sat up straight, her mouth dropping open, just for a moment, in surprise. The peddler—this sketch was of the peddler, Joel Shiloh!

"No," said Derora, in disbelief, even as she studied the drawing. Same strong jawline and square chin, same direct gaze and straight nose. The hair was shorter—

The bold-faced print above the likeness drew Derora's attention, she read it with a rising sense of excitement.

Have You Seen This Man?
Five Thousand Dollar Reward Willingly
Paid. Contact Adam Corbin
Port Hastings, Washington.

"Port Hastings," Derora repeated to herself, and then she studied the sketch again. *Was* this a picture of the peddler who called himself Joel Shiloh or wasn't it? The resemblance was striking, but it could be only that, a resemblance.

She got her spectacles out of the drawer in her bedside table and put them on. "My goodness," she muttered, staring at the drawing in the newspaper and thinking of the places five thousand dollars could take her, all of them far from plodding Simpkinsville, thank you very much. "If you're not Mr. Joel Shiloh, you certainly should be," she told the newsprint image.

Derora closed the newspaper and folded it neatly. Then she removed her spectacles and hid them away again, in the depths of the drawer. Contact Adam Corbin, in Port Hastings, the advertisement had said. But how? It was Sunday and the telegraph office would be closed. . . .

She rose from the bed, dressed, and groomed her hair. Andrew McMichaels, the telegraph operator at Western Union, was a friend of hers. Surely she could prevail upon him to send a wire; this was an emergency situation, after all.

What if she were wrong, though? What if Joel Shiloh were not the person this Adam Corbin man was seeking?

Derora unfolded the newspaper again, turned to the advertisement, and studied it. Then, on a hunch, she searched through the Portland paper, too. The advertisement was there, but it gave no further information, for it was an exact duplicate. In *The San Francisco Chronicle*, however, she found a slight variation in copy. The blurb above the sketch read:

Missing. Keith Corbin. Likeness Below.

And under the image—Lord, but he did look like Joel Shiloh—was the same offer of a reward.

Derora sat down at her dressing table, staring at her own image in the mirror but not seeing it. Five thousand dollars, she thought. Five thousand beautiful dollars.

The decision was made. She would wire Port Hastings, that very night. If she was wrong, if this peddler was not Keith Corbin, well, anyone could make a mistake. She would have lost nothing but the cost of sending a single wire. Time was of the essence—how long would it be before someone else noticed the similarities between the drawing and Joel Shiloh? Suppose someone beat her to that reward?

Yes, indeed, time was of the essence.

Chapter Four

EMMA LOOKED VERY PLEASED. "TESS, PAPA HAS ALREADY developed your photographs," she said, scurrying along beside her friend as she wheeled her bicycle into the little stable behind Derora's house. "I have them right here, in my bag!"

Tess leaned the bicycle against an inside wall and tossed her head, so that her hair flew back over her shoulders. After eating lunch, she had taken the photographic plates to Mr. Hamilton, Emma's father, and asked him to process them. Then, because she couldn't bear to sit still, she had pedaled off into the countryside. Knowing where Joel Shiloh was camped, she had, of course, ridden in quite the opposite direction.

"Let's see them," she said casually, walking back out of the rarely used stable—Derora did not own a horse or carriage—and into the late afternoon sunshine.

Emma was eager to hand the four-by-five-inch photographs over and obviously disappointed in the idle manner in which Tess flipped through them. There was a lilac bush, just blooming. There was a riverboat, passing blurrily by on the Columbia. There was Mrs. Swendhagen's hopelessly ugly baby. There was Tess, herself, standing in front of the peddler's wagon, his hat on her head, an idiotic smile on her lips.

And there was Joel. Only one of the two plates she had used had turned out, but the likeness was a good one, clear and fairly pulsing with the distinct personality of that difficult, audacious, and completely wonderful man.

"Tess?" Emma whispered. "Is something wrong?"

Tess could not raise her head, but she did manage to shake it. "No. No, nothing is wrong."

Emma was instantly mollified, for once. "I've got a surprise for you, Tess," she said, with proper mystery and relish. "Guess what it is!"

Tess tucked the photographs carefully into her skirt pocket and lifted her head, meeting Emma's eyes, praying that her friend would not notice the shimmering mist in her own. "You know I hate to guess," she answered. "Tell me!"

Emma beamed. "Tickets! Tess, I have tickets to the show on the riverboat—Mr. Roderick Waltam gave them to me himself!" She paused, considering, her eyes shining. "I think he likes me," she added, at last, in a shy voice.

Tess linked her arm through Emma's and ushered her

toward the kitchen door, failing to mention that Mr. Roderick Waltam had spent the night with Derora. "Let's have some teacakes—there are some left from last night, I think. When is this show, anyway?"

"Why, it's tonight!" cried Emma, all ashiver at the very prospect. "It's going to be spectacular, Tess! You will go with me, won't you? Please?"

For once, Juniper was not in the kitchen. Tess put on a pot of coffee and, as Emma settled herself at the round table with its checkered cloth, took the remaining teacakes from a tin box on the counter. "Of course I will. What kind of show is it, Emma? A play? A musical review?"

Emma reddened a little and lowered her voice to a confidential whisper. "It's burlesque," she admitted. "I told Mama and Papa it was a rendition of *Macbeth*—I do hope neither of them see the bills the company has been posting around town."

Standing at the stove, Tess looked at her friend and shook her head. "Emma Hamilton, you amaze me sometimes. Lying to your mother and father! It's a wonder you haven't been sent off to boarding school long before this."

Emma shifted in her chair, her plump little body stiff with determined defiance. "Are you going with me or not?" she demanded.

Tess retorted with a question of her own. "Don't people take their clothes off in burlesque?"

"I don't know," Emma answered, with a converse sort of certainty, "but I surely intend to find out."

"Your parents will be furious!"

Emma shrugged. "For an hour, a day, a week. But

I'll remember seeing a show on a real riverboat all my life! No matter what they do to me, it'll be worth it!"

The coffee came to a boil, and Tess reached for a potholder before grasping the handle, filling a cup for Emma and one for herself. In a way, she agreed with her friend—interesting experiences were rare enough in Simpkinsville, and something as wondrous as a professional burlesque show would probably be well worth the average punishment.

"I told Mama I'd be spending the night here," Emma imparted, as she was about to leave. "That's all right, isn't it?"

Tess nodded. Derora would not care, as long as she was up and about her chores first thing the next morning. Her only reservation was that Roderick might spend the night again and shatter the romantic fancies Emma was no doubt entertaining.

"I'll bring my things over after supper, then," Emma said, again speaking in a conspiratorial whisper. "The show begins at eight."

"Eight," confirmed Tess, hiding a smile. When the door closed behind her friend, she immediately plunged a hand into her pocket and drew out the photographs. Laying the one of Joel Shiloh on the table before her, she cupped her chin in her hands and tried to will herself into it. She would travel with him, as his wife, selling medicines from door to door, farm to farm, lumbercamp to lumbercamp. They would have a cabin for winter, a cabin with gingham curtains at the windows. And perhaps a plump baby would play on the hearth. . . .

"You're as bad as Emma," Tess scolded herself

aloud, putting the photograph back into her pocket and standing up. Full of silly dreams, that's what she was. And the reality was that Joel Shiloh would go away and she would stay here, dusting and cooking and changing bed linens. Occasionally she would hear a lecture. She would take her photographs and ride her bicycle—dear Lord, she would go mad if she couldn't do those things—and eventually she would be married, probably to an ordinary, hardworking man like Mr. Wilcox, the boarder who worked in the sawmill.

Patently depressed, Tess cleared away the cups, put the few teacakes that had not been consumed back into the tin breadbox, and went upstairs to her room. She had barely had time to hide away the cherished photograph of Joel Shiloh when a furious tapping sounded at her door.

"Tess!"-cried Derora, from the hallway, "open this door!"

I wouldn't have thought she'd miss a few teacakes, Tess marveled to herself as she obeyed. Derora looked outraged, but it was a studied sort of look, like Roderick Waltam's smile.

"What's going on between you and that peddler?!" her aunt demanded, waving an exact duplicate of the photograph Tess had just secreted away in her bureau drawer. "And where is he, anyway? I haven't seen him since this morning!"

Confused, Tess resisted an urge to snatch the picture from Derora's fingers, and said, "He's gone."

The color beneath Derora's rouge seeped away, leaving the cosmetic to stand on its own. "Gone?" she echoed. "Gone where?"

"B-Back to his camp. He said it would be b-better if he left—"

Considering that she might well have been done out of a night's room rent, an event she wouldn't take lightly, Derora seemed strangely relieved. A fact which made her question that much more of a shock. "Have you been dallying with Joel Shiloh, Tess?"

"D-Dallying?"

"Don't be coy, my dear. You know perfectly well what I mean. Did you allow that man to take liberties with your person?"

Coming from Derora, such a suggestion was indeed ironic, but Tess wouldn't have dared to laugh. She wasn't inclined to anyway; she was too insulted. "I most certainly did not," she said, holding her chin high.

Derora further surprised her niece by giving a high, trilling burst of amusement. "I thought you might have taken that free love lecture seriously—don't try to deny that you heard it, Tess, because I saw you sitting there with that Hamilton girl—and it's obvious that you're taken with Mr. Shiloh or there wouldn't be a photograph like this one, would there?"

Tess reached tentatively for the picture, Derora withheld it.

"Oh, no. This is mine. Do you realize what a scandal this could have started, Tess? Why, if Mr. Hamilton hadn't warned me—"

"A simple photograph?" Tess broke in, in angry wonder. "How could that start a scandal?"

"It implies improper familiarity, Tess!" snapped Derora, impatient now, red with conviction.

"You're a fine one to talk about improper familiarity!" Tess burst out.

She was immediately and soundly slapped for her trouble. "I will not endure such insolence, Tess, not for one moment! If it hadn't been for Mr. Beauchamp—may he fry in hell—and myself, you would have been alone in this world! Alone. May I remind you that we took you in, that we gave you a home after your dear, foolish mother lost her mind?"

Dear, foolish Mother. How Tess missed her, how she wished that they had never come to this place, hoping to make a new life. If they'd stayed in St. Louis. . . .

But they hadn't. Mr. Asa Thatcher, Esquire, her mother's lover, had grown tired of his mistress and turned her out of her gilded cage, along with Tess, his illegitimate child. It had all been handled by minions, of course, clerks from his law firm. Olivia Bishop had had no choice but to pawn what remained of her jewelry, garnered during the days of favor, and buy train tickets for herself and her daughter.

. Olivia must have loved Asa Thatcher, dour curmudgeon that he was, for even in the West, where men were anxious to court so lovely a woman, even willing to overlook her past, she had not thrived. No, she had written long letters to Asa, Olivia had, and when there were no answers, she had sighed and shed tears and gradually faded away into a staring silence that excluded the rest of the world.

Tess shook away memories of her unconventional mother and swallowed hard. As a substitute parent, Derora had been cold and largely disinterested, but she had provided food and shelter for her sister's love child. She had seen that her niece finished school, and after that she had given Tess work to do, there at the boardinghouse, instead of marrying her off or simply turning her out. Furthermore, she had settled Olivia in a good hospital in Portland.

"I didn't mean to be ungrateful, Aunt Derora," Tess said quietly. "I'm sorry."

"You should be," came the clipped response, and Derora turned and swept away, skirts rustling, the photograph of Joel Shiloh still in her possession.

Tess hadn't much spirit for attending a burlesque show, even if it was being performed on a riverboat. She wanted to rush to Joel Shiloh, like a wanton, and ask him to take her with him wherever he might travel. But she had promised Emma that she would go, and she intended to keep her word.

Roderick disliked sharing his quarters on the *Columbia Queen* with the likes of Johnny Baker, a common, pimply roustabout, but there was nothing for it. Work was work, and it was a rare enough quantity, for an actor at least. Nights like the one just past, spent in Derora Beauchamp's bed, went a long way toward making life bearable, though he would have preferred to pass the time with the lady's niece.

Tess. He smiled, mentally tasting the name, as he applied a blackface for the first performance. The roustabout stood behind him, watching the process with an avid sort of fascination.

"Last night must have been pretty good, huh?" leered the weasel. "I noticed you was gone."

Roderick glued a bushy white eyebrow into place. "Nothing much gets by you, does it, Baker?" he asked, dismissing the man even as he spoke. He'd given Emma

Hamilton two tickets to tonight's performance, an indulgence that had cost him dearly. Would the little chit have the sense to offer the extra one to Tess?

He glued on a second eyebrow. "I'd like this room to myself tonight, if it's all the same to you," he said to the pockmarked face reflected beside his own.

Baker looked lewdly delighted. "You bringin' a woman here?"

Roderick resisted a temptation to roll his eyes in overt disdain. It wouldn't do to offend the weasel, not now. "Yes," he said, affixing a false mustache to his upper lip. The greasepaint made it hard to keep the thing in place. "Maybe you'd like to spend the night in town or something." Or anything, he added mentally. Just so long as you're gone before I bring Tess Bishop below deck.

"I ain't got no money," complained Baker.

Roderick sighed. He'd half-expected this development. "There's a five-dollar goldpiece in my other coat. Take that."

Baker's unfortunate complexion was mottled with pleasure. "Thanks," he said adoringly. Sometimes Roderick wondered about him.

"Think nothing of it," Roderick replied, in blithe tones. What an actor you are, he said to himself, as Baker plundered the pockets of his extra coat for the last cent he had.

After the roustabout left, he checked his makeup, made minor adjustments to his cutaway satin coat. Damn, but he was handsome, even with his face blackened with greasepaint!

* * *

Tess and Emma boarded the showboat among a throng of other people, trying to appear casual. It was unlikely that they would encounter Emma's staid and steady parents in such a place, but they could run into Derora, and that would be almost as disastrous.

The show itself was to be held in the vessel's gaudily decorated salon, where there was a stage framed with elaborate gilt curlicues and draped in red velvet curtains. Paintings of nudes covered the walls, and there were crystal chandeliers hanging from the high ceiling, where plump, painstakingly carved cherubs cavorted.

Rows of seats, upholstered in velvet to match the curtains, faced the stage, and Emma and Tess found themselves very close indeed—one good stretch and they could have touched the footlights!

"Front row seats!" whispered Emma, beaming. "Didn't I tell you that Roderick likes me?"

Tess bit her lower lip. Even though Mr. Waltam had fixed her bicycle wheel—a kindly gesture indeed—there was still the fact that he had passed the night with Derora. That had to be borne in mind. "Emma, he's an actor," she retorted, hoping to dissuade her friend from further infatuation. "They are not reliable people, you know."

"No, I don't know!" snapped Emma, with spirit. "I've never met an actor before! Have you?"

The gas-powered chandeliers dimmed. "Yes," she said tightly, after a moment of prideful hesitation. "My mother was an actress, in St. Louis."

Emma was gaping at her, Tess knew that without

looking. "What?!" she hissed. "Tess Bishop, you never told me that before!"

"There are a lot of things I've never told you," Tess responded evenly. "Now, hush up and watch the show!"

And what a show it was. It began with a colorful song and dance number, the music supplied by a small orchestra seated on a balcony at the back of the salon, with Roderick Waltam as the central performer. He sang and played a banjo quite creditably, his face painted black, while a bevy of women in similar makeup danced and sang all around him.

Following that was a Parisian number—surely these were different players, for there had not been time for them to change their costumes and remove their greasepaint—and then a skinny little man in a plaid suit and a bowler hat comically like Joel Shiloh's came out onto the stage and told stories that made the women titter and the men guffaw.

And after the jokester came a woman dressed in glowing velvet and wearing pearls in her hair. She was Anne Boleyn, locked in the Tower of London, facing her imminent execution with a bemused sort of valor that brought tears to Emma's eyes, and to Tess's.

The doomed queen received three curtain calls, along with several coarse proposals from the back of the salon, and the audience did not like parting with her. They were of a somewhat grudging mind when a perfectly groomed Roderick reappeared, without his greasepaint and cotton eyebrows, to sing a series of touching Irish ballads.

His voice was a clear, heart-wrenching tenor, and one look at Emma told Tess that if this showboat didn't chug away down the Columbia soon, there would be trouble of a serious nature.

As the lights came up, indicating that the show was over, the applause was thunderous. Tess clapped half-heartedly, watching Emma instead of the players taking their bows. She had decided to enlighten her friend, with regards to Roderick Waltam, and was just opening her mouth to do so, when a heavy hand fell upon her shoulder.

Tess turned, startled, and looked up into the face of Mr. Wilcox, the millworker who boarded at Derora's.

"Miss Bishop," he began, drawing his hand back at the sudden realization that he'd taken an improper liberty. "Miss Bishop, I brought a message for you, from Juniper. She says come home, right away quick, because Mrs. Beauchamp's done hurt herself and she's askin' for you."

Tess swallowed hard, bolted to her feet. "How badly is my aunt hurt, Mr. Wilcox? What happened to her?"

Sympathy moved in Mr. Wilcox's face, gentling his coarse features somewhat. "I don't think it's real bad, Miss Bishop—there's a lot of carrying on, though, that's for sure. Near as I could tell, Mrs. Beauchamp fell down some stairs and twisted one ankle."

For all the quiet antipathy that kept Tess and her aunt at an emotional distance from each other, Tess was frightened and worried. "Come on," she said to Emma, impatiently. "We have to go."

Emma chose then, of all times, to be stubborn. "Not me. I'm staying."

"Emma Hamilton, I have no time to argue with you! You come with me or I swear I'll send word to your papa that you're here!"

Emma folded her arms. "Do your worst, Tess Bishop. I'm seventeen years old and I'm perfectly capable of taking care of myself. If you tell my papa, just don't expect to call yourself my friend ever again."

Tess had no time, or patience, to stand there arguing with Emma, and no desire to lose the only real friend she had. "Promise me that you'll stay away from that actor!" she pleaded, and then she rushed out of the salon, Mr. Wilcox clearing the way through the crowd ahead of her. She hadn't been able to extract a vow from Emma; she would just have to trust the fates to watch over the little idiot.

Derora was pale and pinched, her swollen ankle propped up on a stack of pillows. At the sight of Tess, she ordered the fluttering Juniper out of her chambers.

"Are you all right?" Tess asked, standing beside the bed where her aunt was ensconced like an ailing queen. "What on earth happened?"

"I tripped on the stairs and fell," was Derora's composed, if slightly hushed, reply. "And, my dear, it couldn't have happened at a worse time!"

As far as Tess was concerned, there was no such thing as a good time to fall down a flight of stairs, but she sensed from her aunt's manner that it would be unwise to express that opinion or any other. "How can I help you?" she asked softly.

Derora smiled, reached out to clasp Tess's hand and squeezed it between both her own. "Dear child. Sometimes I'm too harsh with you, I know. I don't mean to be."

Tess simply waited, making no attempt to withdraw her hand from Derora's. Had there been word from the hospital, in Portland? Was Derora preparing her for bad news about her mother?

Derora let go of her hand and took up a folded newspaper from the bedclothes. "I have no choice but to enlist your help, Tess. There is five thousand dollars at stake, and time is of the essence—I'm sure it's only a matter of days or even hours before someone else sees this."

Tess took the newspaper, looked at it in confusion and then thunderstruck amazement. "Joel! That's Joel Shiloh!" she breathed, her eyes moving over the sketch.

"Then I'm right," sighed Derora. "I feared that I might have been mistaken."

Scanning the copy printed with the drawing, Tess knew a sinking sensation. She had been right, in her half-formed suspicion—Joel was not Joel at all. He was a Corbin. The name printed on the front of the Bible she'd seen in his wagon leaped into her mind. Keith Corbin.

She sank into the chair at Derora's bedside, her heart pounding. Why had he lied about his name? Why was he hiding from his family? Moreover, why were they so anxious to find him that they would offer such a staggering sum of money for word of his whereabouts?

"We need that money, Tess," Derora said, in quiet, determined tones. "Frankly, I didn't intend to share it, but now I must have your help."

Tess let the newspaper lie in her lap, her hands folded over it and trembling. "Y-You plan to collect this reward?"

"Of course I do! Five thousand dollars is a great deal

of money, Tess. Think of the care you could provide for your dear mother, with your share of it. You could even settle in Portland, find yourself some sort of employment there, and be near her—"

"But J-Joel must have some reason for evading these people. It must be a very good reason—"

"What do I care what his reasons are? I could get away from this rough town, from this roominghouse. I could travel, make a new life for myself!"

Tess lowered her head. Derora had been paying for her sister's care in that Portland hospital all this time, in lieu of paying Tess full wages. What would happen to Olivia if Derora no longer sent those monthly bank drafts? "M-My share would be enough to keep Mother, to pay for her care?"

"I will give you half the money, Tess. Twenty-five hundred dollars should keep her for a good long time and allow you to settle yourself in very nice circumstances in the bargain."

Tess's throat was tight. What a choice this was. She could abandon her mother to God knew what fate, or she could sell out the first man she had ever loved. Oh, yes, she loved Keith Corbin, loved him fully. Hopelessly. She guessed she had from the moment she'd first seen him. "What would you have me do?" she whispered.

"Just this. Go to the telegraph office and force them to open up—I don't care what you have to tell them, just so you get them to send a wire to this Adam Corbin person, tonight. There isn't a moment to spare, Tess. It won't be long before someone else sees one of these advertisements and recognizes our friend, 'Joel.'"

"S-Suppose Keith's family wants to hurt him—suppose—"

"That's his problem," said Derora, with a sigh of resignation. "Do as I tell you, Tess—for my sake and for your mother's."

Tess rose out of her chair, carrying one of the newspapers under her arm, walking blindly toward the door. The last time she had visited her mother—it had been nearly a year now—Olivia hadn't even known her. The woman's mental state was such that she could only stare vacantly; she did not feed herself, she did not speak, she did not react to the speech of others. How could Olivia survive outside that clean hospital with its kindly staff?

"Hurry," prompted Derora, and Tess stepped out of the car and onto the little wrought iron porch. It was dark now, and frogs and crickets were singing their spring time songs.

Tess went to the stable, wheeled her bicycle out, put the newspaper into the wicker basket affixed to the handlebars. Send a message. She was to knock at the door of the telegraph office until someone answered, and then she was to send a message. . . .

There were tears pouring down her face by the time she reached the moonlit road. Perhaps that was why Tess went the wrong way, why she headed out of town, not toward the telegraph office, but in the direction of the peddler's camp.

It was very late and he was sitting by the campfire, just staring into the flames, his bowler hat at his side.

"Mr. Corbin?"

Broad shoulders stiffened, he turned his head swiftly.

Was it Tess's unexpected appearance that jolted him that way, or was it the sound of his real name? She didn't know, didn't care.

Instantly, Joel—no, she must remember that he was Keith, not Joel—was on his feet, towering over Tess, his whole body tense. Wary. "What are you doing here?" he bit out, and she couldn't tell whether he was angry or just surprised.

The tears she had managed to control during the ride out into the country—of which she had almost no memory—were sliding down her face again as she extended the newspaper. "Read for yourself."

Keith took the tabloid and bent closer to the firelight, in order to scan the large advertisement. A hoarse swear word was his comment.

"My aunt sent me to w-wire your family. She wants the m-money. . . ."

He stood very still. "And you double-crossed her. For me. Why did you do that, Tess?"

Tess dashed at one of her cheeks, but the gesture did little good, for the tears kept coming. "I don't know," she said, finally. "God help me, I don't know. My mother—my poor mother—"

Keith drew her close, held her as though she were a child. "What about your mother, shoebutton?" he asked. "What about her?"

Tess could not give an answer.

Chapter Five

IT TOOK ONLY MINUTES TO GATHER UP THE POT AND KETTLE he'd used to prepare his supper, to hitch the mule to his wagon, to put out the campfire. During those minutes, Keith Corbin damned the two brothers he would have died for. Good God, why didn't they just leave him alone? They were both intelligent men; surely they knew that when he was ready, he would come back.

He paused, aware of Tess, more aware of her, in fact, than he had ever been of any other woman. She was standing beside the wagon, watching him, the bright moonlight giving her a luminous, angelic appearance.

"I want to go with you," she said.

Keith had been checking the mule's harness; the warm, dusty hide of the beast rippled beneath the palms of his hands. "No."

"I can't go back," she insisted. "Aunt Derora wants that reward money. Once she knows that I've betrayed her, she'll throw me out. I won't have a job. My mother—my mother will—"

Keith turned to face the urchin-child squarely, again silently cursing his brothers. For two cents, he'd let them find him. And when they did, he'd break their necks.

A half-smile curved his lips. It would serve Adam and Jeff right if they paid five thousand dollars to have their asses kicked. "Tell me about your mother," he said aloud.

Tess had managed to regain her composure; her shoulders were straight, her chin high. She hadn't worn any kind of wrap over her calico dress, and she was rubbing her upper arms with both hands in an attempt to keep warm. "She was an actress, in St. Louis. She was also the mistress of a man named Asa Thatcher, a lawyer. Very successful." She stopped and her face hardened; Keith saw, even in the relative darkness, a flash of rancor in her wonderful green-brown eyes. "One day, Mr. Thatcher—yes, if you're wondering, he was my father—decided that he didn't want to keep Mother and me anymore. He sent people to evict us from our house, and we came out here because we didn't have anywhere else to go.

"Mama was young and pretty, and she could have gone on being an actress, found a husband or at least another lover, but she didn't. She just faded and faded until one day Aunt Derora and I had to take her to P-Portland and put her in a hospital."

Keith ached, thinking of his own bright, beautiful mother, with her wicked wit and her outrageous political and moral opinions. He tried to imagine Katherine Corbin in an asylum and failed completely. "She's there still?" he asked, in a raspy whisper.

Tess swallowed visibly and nodded. She was shivering now, and Keith went to the rear of the wagon, got out a suit coat for her to wear. The way she looked with that oversized and obviously masculine garment draped over her shoulders made him ache inside.

She didn't say that she had risked her mother's welfare to help him, but, then, she didn't have to. Again he considered driving Tess to the telegraph office himself and then just sitting back and waiting for one or both of his older brothers to show up. And when they did—

But he didn't take to the idea; it was like a chess game, this situation. And if he let Adam and Jeff find him, he would be moving his king into check, so to speak. Letting them win. The fact that it had cost them five thousand dollars to do it would be of no comfort at all; that was pocket money to them. And even if he smashed their arrogant, aristocratic Corbin noses—a prospect he relished—they would still have found their little lost brother. It was that which rankled, when all was said and done.

And there was this moon-nymph. She had sacrificed practically all there was to sacrifice, in an effort to help him. How could he send her back to face her aunt's wrath and still live with his conscience?

Besides, if he were to be honest with himself—and he tried to be—Keith had to admit that he found the prospect of traveling with Tess more than appealing. Since leaving the boardinghouse, in fact, he'd done little but brood about her. And want her.

Did she know what would happen if they were alone together, on the road? Did she sense how badly he wanted her?

"Will you take me with you or not?" she demanded, her chin still up, her voice shaky.

Keith reminded himself that Tess believed in free love, that she even purported to practice it. She had given herself to men before him, and she would give herself to men after him, no doubt. So why shouldn't he avail himself to the pleasures her lush body promised?

Mingled with the desire that raged within him like an inferno was a cold, bitter anger stemming from the knowledge that he would be neither the first nor the last man to possess her.

"I'll take you to Portland," he found himself saying. "I've got to go there for supplies anyway."

Color pooled in her cheeks and then drained away, and her eyes widened. "My camera!" she breathed. "I left my camera in my room—"

"We'll go back for it, then," Keith offered, to his own amazement, and then he was putting that ridiculous bicycle of hers into the back of the wagon, lifting her into the seat.

"But my aunt—"

"It's late. She's probably asleep. You can get your

72

camera and whatever else you want and then we'll leave."

Portland. Was he crazy? Why had he offered to take her to Portland, of all places? Showing himself there was almost as foolhardy as turning up in Seattle or Port Hastings!

But Keith knew why he was taking Tess to Portland, despite the fact that it was one of Jeff's favorite harbors, a place where the Corbins were widely known. He had to risk losing the game, risk being recognized, because Tess had risked so much for him. Because her mother was there.

They reached the roominghouse within the hour, and it was, to all appearances, completely dark. Still, Tess seemed nervous, hesitant.

"She must suspect something by now," she breathed, her small hands knotted in her lap, her shoulders slumped beneath the suit coat Keith had loaned her. "She would expect me to wait for a reply from your family and then report to her."

"Do you want me to go inside with you, Tess?" He had not planned to make that particular offer, it just sprang to his lips.

She shook her head, drew a deep breath, and jumped nimbly down from the wagon seat. "You'll wait for me?"

For some reason, it hurt Keith that she would ask him that. His jawline tightened and he whispered, "Yes, damn it!"

Tess hesitated another moment and then turned and sprang over the gate, like some gangling boy. She was a shadow, scurrying up the walk, opening the door so quietly that Keith didn't hear it from the wagon.

In her bedroom, Tess looked out the window and saw what she had feared—a lamp flickering in the southern car, where her aunt's room was. Derora was waiting up, probably watching for any sign of her niece, no doubt suspecting betrayal already.

There was no time to pack all her clothes—Tess dared only to fill a small valise with a nightgown, some underthings, two practical dresses, and the photographs she had taken. She abandoned all but the one of Keith, taken beside his wagon, one of her mother, and one of Emma.

Emma! Where was Emma? She was supposed to spend the night here, Tess remembered suddenly, and the show on the riverboat had been over for hours. Where was that silly little monkey? Not, please God, with Roderick Waltam?

Tess sighed, clutching her camera and the valise, making her way quietly out of her room and down the dark stairs. Surely Emma had had the good sense to go home, where she belonged. She wouldn't have come here, to the roominghouse, because she'd been miffed with Tess. That was it. That had to be it.

Joel—no, Keith—was waiting just where Tess had left him. She felt a thrill of anticipation as she hurried toward him, a sensation of impending adventure. Which was odd considering the rashness of the whole situation.

He tucked her things beneath the wagon seat and smiled at her, his teeth catching the moon's light, and the expression in his eyes was at once mischievous and wary.

"Ready?" he asked.

"Do I have a choice?" she retorted, impatient to be gone.

"I guess not," he replied. And when they were outside of town again, on the road to Portland, he stopped just long enough to light the lamps on the sides of the wagon.

The light danced ahead of them on the crude, rutted road, like a golden specter, and Tess was suddenly very tired. Knowing better, she rested her head against the peddler's hard, sturdy shoulder all the same. And she slept.

It bothered Emma, the way Roderick kept scanning the salon with those wonderful brown eyes of his. She had a feeling that he was only half listening to her.

"I was married to an elephant for three years," she said, to test him. "We were very happy together."

"That's nice," Roderick muttered, looking annoyed and rather disappointed, too.

He was searching the salon for Tess, of course. Emma was all too used to that, men cozying up to her just so they could be close to her best friend, and she was sick of it. Maybe she wasn't as pretty as Tess, maybe she wasn't as bright, either. But she had better bosoms and rounder hips and she never went around with her hair flying in the breeze, like a hussy. She would make some man a good and fruitful wife.

Like this one, for instance. Emma imagined herself traveling with Roderick, keeping his costumes in order,

helping him to learn his lines and the lyrics to new
songs.

"Tess is gone," she said, watching Roderick's instant
reaction with a sort of bitter satisfaction. "She and that
peddler are eloping tonight, you know."

Roderick was as white as the alabaster urn Emma's
mother kept on the parlor piano. "No," he choked out.
"No, I didn't know—"

Emma smiled. Tess was going to kill her for this, but
that would be tomorrow or the next day, wouldn't it?
"In the family way," she confided, in a stage whisper,
warming to the lie because it was so deliciously outrageous. "There was simply no time to spare!"

"She didn't look—"

"Oh, but she is, you know," said Emma sagely.

"My God," said the actor. And then he visibly
reassembled himself; it was a fascinating process to
watch. He stood straighter. He smiled. And the color
flowed back into his handsome face. "What was your
name again?" he asked, attentive now.

Emma was pleased to tell him.

Toward dawn, they stopped. Still far from Portland—
it would take another two days to reach that city, by
Keith's calculations—they were also a good, safe distance from Simpkinsville.

Tess was sound asleep. She stirred slightly but did not
awaken when Keith lifted her down from the wagon
seat and carried her around to the back. There, he put
her in the bunk, struggled with the tangled blankets,
and finally tucked them in around her.

Looking down at her now, he found it almost impossible to believe that this was a woman who practiced

free love. She seemed so innocent, so small. So vulnerable.

Keith left the wagon abruptly. Making love to Tess Bishop was inevitable; he knew that he would, and soon. But, for now, he wanted to let her sleep. Wanted to go on pretending she was all that she seemed.

He built a fire, unhitched the mule, and tethered it where there was grass to graze upon, brought it water from the nearby creek and a ration of feed from the wagon.

He was brewing coffee and reflecting on life in general when Tess appeared, looking sleepy and flushed and more like a child than ever. Her calico dress was wrinkled; her hair fell in gleaming tumbles to her waist.

I love you, he thought. And then he caught himself. I don't. I loved Amelie. I will always love Amelie.

"Good morning," she yawned, putting one hand over her mouth. "Where are we?"

His mouth quirked, he knew he gave the appearance of idle amusement. Which was odd because inside he felt a sort of happy hysteria. "Oregon," he retorted.

Apparently she was one of those people who do not feel agreeable upon awakening. "I know that!" she snapped, sitting down on the upended chunk of wood he had set out for her, near the fire. "I meant, how far are we from Portland?"

"Two days." Some wicked part of his nature made him add, "And two nights."

She blushed and lowered her eyes, giving no answer.

"Do you really practice free love, Tess?" What made him ask that? Keith could have kicked himself.

Tess met his gaze; the color in her cheeks was metered by her heartbeat. "Yes," she said stubbornly.

"I think you're lying." He was grasping at straws. He knew that. Why had he brought this subject up in the first place?

Her lower lip trembled almost imperceptibly. She knew what was going to happen between them as well as he did, and it seemed to him that she was frightened by the prospect. Or was it merely that she found him wanting in some way, found him less appealing than previous lovers?

The idea was annoying.

"Well?" Keith prompted.

She looked away. "I don't want to talk about it. I'm hungry."

He got up, glad for something to do, and brought back hard bread and a couple of withered apples from the wagon.

Tess's delightful, annoying nose crinkled.

"You expected bacon and eggs?" he drawled, mad at her. "Welcome to the open road."

She made a face at him, but she ate her share of the bread and most of the apple with amazing appetite. That done, she went off into the bushes beside the creek and was gone so long that Keith had to pace to keep from going in search of her.

When Tess returned, her face was pink with cold and still moist from a dashing of creekwater and her hair was done up, too.

Keith glared at her, his fingers aching. And then, surprising himself as much as Tess, he strode over to her and unpinned her hair, so that it fell about her shoulders in shimmering waves and curls, catching the early morning sunlight, smelling of fresh air and wood-smoke and castile soap.

It seemed natural to kiss her, and he did, cautiously at first and then with a hunger that was so intense that it could not be denied. Tess swayed—or was it he that was unsteady? He couldn't tell.

The onslaught of emotion washing over Tess in the wake of that kiss was devastating, buckling her knees, causing her to waver dangerously. When Keith took his mouth from hers, it was as though he had taken some deep and integral part of her away, too. To keep for always.

"Good Lord," she breathed.

"My sentiments exactly," he replied. And then, without waiting for another moment to pass, he lifted Tess into his arms and carried her toward the wagon.

They both got inside somehow; Tess didn't remember the mechanics of it. She could barely breathe, after all, let alone think.

The interior of the wagon was shadowy. Keith closed the door, lit a lamp—the movements seemed almost simultaneous.

Tess was frightened, and yet she felt she'd been born for what was about to happen—whatever it was. Despite the unconventional home in which she'd been raised, despite the daring theater people who had been such frequent guests in Olivia Bishop's St. Louis town-house, despite the racy French novels she'd been allowed to read from a scandalously early age, Tess didn't know what to expect. Not beyond the most rudimentary basics, that is.

Keith approached her gently, tangled his fingers in her hair, kissed her again. This time his tongue made no fierce invasion; his lips were tentative upon hers. Cautious and warm.

"Tess," he said presently, in a distracted whisper. "Tess."

She shivered in his arms, wanting to give herself, not knowing how. But when his fingers came to the buttons of her prim pink calico dress, she closed her eyes and tilted her head back, tacitly willing.

"Tess?" he said again, and this time he was asking her permission.

"Yes," she whispered. "Oh, yes."

Keith opened her dress—or was he Joel? She couldn't remember. He was displacing her plain muslin camisole now, baring breasts that no man had ever dared to touch before.

"Open your eyes," he ordered gruffly.

Tess complied, but she was dazed, barely able to see.

"You are so beautiful, Tess. Do you know how beautiful you are?"

The words, spoken so softly that they were hardly audible, seemed to deepen the trance. Tess swayed on her feet, was both grateful and surprised when she felt herself being lowered to that narrow, rumpled bunk.

"Do you?" he persisted, and his mouth was near her nipple now—she could feel his breath there, seeking, warming, making the nubbin tighten to a buttonlike hardness.

Tess could not answer; everything within her was attuned to the fate of that one yearning nipple. The best she could manage was a soft, despairing groan.

Keith chuckled and took the pulsing morsel between gentle teeth.

A massive shiver of need shook Tess; she clasped

both hands behind the peddler's wheat-gold head to hold him close. She could not see clearly, though she was sure her eyes were open—the wagon seemed to be spinning in some unseen storm.

"Joel—Joel—"

He was suckling at her breast now, drawing gently, nibbling. "Keith," he corrected her. "Do you want me to stop, Tess?"

"N-No—"

Keith progressed to her other breast, kissing it. Circling the nipple with his tongue.

Silver flecks seemed to fill that shoddy little wagon, dazzling Tess—were they a part of that strange storm? Did they come from within her, or from without?

"Ooooh," she moaned.

He took away her dress, her camisole, her drawers. She was conscious of that, and yet it seemed to be happening to another person, not to herself. And then he was naked, too; his clothes had dissolved away, become part of the silvery mist.

"T-Take me," she said.

"Not yet," was the rasped answer.

And then she was losing her grasp on him, he was moving down her body, kissing his way over planes of satin, searching for silk. Finding it.

He sought the hidden rosebud and found that, too, making it blossom.

Tess gave a great cry of tenderness and fear, he soothed her with his hands, stroking her smooth thighs, her hips, her waist, and ribcage. And while his hands tamed her, his mouth turned her to a wild thing, writhing, making a low, whining sound in her throat.

He was her lover, he was her tormenter. He held her

earthbound, he made her hips fly in a savage bid for heaven. He kissed her, he feasted upon her until a terrible, wonderful quivering began within her, culminating in a tender explosion that left Tess Bishop forever changed.

Her fingers were limp in his hair, her breathing was ragged, her flesh was moist. He nipped the inside of her thigh gently, then moved up her body again and kissed her.

He entered her with a motion that was at once swift and tender, and Tess cried out because there was a stinging sort of pain.

Keith stiffened upon her, his eyes hot with passion and anger and shock. Lest he withdraw, she clutched at him, lifted and lowered her hips as she had when he'd been pleasuring her moments before. Every instinct demanded that she keep him near.

There was a certain satisfaction in the moan the motion wrung from him; he tilted his head back, closed his eyes. His throat worked. "You—little—witch—"

Tess smiled sleepily. She had him now, she could control Keith Corbin as surely as he had controlled her seconds before. The pain was gone, replaced by a feeling of lush need, and she continued to feed the sweet torment she saw in his face.

"Oh—God—" he muttered, his features taut now with the effort to deny what his body was demanding. "Tess—"

Slowly, smoothly, taught by instinct and guided by her own piercing pleasure, Tess moved beneath him. To her bedazzled delight, his powerful body was now in submission to hers, following her lead. He groaned again and began to move as she moved. And he caused her to need as he needed, something she had not anticipated.

Their bodies were entwined, straining now in some desperate quest. Tess's triumph was a brutal thing, shaking her very soul, flinging her high with the raw power of an angry sea, leaving her to weep in wonder as she fell from heights she had never before imagined.

"Joel!" she cried, as she soared and as she tumbled.

A moment, no, a fraction of a moment, later, his steely frame tensed with a violent magnificence; he groaned as if in a fever and shuddered upon Tess, spilling sacred warmth inside her. But the name he called was not her own. No, it had sounded like "Emily."

It was a sudden wounding, all the more brutal because of the tender, sweeping glory that had gone before. Tess's eyes filled with tears, blinding her as the silvery storm had blinded her before.

He lay upon her, gasping, unable to rise, for some moments. But she could feel his anger.

She wanted to scream that she hated him, but she could not manage so much as a whisper, for her throat had closed tight, keeping in the hurt.

Presently, Keith gathered the strength to raise himself, to withdraw. His breathing was ragged, his flesh, like Tess's, was damp from the exertion. As though begrudging her so much as one kind word, he glared at her and then turned away to dress.

He wrenched on his trousers, his socks, his boots. Tess thought his shirt would tear in two, so great was the force with which he pulled it on. And still she could not move, could not speak.

He turned, buttoning his shirt, his azure eyes flashing

with quiet disdain, his jawline set. It was as though by glaring at Tess he could make her disappear.

She could not bear the expression on his face and lowered her eyes. She saw the ring then, the gold wedding band hanging from a chain around his muscular, sun-browned neck. Married. Dear God in heaven, he was married!

Suddenly, Tess's voice was back. "You bastard!" she screamed, bolting upright in the bunk, reaching for her own camisole, her drawers, her dress, all of which had been tossed onto the floor. Her gestures were feverish, frantic, and awkward.

Keith didn't even attempt to button his gaping shirt, cover his gold-matted chest or that damnable ring. He put his hands on his hips and watched Tess coldly as she wriggled and fretted her way into her clothes.

"How could you?" she hissed, watching him through a mist of angry, wounded tears. "How could you?"

His contempt was tangible in that tiny wagon, almost an entity in its own right. "How could I what?" he allowed at last, in a fierce rasp.

Tess's teeth were chattering now, even though she wasn't cold. No, if anything, she was burning up. With shame, with revulsion, with pain. "How could you betray your wife?!" she sobbed, horrified at what he had done, what she had done, what they had done together.

"My wife is dead," he answered, quietly ferocious. And then he was opening the wagon door, jumping to the ground. The door slammed into the framework and then creaked accusingly on its rusty hinges.

Tess no longer tried to dress, to think, to understand. She covered her face with both hands and allowed herself the luxury of a noisy cry. She sobbed. She cursed. She wailed.

Even so, she could hear Keith outside, carrying on a rage of his own. The mule brayed repeatedly. The man bellowed a series of senseless epithets, and something made of metal clanged against the side wall of the wagon.

Tess was sure it was the dishpan. The same dishpan this maniac had flung at God only two days before. At God! She was alone with a madman, on a little traveled road, and there was no going back, no escaping.

And, remembering that she had given herself to that madman, writhing and tossing like a wanton all the while, Tess threw back her head and gave a shriek of fury that silenced both Keith Corbin and the mule.

Chapter Six

HE WAS STOMPING AROUND THE CAMP IN A LITTLE-BOY fury, finding the harnesses and hurling them in the direction of the mule, grasping the coffeepot and burning his fingers on the handle. Despite her wounded pride, Tess felt a mischievous sort of tenderness as she watched him.

"Don't jump in the creek," she advised, as Keith cursed and shook his seared hand in the air.

He seemed to forget his injury then. How still he stood, watching Tess, his eyes a pale and molten blue. "Why?" he rasped.

"What do you mean, 'why'? It's foolish to leap into

icy streams—I would have thought you'd learned that from the last time."

Keith's jaw was rigid and his eyes flashed. Apparently her reference to the day they'd met had not lightened the moment. "I don't make a practice of deflowering virgins, Miss Bishop," he said coldly. "Why the hell did you let me think you—"

"I wanted you to see me as a woman, not a girl," she answered reasonably, approaching him now, taking his hurt hand in her own, bending her head to examine the damage. It was miniscule.

"Did it ever occur to you that you were playing with fire, as the saying goes?"

She looked up at him then, impishly. "I'm not the one who got burned," she pointed out.

"That remains to be seen, doesn't it?" he countered immediately, and though he made no move to withdraw his hand, his mood was still unfriendly. Distant. "Suppose you're pregnant?"

Tess was terrified by the prospect, but she was damned if she was going to let this rounder know that. "My mother was never married," she reminded him. "I've lived in unconventional circumstances from infancy." She paused, orchestrated a shrug. "If I had to raise a child alone, I guess I could do it."

"Your logic has one glaring flaw," he said, bending close, his imperious nose not even an inch from Tess's. "The child in question would be mine as well as yours. Do you think I want my son or daughter raised by a free lover?"

Maybe she was an actress, like her mother. In any event, Tess managed to hide the pain his words caused her and even smile. "Maybe Mrs. Hollinghouse-Stone didn't convert me, but you did," she said, knowing that she was galling him and glad of it. "I liked what happened in that wagon a few minutes ago. I liked it very much."

"That was obvious!" Keith bellowed. "Don't you know anything? Virgins are supposed to weep for their lost virtue, not come right out and say they liked it, for God's sake!"

Tess shrugged again. Now that she had the emotional upper hand, it was easy to overcome her pain and her injured pride and goad Keith Corbin as he deserved. "I plan to practice it from now on," she said, delighting in the stricken rage that moved in his maddening, magnificent face. "Portland is a big city, and I suppose there will be all kinds of opportunities—"

He grasped her shoulders, gave her a hard shake, abruptly let go again. A flicker in the sky-blue eyes indicated that he was wise to what she was doing. "You can plan on practicing free love between here and there, at least," he said.

Tess's mouth dropped open; it was a moment before she could regain her composure. If ever there was a time to change a subject, that was it. "Tell me about Emily."

"Who?"

A flush of remembered shock tingled its way up Tess's neck and into her face. Nothing except her mother's swift slide into madness had ever stricken her the way the sight of that wedding ring had, the way his cry of another woman's name had. "Your wife," she said. "You called her name when—when—you called her name!"

Keith turned away, and his shoulders tensed beneath his shirt. "No."

Tess rounded him, looked up into his face. "Yes," she argued. "I told you about my mother and everything else. It's only fair that you tell me about your wife. And while you're at it, Mr. Joel Shiloh-Keith Corbin, you can just explain why your family is so desperate to find you that they'd offer a reward like that!"

"Get in the wagon," he said, avoiding her eyes.

"No. Not until you answer me."

"Fair enough," he said, striding off toward the wagon, where he proceeded to hitch up the now-nervous mule.

Surely he couldn't intend to forsake her, out here in the middle of nowhere? Tess became so incensed at this thought that she picked up her skirts and marched over to where he was working, the muscles in his arms and shoulders moving in jerky, furious motions.

"You would desert me here, after what you just did?" she demanded.

"Desert you? Lady, I'd like to kill you."

Tess withdrew a step. Then she realized that this man, for all his apparent madness, would never kill anyone. There was a fundamental goodness inside him, a deep if reluctant sort of integrity that set him apart from every man she had ever known. "Tell me about Emily," she insisted.

Keith did not look at her. He went so far as to stoop and pass beneath the mule's belly to stand on the other side of the beast. "Her name wasn't Emily," he said, with a hoarse sort of tenderness that left a scar deep in

Tess's heart. "It was Amelie. She was killed moments after we were married."

Tess swallowed hard, hurting for his loss even though she had never felt more jealous. "I'm so sorry," she whispered, and it was the truth. "How did it happen?"

Keith stopped then; bleak blue eyes pierced Tess over the mule's back. "There was an explosion. Somebody had laid charges of dynamite inside the church. The ceremony was outside—if it hadn't been, everyone there would have died. The bell—the bell struck Amelie and she was killed."

Tess put one hand over her mouth and turned away for a moment as an album of horrible images flipped through her mind. "Dear God."

"There is no God," Keith said coldly, and the subject was closed.

They traveled through the morning in silence, coming to a small town at midday. Keith stopped the wagon on the main street, which was little more than a logging trail, and proceeded to sell bottles of laudanum and castor oil and hair dressing with an exuberance that stunned Tess, considering his earlier mood. He drew people from every part of that tiny community, people of all sizes and shapes and ages. Those who had money spent it happily.

Tess watched and listened, wondering all the while. Peddlers were a gregarious lot, as a rule—they had to be if they were going to earn any kind of living. But Keith Corbin spoke with an authority that went beyond that; he led easily, deftly, as though it were a game to him.

"Where did you go to school, anyway?" Tess asked, when most of the medicines had been sold and they were sharing a hearty restaurant luncheon on the proceeds.

He smiled at her, reaching across the checkered café tablecloth for the salt shaker. "Oxford," he replied blithely.

"Oxford?!" Tess could barely believe it. The piece of pork chop she'd just stabbed with her fork hung in midair. "The one in—"

"England," Keith supplied. Damn him, he knew he'd presented her with another mystery, and he was enjoying her puzzlement.

"Why do you sell medicine, for heaven's sake, if you went to Oxford?"

Keith held up a spoonful of mashed potatoes. "To eat," he answered.

Tess was wild to know more, to know everything. But she realized that Keith wasn't going to tell her, and she wasn't going to beg. She shrugged and concentrated on finishing her meal.

Derora Beauchamp was quietly, coldly furious. Though her ankle throbbed every step of the way, she made her way up the stairway and into Tess's room.

Sure enough, her niece's best dresses and camera were gone.

A tearful Juniper appeared in the doorway, wringing her hands and a corner of her apron into a tangle. "She ain't here?" the woman mourned.

"Juniper, Tess obviously is not here." Derora glared speculatively up at the ceiling. "She's run off with that good-looking peddler," she mused. But then she got a hold of herself and met her housekeeper's eyes. "Did you send the wire?"

Juniper nodded. "Yes, ma'am, I did."

"There may still be a chance of finding them," Derora pondered aloud. "Has there been a reply yet?"

"No, ma'am. The boy said he'd bring it by when it came. Mrs. Beauchamp—"

Derora's ankle hurt, and she was, thanks to that ungrateful snippet of a niece of hers, out a staggering sum of money. "What, for heaven's sake?" she snapped impatiently.

"There's a man downstairs, askin' for Miss Olivia."

"Did you tell him she isn't here anymore?"

Juniper shook her head.

"Oh, bother," sighed Derora. She did get tired of dealing with Olivia's persistent suitors. After all, the woman was mad as a hatter. Why did they even want her, given that she could do nothing, nothing at all, besides stare into space?

Limping down the stairway, spurning Juniper's anxious attempts to help, Derora considered her sister. The dear fool, even as a child she'd been odd, Olivia had. Claiming she could talk to Uncle Henry, see and touch him, and this years after he'd died, for pity sake. Going mad over one man, when hundreds wanted her.

She reached the bottom of the stairs and curved one arm around the newel post, to steady herself. Asa Thatcher hadn't even been handsome—rich, yes, but not handsome. From his photographs, which Olivia had mooned over for hours on end, Derora would have called him homely, in fact.

A tall, cadaverously thin man stood near the parlor fireplace, wearing a somber but well-made suit. His arms appeared too long, his hands were positively matted with dark hair to match the thick thatch on his head.

"May I help you?" Derora ventured, testy from the pain in her ankle and the loss of the reward the Corbin family was offering for the return of their lost sheep.

The man turned and Derora knew a moment of jarring surprise. Bleak brown eyes studied her from beneath bushy black brows, set on a gaunt, almost skeletal face. Dear heaven, but that fellow did resemble—who did he resemble?

"I seek Miss Olivia Bishop, please," he said, "My name is—"

Derora recognized him and wondered how on earth such a man could have fathered a beauty like Tess, won such lasting devotion from her scatter-brained but devastatingly attractive sister. "Asa Thatcher," Derora broke in.

A slight nod was offered, followed by a weary sigh that suggested constant, fathomless pain. "I have traveled a good many miles, madam," he said. Abraham Lincoln, that was who he looked like. Abraham Lincoln. "Tell me, please, where I might find my—where I might find Miss Bishop."

Derora bore no particular rancor toward this man. She felt that Olivia, by dallying with a married man, had gotten pretty much what she deserved. But she took a certain pleasure in answering, "I'm afraid I have distressing news for you, Mr. Thatcher. My poor, dear sister has been confined to an asylum for some years now."

Asa looked as though he'd been struck a shattering blow. He braced himself against the mantelpiece with one arm and lowered his head for a moment. Dear Lord in heaven. What had bright, laughing, beautiful Olivia seen in this dreary fellow?

"Where?" he rasped finally. "Where is this—this place where they keep my Livie?"

The emotion in his voice gave Derora pause. She had always assumed that he had toyed with her sister, used her. Not once had she considered the possibility that he might return the tiresome sentiment that Olivia had borne for him. "The hospital is called Harbor Haven, and it is in Portland. I can give you the address if you'll give me a moment to look it up in my—my accounts."

Asa Thatcher was no fool, that was clear. He caught Derora's implication, subtle as it had been. "You've paid for Livie's care, then?"

No need to mention that Tess had, in effect, worked for the money. After what that little chit had done, why make her look good to her neglectful father? "Yes," she said evenly, "and I don't mind telling you that that care has been costly indeed, Mr. Thatcher. And then, of course, there was your daughter—"

The homely man brightened visibly; the mention of Tess seemed to renew him somehow. "My daughter. She is here, at least?"

"I regret to tell you that Tess has—has left us."

Asa swayed, paled. "Left you?" he echoed, in hollow tones.

"Oh, my dear man—I'm sorry." Derora hastened to approach her guest, take his skinny arm in her own. "I didn't mean that our Tess had departed this earthly life! She's well." She maneuvered the shaken man toward a chair, into which he fell gratefully. "I merely meant to say that—well—she's run off. With a man."

Asa covered his scarecrow face with one gaunt, bony hand, and his sigh was a hoarse one. "Does she love this fellow?"

Derora went to the sideboard and took a decanter of brandy from among the porcelain shepherdesses and framed photographs that cluttered its top. She poured a generous portion and handed the glass to her guest. With a sigh of her own, she sank into a chair facing Mr. Thatcher's. "Tess has—will you forgive me—a way with men. She quite bewitched this peddler and—"

"Peddler?!" rasped Asa Thatcher, with startling spirit. "My Tess, my beautiful Tess, has taken up with a peddler?"

Derora lowered her head to hide her smile, entwined her hands, ladylike, in her lap. "I'm afraid so, Mr. Thatcher." When she looked up, her eyes were filled with tears and her smile was gone, for Olivia was not the only natural actress in the Bishop family. "As God is my witness, sir," she choked out brokenly, "I tried to carry on after Olivia—after our sweet Olivia collapsed, but—being alone myself—being poor—"

"I understand, dear lady," Asa Thatcher comforted her gruffly. "I understand. Burdens that should have been mine were thrust upon you. I have only myself to thank for the state of my family."

And me to thank for the roofs over their heads and the bread in their mouths, Derora thought fiercely, though, of course, she would not say such a thing aloud. "We all do what we must, Mr. Thatcher," she said softly. "We all do what we must."

Asa had already downed his brandy; now he thrust his skeletal frame out of his chair with determined energy. "And I must gather my sheep," he said. "Tess was always close to her mother. It would be my guess that, in finding the hospital where Livie stays, I'll also find my daughter."

Derora thought quickly. "You'll—you'll give them both my love, won't you?"

It was just the right measure of tender concern, of long-suffering devotion. Asa Thatcher smiled and reached into his suitcoat for his wallet. He gave Derora a respectable sum of money for her care of Tess and promised to wire his bank in St. Louis for more, this last meant to compensate her for the cost of Olivia's confinement.

Derora deliberately widened her dark eyes. "Oh, but it's too much, Mr. Thatcher," she lied. "Olivia is my sister, after all—it was my duty—"

Asa was already on his way to the door. "The duty was surely mine, dear lady. How I wish that I had undertaken to fulfill it more wisely."

It took all Derora's self-control not to laugh and crow and count through that thick wad of currency again and again, to remain circumspect and dignified. But if her composure was false, her curiosity was not. "Mr. Thatcher, you love my sister very much, don't you? Pray, tell me why you turned her and Tess out so—so abruptly."

Thin shoulders moved in a broken, despondent sigh, memories filled the sunken eyes. "My late wife did that, with the help of our daughter, Millicent. I had no knowledge of it until it was too late."

"You mean, they sent Tess and Olivia away? It wasn't your doing?"

"I would sooner have parted with the breath in my

lungs than given up my Livie or our little girl. But I was away from St. Louis on business, and it was regrettably easy, apparently, for my wife's attorneys to convince Livie that the order came from me. When I returned from New York"—Pain, real and ferocious, moved in his plain-featured face—"they were gone."

"The letters," Derora remembered suddenly. "Olivia wrote you letters, and so did Tess."

"I received no letters," Asa said flatly, and Derora believed him. "It was only after my wife's death—a scant two weeks past now—that I found out what had happened. My daughter, Millicent, had fallen in love, and this worthy emotion had sparked some pity in her, some sense of compassion. She told me that she and her mother had intercepted the letters and burned them."

"My God," breathed Derora, remembering how Olivia had despaired, how Tess had hated.

Asa took her hand, squeezed it. "I must go now and find my dear Olivia. Thank you, madam, for your unfailing kindness throughout."

Derora remembered the bills clenched in her hand and beamed. "You are most welcome, Mr. Thatcher," she replied, with the utmost sincerity. "And God speed you on your journey."

Thatcher smiled his forlorn smile, and then he was gone.

Juniper stood, wide-eyed, in the dining room doorway. "That man was the spittin' image of Abe Lincoln!" she cried.

Derora lifted the bills, fanned them out in front of her face to be properly admired. "How would you like to own your own roominghouse, Juniper?" she sang.

"Five dollars down and five dollars a week and, my dear, this dreary place is yours!"

"Sold!" said Juniper, with feeling.

Tess did not begin to worry about the night to come until they were well away from the little town where Keith had sold virtually his entire stock and making camp in a verdant, wildflower-strewn clearing beside a pond.

The sky looked angry and too dark for a spring evening; there was a storm coming. The mule, tethered where he could graze and drink from the pond at will, was fitful despite the copse of wild birch trees that would shelter him.

Tess leaned against the wagon, her arms folded, her eyes wide and wary, watching Keith lay rocks in a circle, gather sticks, and start a fire.

"Are you going to help me, woman," he demanded, with a good-natured sort of impatience, "or just stand there gawking?"

"It's going to rain," Tess fretted, glancing ruefully up at the sky.

Keith shrugged, still grinning. Damn him, he knew what was worrying her, but he offered no reassurance. Oh, no. He just passed her, leering a bit as he went, and climbed into the back of the wagon. After a noisy search, he came out with a strip of canvas wound around four long wooden poles.

Smiling to himself, he proceeded to set up a crude sort of canopy that would keep the fire from going out, should the sky make good on its promise.

"What's so funny?" Tess demanded, tired of his smug smirk. There was a limit, after all.

"You are," he answered expansively, grasping one of the poles that held up the canopy and giving it a shake to test it. "Drag a log over here, will you? We're going to need more wood."

"Drag a—"

"Well, you don't expect me to do everything, do you? You've got to pay your way in this world, Tess. Pull your own weight, as it were." His blue eyes swept over her, appreciatively mischievous. "Such as it is, anyway," he reflected, at length.

"If you think, for one minute, Mr. Keith Corbin, that I am going to—"

Keith folded his arms, the bowler hat at a cocky angle on his cocky head, his azure eyes twinkling. "I thought you believed in free love. Don't you want to save the world, Miss Bishop? Don't you want to end war and hunger and poverty by giving yourself to me?"

Tess colored richly; she hated herself for blushing but she couldn't help it. "How would that end war and hunger and poverty?"

"Exactly my question. But that's what you free lovers believe, isn't it? Here's your chance to strike a blow for universal peace. Are you going to miss it?"

"You lecher. You're not concerned with 'universal peace'! You're concerned with your own p-personal satisfaction!"

"Aren't we all?" he countered, and though he didn't move, it was as though he had shrugged.

Tess wanted to claw his eyes out. "I'm not," she said loftily.

"Nevertheless, Miss Bishop, I'm going to make love to you tonight. I'm going to—"

"You're not going to do anything to me!"

He only laughed.

And because Tess knew that her body would override her will if that insufferable man so much as kissed her, she turned and flounced off into the trees to find the log he'd asked for earlier. Maybe the effort of chopping it into firewood would exhaust him.

She found a fallen birch bough, and, as she dragged it back toward the camp, Tess reflected, huffing and puffing, that it might be she who was exhausted, and not Keith.

Sure enough, he chopped the huge limb into suitable pieces without even working up a sweat. Tess sat bleakly under the canopy, watching him while she stirred the stew they'd bought at the restaurant in town.

After washing up with disturbing industry—he removed his shirt if not that insufferable hat—at the edge of the pond, Keith joined Tess at the fire and sat down on the ground, cross-legged like an Indian.

He ate his share of the warmed-over stew with good appetite, his eyes seldom straying from Tess's slightly pinkened face.

"What more can a man ask?" he finally observed, philosophically, setting his metal bowl aside and settling back against an empty laudanum crate with a sigh. "A snapping fire. A hot meal. And a woman. What else could I want?"

For her part, Tess wanted a hot bath, a shampoo, and perhaps a cup of tea, but she mentioned none of those things. After all, it wasn't Keith's fault that she was without such comforts; forsaking them had been her own idea.

"You definitely have a fire," she pointed out, determined to keep her temper, "and you've had a hot meal.

100

But you will not have a woman, Keith Corbin. Not this one, at least."

"Why not?" He was still teasing her, but there was a gentleness in his voice now.

Tess couldn't help it; tears slid down her cheeks, tears of weariness, confusion, and hurt. "Because I'm sore," she said honestly. "I was, after all, a virgin."

The azure eyes, so mischievous before, seemed to caress her now, to console her. "Why didn't you stop me, Tess? Why didn't you tell me?"

Tess lowered her head, dashed away the foolish tears. "I guess I wanted—I wanted you to take me."

Keith made a sound of gentle exasperation, but no move to touch her. He seemed to sense that she could not have dealt with that, not at that moment, anyway. "You know something, shoebutton? You're the most confusing woman I've ever met. When you could have told me that you were a virgin, you didn't. And now, when it would preserve your pride to say I forced you—"

Tess met his gaze instantly. "But you didn't force me! I—I was willing—"

"Most women wouldn't admit that." Now, he moved closer to her, set the bowler hat on the top of her head, smoothed her hair with an unbelievably gentle hand. "Tell me just one thing, Tess. When you said that you liked making love, were you just trying to get my goat, or did you mean it?"

Again, she averted her eyes. "I meant it," she admitted. "It was—well—do you think it would be like that with any man?"

He slid an arm around her shoulders, held her in a comforting, undemanding way. His shirt was not fully buttoned, though he had had the decency to put it on again after washing, and she could feel the warm, hair-roughened hardness of his chest against her shoulder. "I hope not," he said, in a faraway voice.

The sky rumbled above them, threatening mayhem, and a cool wind made the birchwood fire dance in its circle of stones.

"I do wish I could take a bath," Tess wailed softly, despairingly, for want of something better to say.

Keith laughed gruffly and hugged her. "Then a bath you shall have," he said.

Tess watched him in love and wariness and wonder as he filled a large kettle with pond-water and then set it over the fire to heat. What an enigma this man was, shouting at her, teasing her unmercifully, baiting her. And then going to such effort to provide her with hot water for a bath.

It was going to be awful, giving him up, saying goodbye to him. It was going to be impossible. And yet, when they reached Portland, Tess knew she would have to do just that.

Chapter Seven

ASA THATCHER HAD HAD ALMOST ALL THE SHOCKS HE could bear during the past hour—his beloved Olivia in an insane asylum, his Tess cavorting with a common peddler! Asa was not a comely man, but he was a wise one, and he knew the state of his family was a shame that belonged at his own doorstep and no other. With one clenched and weary fist, he struck the steamboat's railing in what was, for him, a wild gesture of anguish.

There had been no trains leaving that sleepy little Oregon town that afternoon, not even the one he'd arrived on. And so he had bought passage on this vessel, the *Columbia Queen,* the craft was called. It was a gaudy showboat, but that didn't matter to Asa. No, all he cared about was reaching Portland as soon as possible.

The captain, who was something of a showman in the bargain, had assured him that they would put into port in that coastal city early the next morning.

Asa sighed, scanning the river—it was the color of worn jade—and the rich timberlands that edged it. What a fool he'd been all these years, taking Olivia and Tess for granted, staying in a marriage that had made both him and his wife miserable. Please God, if he could reach his Livie, if he could have a second chance with her—

There was some kind of ballyhoo going on on the ship's ramp, and Asa turned, mildly curious, to see what was happening. A young woman was sobbing that she'd been besmirched, used; it was all very dramatic. But it was her tall and handsome swain that gave Asa pause. Was that—? But no, it couldn't be?

It was. It was Rod.

Asa considered and then approached his son. Truly, this was a day for surprises.

"My papa will make you marry me!" wailed the girl, a small, plump, red-headed bundle of outrage and betrayed virtue. "You can't just sail away from what you've done, Roderick Waltam!"

Asa sighed. So he was still up to his old tricks, was Rod. And using his mother's maiden name. "Asa Thatcher, Jr.," had never been good enough for him—he'd amended it to Asa Thatcher II while at Princeton and that hadn't satisfied him, either. Finally, he'd dubbed himself "Roderick," sometimes retaining his rightful surname of Thatcher, sometimes calling himself Waltam.

"Rod?"

He turned, faced his father, speechless with surprise. Color moved up the handsome face inherited from the more comely Waltams, faded away again to a striking sort of pallor. "Father?"

The steamer's whistle blew, and, having no real choice, the young lady stormed down the ramp to the shoreline.

"My papa will find you!" she screamed, from the riverbank. "Mark my words, Roderick Waltam—"

Her voice faded away into silence as Asa Jr. and Asa Sr. stood on the slippery deck of that riverboat, staring at each other.

"Mother is—" Rod began, hoarsely, after some considerable time.

Asa took his son's arm, ushered him back to the railing, where they could talk as the steamer moved out into the river in a graceful arc. "She died two weeks ago," he said, when the time was right.

Rod was recovering himself. "How did you find me?" he managed to ask.

"It was an accident," Asa confessed, in his straightforward way. "But I'm glad of it. That girl back there—"

Incredibly, Rod grinned. "Emma. Isn't she something? I've never met anyone quite like her."

Asa bit back a lecture on the proper treatment of women. Who was he to talk, when he had driven Livie to madness by his own indecisiveness? And Tess—well, God knew what would happen to Tess.

Rod watched the distant figure that was Emma—she was like a furious little mudhen, pacing the riverbank, waving one fist in the air—until she and the town disappeared from view. And it seemed to Asa that his son bore a certain fondness for the girl.

"Mother suffered?" the younger man asked, at great length, his expression serious again.

"No," Asa was relieved to answer. "She died very suddenly, in her sleep. You might have written home once or twice, Asa—we were worried about you."

The flawless face hardened. "My name is Rod," he pointed out. "And I wanted nothing further to do with any of you, so why should I have written? You cared for nothing but your work and that mistress of yours, whoever she was. And Mother and Millicent spent their days trying to find her and destroy her."

Asa sighed and braced himself against the railing, suddenly weary almost beyond bearing. Suppose, after all this, he could not reach Olivia with his love? Suppose she could not or would not become her old self?

"Who was she?" Roderick asked grudgingly.

"An actress," Asa answered. "Her name was—is— Olivia Bishop." Now, he met his son's angry eyes. "I love her very much, Rod. She bore me a child."

Rod was white as parchment; Asa had not expected the news to be quite that much of a shock, all things considered. "Bishop," he muttered. And then he added, more to himself than to Asa, "No. It couldn't be."

Asa gestured toward the town; only the lumbermill, with its screaming saws and log booms, was visible now.

106

"She came here, my Livie, after your mother and sister drove her out. Here to this very town."

"Her child," Rod gasped out. "Your child—"

Asa could smile at the thought of his daughter; it felt good to tell someone about her. To speak of her proudly. "Tess," he began. "Rod, you'll like her. She's—"

Rod was grasping the railing in white-knuckled hands and looking as though he might swoon right to the deck with all the drama of an old maid trapped in an opium den. "My God!" he breathed.

It seemed to Asa that his son was overreacting to the news; after all, Rod was a grown man now. Certainly old enough to understand that men sometimes had mistresses and sometimes fathered illegitimate children. "Rod?" he prompted, concerned.

"I met Tess," Rod managed to say, more composed now. "She's beautiful and wild and I wanted her. Thank God, I got Emma instead."

Now it was Asa who was shaken, Asa who was pale and unsteady on his feet. "Can a man get a drink on this boat?" he asked, in plaintive tones.

Emma Hamilton dashed at her tears as she stumbled along the road that led to Derora Beauchamp's roominghouse. Tess would know what to do, Tess always knew what to do. She had but to find her.

At Mrs. Beauchamp's front gate, Emma paused, her shame thick in her throat. Suppose everyone could tell what she had done with Roderick, just by looking at her? Did that sort of wickedness, enjoyable as it was, leave a visible mark on a person?

She gave herself a mental shake. Mercy, she was being foolish. If the sweet-evil things Roderick had done to her, had taught her to do to him, left actual marks, Derora Beauchamp, for one, would be a mass of scars.

Her valise, containing only a nightgown, a toothbrush, and an extra dress, was tucked beneath the swing on the front porch, where she had left it the night before. She had planned, of course, to spend the night with Tess—

Staunchly, Emma turned the bellknob beside the door and waited. The black housekeeper, who secretly frightened Emma in some inexplicable way, answered promptly.

"She ain't here anymore," was the brisk response to Emma's request to see Tess.

Emma swayed, put one hand to her cheek. It felt as cold as that of a corpse. "What—wh-where—" she stammered miserably.

Juniper looked impatient. "Miss Tess done run off with that peddler-man," she said. "Happened last night."

Emma felt sick. She was alone now, alone. Roderick was gone and so was Tess. How could they do this to her?

"You all right, missy?" demanded the black woman shortly.

"I—" Emma turned, like a sleepwalker, and stumbled away from the door. "Yes—I—"

She bent and picked up her valise, aching with hurt, dazed with anger. It was to be expected, Emma guessed, that a man would use her and then leave her

108

stranded, but Tess was supposed to be her friend. How could she go away without even saying goodbye?

Emma's valise thumped against her leg as she went back up the walk to the gate. Tears streaked down her face; she was in dire trouble now, she just knew it. And Tess wasn't here to help her.

Tess had betrayed her.

Emma tried to think rationally. After all, if Roderick had asked her to run away with him, as the peddler had obviously asked Tess, she would have gone without hesitation. How could she blame her friend for a similar action?

With her free hand, she touched her midsection. There was a baby growing inside her somewhere, she was certain of it. How the devil was she going to explain a baby to her mama and papa? How long would it be before the little one came—a week? A month?

Oh, Tess, Emma mourned. Tess, how could you leave now?

She was in the main part of town now; she found her father's shop and rounded it to climb the steep stairs at the back and enter the small apartment where she had lived in sheltered comfort all her life.

Her mother, rolling out pie dough at the table, looked up and smiled her sweet, patient smile. "Hello, Emma. Did you and Tess have a nice time last night?"

Chin wobbling, Emma put her valise on a horsehair settee. I can't speak for Tess, she thought with bitter humor, but I've never had so much fun in my life. "Mama!" she wailed.

Cornelia Hamilton ceased her work, dusted her floury hands on her ruffled apron. Worry leaped in her dark eyes. "Darling—what is it?" she asked, in an alarmed whisper.

She had to tell somebody. She had to. And Tess was gone. Damn Tess, why did everything good have to happen to her? Why did her man have to want her enough to take her with him, when Emma's had sailed blithely away on a riverboat?

"Emma," prompted her mother.

Emma couldn't bring herself to name Roderick as the culprit in the story she was about to tell; mild-mannered as her papa was, an incident such as this one would make him dangerously angry. For all his fickle ways, Emma didn't want that anger directed at her Rod. "Mama," she sobbed, "oh, Mama, I'm so ashamed—I didn't spend the night with Tess—I was with—I was with a man."

The color flowed out of Cornelia's face, disappearing under the prim collar of her green cambric gown. "With a man?" she echoed. "Dear Lord in heaven, Emma, who? What man?"

Emma swallowed hard, sent a silent prayer for forgiveness shooting heavenward, and said outright, "Joel Shiloh. The peddler, Mama. I thought he loved me—I thought he would marry me."

Cornelia sank onto the horsehair settee, waving one hand in front of her face, swaying back and forth in a way that alarmed her daughter. "Did he force you, Emma? Did that awful drummer force you?"

Emma wasn't willing to carry the lie quite that far. "No, Mama," she said, her voice shaking. "H-He courted me. I thought—I believed—"

"Where is he now, Emma? This Shiloh person?"

Emma's tears were real. "That's the terrible part of all this, Mama—he compromised me and then he—and then he eloped with Tess!"

Cornelia was a kindly, rational woman, but she had always had mixed feelings where Tess Bishop was concerned, and Emma knew that. She disapproved of Tess's hair, falling free and wild so much of the time, of her picture taking and her bicycling. And secretly, Emma suspected, her mother resented the fact that everything was always so much easier for Tess than for her daughter.

She saw these feelings moving in her mother's face now. Cornelia stood up, somewhat unsteadily, her lips drawn in a tight line across the bottom of her face, and untied her apron. "We'll just see who comes out of this situation with a husband and who comes out with a tarnished reputation. We'll just see."

Emma watched with wide eyes as Cornelia left the tiny quarters by the outside stairway. She felt sick at what she'd done. Suppose her father went after Tess and Joel Shiloh? Suppose—

It was all too much. Emma toddled into her bedroom, collapsed into her bed, and gave herself up to the worst sick-headache she'd ever had.

Tess made up the bunk inside the wagon as neatly as she possibly could. Then, conscious of the rain that pelted the top and sides of the wagon that sheltered her, even more conscious of the man who was outside in that storm, she stripped off her clothes and began her bath, such as it was.

Keith had provided her with a scratchy towel, stolen,

judging by the monogram, from a hotel in San Francisco, a bar of buttermilk soap, and a washcloth. There was no tub, but the water in the kettle was steaming hot, and Tess was content with that. She dipped the soap and washcloth into the water, lathered them together, and began to wash herself all over. It was a slow, awkward process, washing that way, but it was worth it to feel clean again.

When she had finished, she dried herself with the rough towel and then put on the one nightgown she had brought along, a prim affair with lace ruching on the yoke. She went to the door of the enclosed wagon, opened it, and flung the water out into the gathering darkness. What would happen now? Where was she supposed to sleep?

She cast an anxious glance at the bunk and reddened at the memory of what had happened there. Was it going to happen again?

A part of Tess hoped devoutly that it would, for never had she experienced feelings so gloriously, ferociously pleasurable. It was out of deference to another part of herself, however—a prim and self-rightous part—that she slammed the wagon's door closed.

She went to the bunk, sat down on its edge. She wished she'd aired the sheets before the rain had started, and the quilt, too. Then maybe they wouldn't have the crisp, distinctive scent of Keith Corbin clinging to them.

Tess was tired and sore and very confused. She sighed and crawled into bed, huddling close to the wall, watching as the light of one lantern danced and flickered against the rough wood there.

Presently the door opened, cool, rain-scented air rushed in.

"Tess."

She stiffened. "Go away," she said.

"This is my wagon, remember?" Keith's voice reminded her, not unkindly. "And that's my bed. Therefore, shoebutton, I'm not going anywhere."

She heard the soft rustling of garments being shed and moved closer to the wall. "You could sleep underneath the wagon," she suggested tentatively.

"If you think that's such a grand idea," he sighed, and the mattress gave a little as he sat down on the edge of the bunk, "be my guest. I'm not about to sleep on the ground."

Rain pounded ominously at the roof of the wagon, as if to add weight to his argument. She heard the thunk of his boots on the wooden floor and felt the heat of his flesh through the flannel of her nightgown, even though they weren't touching. Her bottom flexed and then tingled, and she tried to tuck it in a little further. "If you were a gentleman—" she began, desperate now.

There was a clink of glass and a whoosh of breath and the lantern went out, leaving them in complete darkness. Keith laughed. "A gentleman? Me? Who ever suggested such a thing?"

"Certainly not I," observed Tess, trying to melt into the wall.

He laughed again, and then he crawled into the bunk beside her, stretching out with a sigh. He was naked, and every muscled line of him was hard and warm; he was touching her now because the bed was so narrow that even if he'd tried to avoid contact the task would have been impossible.

113

Tess didn't think he was trying, anyway. Her senses leaped, her heart beat a little faster, and the tingling spread from her bottom into every part of her, even her toes, a certain treacherous warmth following in its wake.

"Let's talk," Keith said, after some moments, and from the shifting of his body, Tess knew that he had cupped his hands behind his head.

"About what?" she snapped, angry at herself, at him, at the world.

"Free love," he answered, with a smile in his voice.

Tess was tired of being goaded about that. She sat bolt upright, in her fury, and looked down at him. It was so dark that she couldn't make out any of his features. "All right!" she burst out furiously. "So I didn't have the courage to try it!"

Keith gave a raucous shout of laughter and enclosed her in his arms, pulling her down so that she rested stiffly on his broad chest, her head on his shoulder. The ring he wore around his neck made a painful circle on her cheek and she shifted to get away from it.

"You loved her," she said, staring up at a ceiling she couldn't see.

There was a long, dangerous silence; she felt his arm, curved beneath her, stiffen slightly. "Yes. I loved Amelie," he finally admitted, in a gruff voice that said he still did.

Tears pooled in Tess's eyes; she was glad it was dark and Keith couldn't see them. Soon—perhaps even the next day—they would reach Portland. He would be lost to her then. But Amelie, even though she was dead, would be with him forever, kept alive by the beat of his

114

heart and the ring that hung from that chain around his neck.

I hate her, thought Tess.

"Did you ever make love to Amelie?" she asked, rash because it was dark and because she hurt so badly.

Another silence. She had made another mistake; he was angry. But he finally answered. "No. God knows, I wanted to. Waiting was hard. But she was pure and sweet—"

Pure and sweet. Tess was wounded to the core. Amelie had been "pure and sweet," too virtuous to touch before the wedding night, an angel to be cherished and set upon a pedestal. While Tess, on the other hand . . .

He seemed to sense her feelings. "I didn't mean it that way," he said gently.

"What way?" she hedged testily. Even now, his hand squeezed her right buttock, through the soft flannel, and she wanted him. She hated herself for wanting him.

"Amelie was a different sort of woman," he tried to explain, albeit lamely.

"Virtuous," said Tess venomously. "Certainly above free love."

He laughed, still kneading her bottom with his hand. "Free love. The very mention of it would have sent Amelie into hysteria."

Tess's throat tightened; she didn't speak because it would have hurt and she was in enough pain as it was. Besides, she couldn't think of anything to say that wasn't hateful.

"Tess."

She wouldn't speak to him, she wouldn't.

"Touch me, Tess." His voice was not imperious; if it had been, she would have sat up again and slapped him silly. "Please, touch me. Make me forget."

He was being unfair. He was asking one woman to soothe him while he loved another, dreamed of another. And yet Tess could not deny him. She shifted, so that she was kneeling in the rumpled bunk beside him. She drew back the blankets, stroking the body beneath with her hands.

She felt his muscles flex and ripple as she ran featherlight fingers over his chest, his powerful midsection, his thighs.

"Oh, Tess," he groaned distractedly, "why do I need you so much? Why?"

Her hands moved—she hadn't planned to do it, oh, she truly hadn't—and closed around the magnificent pillar of his manhood.

Keith's cry of surprise and pleasure was beautiful to her; he stiffened and moaned her name.

"What do you want me to do?" she whispered gently. "Tell me how to please you."

He made a soblike sound. "What I did—Tess, oh, Tess—please."

What he had done to her. Of course. She bent her head and her hair spread over him in a silken fan. At her first nibbling taste of him, he arched his back convulsively and cried out.

"D-Did I hurt you?" Tess asked, frightened.

He laughed, a hoarse, pain-filled sound that belied his answer. "No. God, no."

Relieved, she went back to him. His groan and the tangling of his hands in her hair gave her a fierce sensation of triumph, of joy. Something within her sang

116

as she pleasured Keith, growing more and more bold as he began to writhe beneath her and call her name over and over again.

Finally, with a savage upward thrust of his hips, he stiffened and shouted something garbled and senseless and hoarse, and it sounded as though he was weeping as he sank, shuddering, back to the mattress. Tess followed him, ruthlessly holding him prisoner even in his defeat.

"No," he pleaded finally, on a ragged, forced breath, "please—"

In those moments, Tess understood the mysteries of power. She knew why people sought it, fought for it, died for it. She was not going to give it up.

"Tess," he choked out.

She was greedy for the power, hungry for the pleasure that his pleasure gave her. "I want more of you," she released him to say. "Much more."

He moaned, in submission, in anticipation, in hopeless defeat. She tongued him until he was hard again, shifted him somehow until he was above her, beautifully vulnerable. She nipped him and savored him, sampled him and consumed him, and she soared on the wild joy of his surrender.

When, at last, he pleaded, she drove him into an insanity of satisfaction, glorying in his cries. Cries of her name, and not Amelie's.

Much later, when Keith lay on his back, his breathing under control again, Tess reached to touch his face, knowing what she would find. His flesh was wet with tears.

"Why?" she pleaded. "Oh, Keith, tell me why you're—you're crying?"

Keith caught her wrists in strong hands, forced her fingers from his face. And then he rolled away, laying stiff beside her, using his broad back as a barrier.

She was desperate to reach him, for she sensed that it was not anger or hatred that had undone him this way, but something else. "Keith?"

"What?" he fairly croaked the word.

"Are you one of those men who can't let other people see them cry?"

He laughed raggedly and sniffled. "No. It's fashionable in my family."

"Then, what—"

"Why the hell did you have to come along, Tess?" he broke in, in a raspy whisper, rolling onto his back and then his side, so that he faced her now. "Why?"

Tess bristled; she didn't know what else to do. "What an inane question! It isn't as though I saw you in a crystal ball or something, you know, and said to myself, 'Well, here's this crazy peddler, throwing things at God and jumping into creeks because he doesn't have any better sense than to stand in campfires. It ought to be easy to louse up his life. I'll just set right out to do it'!"

"Damn it," he hissed, "I was happy! I didn't need anybody!"

"That's no way to be happy," Tess pointed out reasonably. "Besides, you weren't. You weren't at all. You were hiding. You were running. As far as I'm concerned, you still are."

"Oh, yeah? Well, what the hell do you know about anything?"

If he hadn't been angry before, he was angry now. And that was perfectly all right, because Tess had

118

worked up a fury of her own. "I know how to make you crazy!" she replied acidly. "I know how to turn you inside out!"

The silence that followed was long and it was awful. And it gave Tess plenty of time to regret what she'd said. She was about to say that she was sorry when he suddenly bit out, "That trick works both ways, woman."

Tess tried to melt into the wall again and had, of course, no more luck at it than before. "Good night," she dared to say.

"Good night, hell!" Keith snarled back, and wrenched her onto her back. "I've got plans for you. And we'll see who makes whom crazy, who turns whom inside out!"

Tess pulled the quilt up to her chin. "Leave me alone."

He laughed and got out of bed to light the lamp. Overwhelmed at the sight of his nakedness, despite what she had done in the dark, Tess wrenched the quilt all the way up over her head.

Keith tore it away again and pulled her out of bed to stand before him, trembling with fury and passion, her hair a wild tangle around her face. He looked at her in bafflement and desire, but not in anger, not now. "Come here, Tess," he breathed. "Come to me."

She did—she could do nothing else—and he kissed her, deeply, thoroughly. The spell was cast. When he removed her nightgown and flung it aside, even when he knelt and buried his face in her, she could not protest.

He enjoyed her until her knees were weak, until she trembled, until she tangled her hands in his hair and sobbed his name into the night. And when she could stand no longer, he laid her on the bed, her legs held apart by the broad strength of his body lying prone on her own, and enjoyed her again.

Chapter Eight

HARBOR HAVEN WAS NOT THE FORMIDABLE, GRIM STRUC-
ture Asa had feared it would be. No, it was a pleasant
brick building, flanked by towering pine trees, overlooking Portland's busy harbor.

His heart pounded as he made his way up the wide
flagstone walk and through the front door, beating out
a litany all its own. Livie-Livie-God-let-her-know-me-
let-her-love-me.

There was a broad-faced woman minding the recep-
tion desk, and she looked up at Asa, when he approached, and smiled. Good. This was a friendly place,
a gentle place.

He asked after Miss Olivia Bishop and was led to a sunny room with windows looking out over the blue, blue water. She sat staring blankly, her body small and wasted now, her once-rich mahogany hair streaked with gray, her thin hands folded in her lap.

"Don't expect much now," warned the kindly nurse who had brought Asa to that room. "She doesn't speak to a soul—not even her daughter."

A fist clasped Asa's innards and squeezed until he was breathless. Still, he rounded Olivia's wicker invalid's chair and crouched. "Livie," he said softly.

Her hazel eyes were circled by dark smudges of misery, but there was a flicker of recognition in them.

He took her hands, cautiously, tenderly, into his own. "Livie, I've come to take you home with me."

Olivia's lovely mouth, now thin and colorless, moved slightly, and then her hands rose slowly, slowly, to cup his face. "Asa," she said, in a dreamer's voice. "Oh, Asa."

Asa Thatcher wept without shame, kneeling now, his head in Olivia's lap. "Livie," he sobbed. "Oh, my Livie—"

"There, there," she said softly, her hands moving tentatively in his coarse hair. "Don't cry, my darling—you're here. Oh, Asa, if I'm dreaming, I won't be able to bear it—"

Asa recovered himself somewhat, lifted his head, placed trembling hands upon her precious face. For a moment, he, too, needed reassurance that this was not a dream. "I should have married you long ago," he said hoarsely. "Long, long ago. Will you forgive me, Livie? Will you marry me now, today?"

"Yes, Asa. Oh, yes."

Asa's joy and relief were so great that he could not contain them; he wept again, noisily this time, caring not a whit that Livie's nurse was looking on. Let the whole world see him thus, a broken man who could be mended by only one woman.

Tess was tired and her knees were still wobbly from the shameless, searing passion of the night before. The sun had been golden at the crack beneath the wagon's door before Keith had let her sleep. Oh, she hated him for the paces he'd put her through—again and again he'd driven her to gasping release without ever actually taking her—but she loved him, too.

The ridiculous wagon came to a stop in front of Harbor Haven, Keith put the brake lever in place with a motion of his left leg and smiled down at his indignant passenger.

"I hate you," she said.

"I hate you, too, dear," he replied sweetly. "Except when you wrap your legs around my head, that is."

Tess sprang down from the seat and glared up at him. "You might have a little respect," she fumed. "A little decency—"

He tipped his stupid bowler hat and smirked at her, but the expression in his eyes was tender. "I've got some things to do," he said, as though she hadn't spoken. "I'll come back for you in an hour or so."

"You needn't come back at all, Keith Corbin! If I never see you again—"

Keith sighed. "I know, I know. If you never see me again, it will be too soon."

"If you will just give me my bicycle and my camera, please. And my valise."

He arched an eyebrow, the reins still in his hands. "What are you going to do, put your camera and valise in the basket and wheel the bicycle through the halls of Harbor Haven? If you do, I guarantee they'll nominate you for membership."

Tess wavered, shading her eyes from the bright, rain-washed sunlight with one hand. "Well . . ."

"I'll be back in an hour," he repeated, with the patience of a man speaking to a drooling dullard. And then he drove away, with everything Tess owned in the back of his stupid wagon.

She turned and hurried up the walk to the familiar door of the brick hospital, despairing as she went. How was she going to earn enough money to keep her mother here and support herself as well? How? Tears of regret smarted in her eyes. Derora had been right; she should have sent that wire, collected her share of the reward. If she had, she would still be pure and her mother would be assured of proper care.

Inside the hospital, Tess thrust aside all thought of the mess she'd gotten herself into and approached the desk.

The nurse, Miss Elmore, smiled at her. In fact, she beamed.

"Your mother isn't here," she said.

The first stop Keith made was at the telegraph office, and the message he dictated was terse, blunt enough that even his thick-headed brothers could be expected to understand.

After that, he sent a more polite missive to his banker, requesting funds. Since the bank in Port Hastings had a telegraph of its own, the reply came almost immediately.

PRIVILEGES SUSPENDED ON THIS ACCOUNT.

Furious, Keith crumpled the message that had been hand-copied before his disbelieving eyes and rattled off a retort that made the squirrelly clerk squirm in his swivel chair.

"We can't say that in a wire!"

Keith paced the rough-hewn board floor, his hands in his trouser pockets. And even as he paced, the telegraph began to click out a new message, which the red-faced clerk hastily copied down.

When the clicking stopped, after what seemed like a long time, the squirrel set down his pencil as though it had the weight of a sledgehammer and mopped his brow with a bright red handkerchief. "I don't believe this," he said.

Keith knew that the message was for him, instinct had told him it was. Impatiently, he reached over the high counter and tore the sheet of paper from its pad.

STAY RIGHT WHERE YOU ARE, YOU LITTLE SON-OF-A-BITCH. I'M ON MY WAY TO PORTLAND TO KICK YOUR ASS.
                    REGARDS,
                         JEFF.

Keith wadded the paper and flung it. It bounced off

the clerk's forehead. "How come he can say things like that over the wire if I can't?" he demanded.

The clerk shivered. "I guess you can, if you want to," he conceded.

"Good," said Keith, calming down a little, smiling even. His message was two words long, and it made the clerk groan, but he sent it.

"I'll lose my job for this!" he complained.

Almost instantly, a reply came in.

THANK YOU BUT I LOVE MY WIFE. ADAM AND I
WILL JOIN YOU TOMORROW, GRAND HOTEL. YOU KNOW
THE ROOM NUMBER. JEFF.

It became a game then. Indulging in an evil smile, Keith leaned against the counter and dictated this answer:

I WANT ACCESS TO MY MONEY, YOU BASTARDS.
AND HAVEN'T YOU GOT ANYTHING BETTER TO DO THAN
HANG AROUND THE BANK?

YOU ARE BOTH IDIOTS. THIS COSTS MONEY, DAMN IT.
WILL ADVISE BANK AS REQUESTED. WILL ALSO LOOK
FORWARD TO BREAKING YOUR NECK. ADAM.

YOU'VE GOT IT TO DO, BIG BROTHER.

DO IT I WILL, LITTLE BROTHER.

By this time, the clerk was in a highly agitated state. "Mr. Corbin, I really must insist—"

Keith took pity on the fellow. He paid what he owed

for his share of the telegraphic argument and said, in parting, "I'll be in the Corbin suite at the Grand Hotel. When you hear from my bank again, send a messenger right away."

The clerk's Adam's apple bobbed up and down in his skinny throat. "Yes, sir," he said.

As Keith was opening the door to leave, the telegraph started clicking again. He paused, waiting, a half-grin on his face.

"M-Mr. Corbin?" The clerk called to him with anxious reluctance. "The party in Port Hastings wants you to wait in the woodshed."

Keith laughed, shook his head, and walked out. But his jovial mood faded away as he drove his mule and wagon toward the Grand Hotel. Going there, as ordered, went against his grain, and sorely so. But he had no money left, to speak of, and he could stay in the suite his mother kept for nothing, putting his meals and Tess's on her account.

He went to the Grand, he checked into the family suite. For Tess and only for Tess.

She was sitting on the front step, looking lost and forlorn. At the sight of Tess, Keith forgot the telegraphic row with his brothers, secured the wagon, and hurried up the walk toward her.

"What happened?" he asked, crouching before her, fearing the worst.

Her lovely, elfin face was tear-stained. "He came and took her away. H-He's here, Keith—he's actually here—"

Keith caught her hands in his. "Who, shoebutton? Who's here?"

"Asa—Asa Thatcher—he took my mother—"

He drew her up, supported her when she wavered on her feet. There was no color at all in her face. "That's your father, isn't it?"

Tess nodded distractedly. "Keith, she wasn't well enough to leave—maybe he's going to put her in some awful place—"

Mentally, Keith reviewed what little Tess had told him about her mother and Asa Thatcher. "Did they leave any kind of message for you?" he asked gently, as he lifted her into the wagon seat.

"I'm to meet them at the Grand Hotel. Suite 17."

Keith was reminded of his own forthcoming rendez-vous at the Grand, with his brothers, and he frowned. Damn, how he hated to give in like that, wait there for Adam and Jeff like some errant child sent off to the woodshed. "It seems simple enough, Tess," he said, somewhat shortly. "We'll go there and talk to Thatcher right now. It should be easy enough to find out what he plans to do."

Tess only stared straight ahead, her teeth gnawing at her lower lip, her shoulders and backbone rigid.

She was so wan and fragile, was Olivia. Which was to be expected, Asa thought ruefully, after all she'd been through.

She sat in a plush velvet chair now, her fingers plucking at her skirts, her gaze taking in the elegant sitting room of their hotel suite with a tentative sort of shyness, as though she expected it all to disappear.

128

"I'm truly not dreaming?" she asked again, in a small voice.

Asa wanted to weep. Wanted to shout for joy. Wanted, above all, to make this woman his wife before circumstances could separate them again. "No, my darling. You're not dreaming."

He had explained it all to her, how his wife and daughter had arranged for Tess and herself to be thrown out of their house, how her letters and Tess's had been intercepted and disposed of. Now, he patiently explained it again.

"We can marry?" she asked wondering. It was incredible to Asa that a creature so lovely, so sought after, could love such a man as he.

"This very day," he promised, his voice gruff and near to breaking.

"This very day," she agreed. "But Tess—what about Tess?"

Asa sighed. The situation of his troublesome daughter had been much on his mind. Always she had been the brightest star in his constellation, next to Olivia, of course—good-humored where Millicent was a curmudgeon, reasonably sensible where Rod was a fool. All the same, she had run off with a peddler, hadn't she? "I expect Tess will appear at any moment," he said, deliberately failing to mention the drummer. There was only so much Livie could be expected to deal with, in her present weakness.

Tess swallowed hard, bent her hand into a loose fist, lifted it to knock.

Beside her, Keith gave her a look of tender exasperation and then knocked at the door himself. With vigor. "Chin up, shoebutton," he teased, in a whisper. "This is your father we're meeting, not Genghis Khan."

The door of Suite 17 swung open, startling Tess, causing her heart to rise into her throat and thicken there. Asa was thinner than she remembered, and no more handsome, but he had a new strength about him, a new spirit.

His dark, cavernous eyes assessed his daughter, misted with an emotion that greatly resembled fondness, and then shifted to Keith, taking in his rough clothes, his dusty bowler hat, in the brief flicker of what could not have been more than a moment or so, taking his measure.

"Come in," he said gruffly, stepping back.

Olivia sat in a plush chair, her face bright, her thin arms outstretched. "Tess," she said, in a choked voice.

Tess flew to her mother, into those outstretched arms, falling unceremoniously to her knees before her mother's chair. "Mama—you're well—you're well?"

Olivia embraced her daughter, tangling her fingers in the wild mane of hair. "I'm getting well," she said softly. "Oh, Tess—my lovely little hoyden. Have you no hairpins?"

The reunion was a glad one, made up of tears and questions and soft laughter. And when Tess had been told that Asa Thatcher actually meant to marry the woman who had been his mistress for so many years, meant to take care of her and cherish her as she deserved, she looked around the room and noticed for the first time that Keith was gone.

A sense of quiet despair filled Tess. Had he left, maybe forever, without even saying goodbye?

Asa, who had been standing circumspectly beside the fireplace throughout the exchange between mother and daughter, read the question in her eyes, that was clear. But Tess could read nothing in his.

Minutes later, though, when an exhausted, protesting Olivia had been settled comfortably into bed in another room, he lit a pipe and studied Tess with a kindly concern she had never sensed in him before.

"That peddler. Do you love him, Tess?"

Tess sank into the chair that her mother had just left. She had much to say to Asa Thatcher, all of it unkind, but she would not do battle with him now. Not with Olivia loving him so much that she could be sent into madness and then drawn out again at his whim. "Yes," she said, for there was no point in lying.

"Has he asked you to marry him?"

Tess was losing her patience. Why was Asa Thatcher playing father now, when for five years he had not even cared enough to answer a simple letter? Did he think she'd forgotten the callous way he'd turned them out of their little house in St. Louis, never giving a thought to what might become of them? Maybe her mother could fall back into his arms, like a heroine in a bad melodrama, but Tess wasn't about to. "No, Mr. Thatcher. The last thing Keith wants is to marry me."

Asa drew calmly on his pipe, and it was clear that he

sensed Tess's animosity. But then, how could he not? How could he—even he—not guess that she hated him? "'Mr. Thatcher,' is it? Once, I was 'Papa.' You used to meet me at the streetcar and—"

"Those days are gone," Tess broke in stiffly, sitting up straight, her hands knotted in her lap.

"Certainly you are too big to ride on my shoulder, the way you used to," said Asa, with a gentle, persistent sort of humor. "And I don't blame you for feeling angry with me, Tess. However, if you'll just give me the chance, I can explain everything—about St. Louis and the years when it must have seemed that I no longer loved either you or your mother."

Tess was not going to let him remind her of the days before his betrayal, the happy days when there had been presents at Christmas, fine clothes to wear, endless, exciting rides on the streetcar line. No, she was not going to remember. "We were destitute," she said, not looking at Asa but at a massive cabbage rose woven into the hotel carpet. "If it hadn't been for Aunt Derora—"

"I have recompensed your aunt," Asa put in. "Though, of course, such a debt could never be fully paid. The woman has my eternal gratitude."

Tess's eyes shot to her father's face at this. He had seen Derora then. And her version of the situation had fallen to one side of the truth. She started to tell Asa about the floors she'd scrubbed, the meals she'd cooked, the bed linens she had changed and laundered, to pay for her own keep and her mother's, too, but thought better of it. What did any of that matter now?

"Derora was kind, in her way," she said, and then

there was a short, tense silence, for neither of them really knew what to say to one another.

Asa came up with something. He told Tess how his wife, now deceased, and his other daughter—his legitimate daughter, Millicent—had arranged for Olivia and Tess to be evicted without his knowledge. He told of searching, of hiring detectives. He said that neither Tess's letters nor her mother's had ever reached him; he had learned of their whereabouts only through the repentant offices of one of the culprits—Millicent herself.

Tess fought against it, but she believed him, for the truth was clearly visible in his eyes and in his manner.

"You are a woman now," he said gently, when the incredible tale had been told, "so the time when I might have had influence is past. I mean to marry your mother today, if she's up to a ceremony, and after she's had time to rest and gather strength, I will take her back to St. Louis. She will be presented proudly as my wife. None will ever be able to say that I hold her in shame."

Tess was watching Asa now, overcome. Clearly this man loved her mother, truly loved her. At last, after so many years of scandal and secrecy, Olivia would be mistress of his house and his heart.

Asa filled the silence when Tess could not speak. "You, in many ways, have been as badly treated as my Livie has, but all that is changed now. You are to be legally acknowledged as my daughter, and when Millicent and Rod inherit, you will receive an equal share. If you so desire, you may return to St. Louis with Olivia and me and take your rightful place in the family."

Her rightful place. To live in that sprawling brick

mansion, with its uniformed maids, its manicured lawns and lush gardens! How many times had she stood across the cobbled street from the high gates of Thatcher House and wished that she could enter in, even be welcomed?

"I couldn't," she said.

Asa did not seem surprised. "Very well. You will stay here, then, in Oregon?"

Tess hadn't thought about that, hadn't thought beyond her mother's recovery. There were so many things to think about now. "I don't know. I was going to get a job here, so Mama could stay in the hospital—"

"What about that young man—Keith Corbin? Doesn't he figure into your plans?"

Tess stared at her father in surprise and then realized that, of course, while she and her mother had been greeting each other so joyously, Asa had probably been questioning Keith. "I may never see him again," she said directly. "He promised to see me safely to Portland. That was all."

"I see. Would you marry him if you could?"

Tess's face was alight at the prospect. "Oh, yes!" She paused, remembered the wedding ring Keith still wore on a chain, remembered the name he had cried out in their greatest intimacy. "But he loves someone else, I think."

Asa arched one bushy brow. "Forgive me, my dear, for my bluntness, but you and that young rapscallion have been intimate, haven't you?"

Tess betrayed herself by gaping. By the time she'd closed her mouth and assembled a look of indignation, it was too late.

"Mr. Corbin would have you be his mistress, then, if not his wife?"

The words went through Tess like lances. Never, ever, would she be any man's mistress! "If I can't be his wife, I'll not be his lover, either."

"It's a little late to come to that decision, isn't it? Lofty though it may be, it is a bit after the fact, don't you think?"

Tess drew a deep breath, straightened her shoulders, worked up her courage. "I don't want to talk about Keith Corbin," she said flatly. "He—we—it was all a mistake." She lifted her eyes to her father's gaunt face, struggling to keep her gaze level. "There is a way you could recognize me as your daughter, if you were serious before. I'm not interested in an inheritance or anything like that, but I would like a loan to buy a little shop."

Asa looked interested. "What sort of shop?" he asked, tapping his pipe against the inside of the fireplace so that bright embers of tobacco fell to the bare hearth.

"I would take photographs and develop the plates."

"You're a photographer?" He looked at her with pride and fondness. "How on earth did you manage to learn such a skill in Simpkinsville, Oregon?"

"I take very good pictures, Mr. Thatcher. I-I saved my money for the camera and I know I could process photographs, too, if I only had the materials and an instruction book."

Asa smiled. "Don't you think another sort of establishment might serve your purposes better—a millinary, for example? Or a dress shop?"

Tess shook her head vigorously. "I want to work with photographs."

He laughed, this father she had despaired over and hated and, for all of it, loved. "There will be no loan, Tess. We will buy the shop, you and I, and stock it with all the supplies you'll need. Since businesses rarely pay a profit at first, you will have an account for living expenses, too."

Once again, Tess was overwhelmed. "I couldn't ask you to—"

"Why not, Tess? I am a wealthy man. Won't you let me ease my sore conscience, just a bit, by giving you this small gift? After all, your brother went to Princeton and your sister had the Grand Tour, among other things."

Tess found that the idea of a brother and sister was hard to imagine; though she had, of course, known always of their existence, they were no more real to her than the princes and princesses in the fairy tales she'd read as a child. "If I cannot repay you, I will not accept the money," she said.

Asa shook his head, looking pleasantly baffled. "We'll have to settle that argument later, my dear. I warn you that I am a stubborn man, used to getting my way."

"And I am a stubborn woman," replied Tess forthrightly.

"Perhaps you inherit that trait from me." He paused, smiled. "Thank the Lord in heaven your looks came from your beautiful mother. You might have resembled me, as your poor sister, Millicent, unfortunately does."

Suddenly, Tess was curious about the prince and the princess. She didn't like admitting it, even to herself, but she was. "And my brother? What does he look like?"

Asa drew a wallet from the inside pocket of his suitcoat, rummaged through it, drew out two small, sepia-tinted photographs. There was a third, which Tess guessed was of herself, but he did not offer that one.

She reached out and caught the pictures in one hand, looking first into the unfortunate face of Millicent Thatcher. Her eyes were deep-set and mournful, like Asa's, and her brown hair was drawn back from her face in a knot so severe that it appeared to lift her ears by half an inch. Life, for all her privilege and wealth, had not been kind to Tess's half-sister; that was easy to deduce from her grim expression.

"Millicent recently married a fine man," Asa said quietly. "A missionary doctor with a calling for Africa. I'm certain that my daughter will scare the fear of the Lord right into those natives, whether they want it or not."

Tess smiled and went on to the second photograph, which widened her eyes and made her breath catch. Looking back at her, much younger and much less jaded, but recognizable all the same, was the face of Roderick Waltam!

"It can't be!"

Asa laughed. "Rod's reaction was similar, when he learned that the Tess Bishop he'd met in Simpkinsville was his own sister."

At that moment, as if cued by some unseen prompter, Roderick Waltam strode into the suite, dropped his key into his coat pocket, and smiled acidly at Tess.

"Well," he said, "if it isn't my baby sister. The peddler's woman. Are you his wife now, sweet? I do hope so, pet. Can't have that whelp of yours born out of wedlock, can we?"

Chapter Nine

"YOU WILL NOT SPEAK TO YOUR SISTER IN THAT MANNER ever again!" Asa commanded, in a sharp hiss, keeping his voice down for the sake of the sleeping Olivia.

Roderick, who had been so friendly in Simpkinsville, who had repaired Tess's bicycle, was clearly displeased to find himself in possession of a second sister. He sat down heavily in the chair nearest Tess's and once again smiled that cutting smile. His words, however, were addressed to his fuming father. "I'll say what I please. I don't need anything from you."

"Don't you?" Asa replied, his tone even again, controlled. "From the looks of you, you haven't a penny to your name. How are you going to pay for food and lodging?"

Roderick lost his look of conviction. Tess remembered the way he'd filled his plate after Mrs. Hollinghouse-Stone's lecture that night and deduced that even if he still had his position in the theater company aboard the *Columbia Queen*—and she had a niggling suspicion that he didn't—his earnings were barely enough to keep flesh and spirit together. Before he could say anything, however, there was a distracted cry from the bedroom.

"Asa! Asa!"

Inwardly, Tess smarted a little. Couldn't her mother have called out for her, instead of Asa? Hadn't she been the one to look out for Olivia all this time? But Asa was and always had been first in her mother's life; it was Asa she called for and Asa who scrambled to go to her.

"We knew about her, you know," Roderick said, not looking at Tess, his voice flat.

"Yes, I know," Tess answered softly.

He looked at her then, and his smile was sad, but not rancorous like before. "You were something of a surprise, however. Millicent must have known about you, but I certainly didn't."

"I'm sorry," Tess said. "For the shock, I mean. Roderick—"

"Rod," he corrected.

"Rod, I don't know how to put this but—well—back in Simpkinsville, the night of the show, my friend Emma—"

Color laddered up from under the frayed collar of Rod's shirt. "Yes. Emma." He was gazing at the screen in front of the fireplace now, as though it held great interest for him.

Tess fell back in her chair with a sigh. So it had happened, then—the worst. If only she had made Emma come with her when she left the showboat to go to Derora. "She's young, Rod. And she was innocent."

Rod stood up, went to stand at the hearth, his back to Tess and her subtle accusation. "I've never seen anyone shed innocence quite so eagerly," he replied, at length.

"Her father is a hardworking, decent man, Rod, but he has a terrible temper. If she told him what you did, he'll hunt you until he draws his last breath."

"So she said. Actually, she shouted it from the shoreline."

Had it not been for the trouble Emma was in, Tess would have laughed. She could see her friend in her mind's eye, imagine her umbrage. Unfortunately, she could also envision the pain and confusion Emma had to be suffering—the poor little dreamer, having been raised in such a conventional way, had no doubt been certain that marriage would go hand in hand with surrender. How disillusioned and afraid she must be now. "You might have confined your romantic adventures to Derora," Tess pointed out icily. "To her, making love is a game. To Emma, it was no doubt a proposal, meant to be followed by a cottage, children, and tea roses growing along the fence."

Rod's shoulders stiffened a little, beneath the worn tweed suit coat he wore. "From an actor? She expected that from—"

"Emma would expect that from any man who compromised her, Rod. It was cruel and thoughtless of you to use her like that and then leave her to face the consequences on her own. What if she's expecting?"

Rod whirled to face Tess, his expression grim, defensive. And just a bit remorseful. So he did have a conscience, after all. "You make it sound as though this is all my fault. She could have said no, you know! I wouldn't have forced her—God knows, she all but forced me!"

"Emma was smitten. Bedazzled, if you will. But she isn't the sort of girl you just use and leave behind, Rod." Like me, added Tess, to herself. Had Keith left Portland already?

"While we're on the subject of morality, sister dear," Rod parried imperiously, "where is this itinerant husband of yours?"

"Husband?"

"Emma said you had eloped with that peddler—Joel Something-or-other. She also said that you were carrying his baby. Given those facts, I find it most interesting that you have the gall to sit there and lecture me."

"She said that?!" cried Tess, in a startled undertone.

"Is it true?" The flush of triumph glowed in Rod's delicate cheekbones.

"Of course not!" Tess caught herself; memories of all she and Keith had done, in the privacy of his wagon, lay jagged in her soul. She had no right to moral outrage; she had run away with Keith in the dead of night and she might well be pregnant. Unwittingly, except for the part about the elopement, Emma had told the bitter truth. "She had no right," she finished, sounding feeble now.

"You'll follow in your mother's footsteps, then, and be the peddler's mistress. Of course, your circumstances will be considerably different from hers. My father, after all, was and is a rich man. I would think the charity of a medicine man would be lacking—"

Tess stood up and slapped her half-brother soundly across the face. To his credit, he gave no indication whatsoever that it had occurred to him to slap her in return.

"Did I strike a little too close to the truth, Tess?" he asked, and those words had the effect of a blow. "You don't want to be kept by a man, the way your mother was, unless I miss my guess."

Tess was shaken and more than a bit sick. She subsided to her chair again and breathed deeply in an effort to force back the tears smarting behind her eyes. "Did you know that your father invited me to live in the family home in St. Louis?" she asked, a few moments later. "I refused and now I'm glad. I wouldn't ever hear the end of how my mother was a bird in a gilded cage, would I, Rod?"

The despondency in her voice must have softened Rod; he went back to his chair and folded his hands and his manner was almost gentle. But then, he was an actor. "You would not be happy in St. Louis," he said at length. "Women like my mother and sister would make your life a constant misery. They would never accept you in a million years. You're a threat to them."

"My mother won't be happy there, either," Tess mourned distractedly.

"If my father loves her as much as he says he does, he'll present her properly and then take her elsewhere. I met Olivia only briefly, but any fool would know that she's too fragile to deal with that special brand of feminine hatred."

Tess felt an abject need to change the subject. The past few days had been so upsetting, so full of shocks and sweet surprises, pain and joy. She was hungry, and she needed a hot bath and a long nap and time to absorb everything.

When Asa returned from the bedroom—he explained that Olivia had had a bad dream but was now sleeping comfortably—he pointed out that the suite had been chosen because it would accommodate all of them. Tess was shown to her small room, and her heart lightened at the sight of it.

Down the hall was a bath, complete with hot and cold running water, wrapped cakes of buttermilk soap, and enormous damask towels, and Tess indulged at least two of her needs by taking a long, luxurious soak and shampooing her hair. She felt sleepy and renewed as she draped herself in a man's plaid flannel robe, discreetly loaned to her by Asa, and hurried back to her room.

There, on a service cart, was a tray bearing a steaming teapot, utensils, and a plate covered by a silver dome. Tess lifted the dome, and a delicious aroma filled the air—biscuits drenched in gravy. Fried chicken. Fresh green beans. Her stomach grumbled, and, as she sat down on the edge of her bed to eat, she reflected that, given this wonderful meal before her and the luscious bath she'd just taken, she might have been sublimely happy.

If she'd never heard of, let alone met, Keith Corbin, that is.

After devouring the food, Tess had a cup of tea. Then she wheeled the service cart out into the hallway closed her door again, took off the borrowed, tobacco- and cologne-scented robe, and crawled into bed.

A sweet, dreamless sleep rose up around her, like a fog, and when she awakened, twilight was gathering at the windows and a plump woman dressed in rustling sateen was standing at the foot of the bed.

Tess was startled and she gasped and put one hand to her chest. "What—who—"

"I'm Mrs. McQuade," said the woman, her voice at once boisterous and pleasant to hear. "I own the mercantile across the street—run it myself,"—here a long-suffering sigh—"now that my poor Alexander has passed on to his reward."

"Oh," said Tess, the bedding pulled up under her chin, not much more enlightened than she had been before.

"I'm here to show you some dresses and things. Got them right out there in the sitting room." Mrs. McQuade sniffled, wiped away a moist memory of her departed Alexander, and beamed. "That papa of yours is a generous man. I'm supposed to outfit you and the lady as fast as I can, and no expense spared, neither!"

Asa wanted to buy new clothes for her. Tess bit her lower lip and wondered how to phrase a polite refusal. It was perfectly fine for him to provide for Olivia, but she was not his responsibility, not to such an extent as this.

"I'm not supposed to let you say no," put in Mrs. McQuade, lowering her voice to a confidential level.

"And if the truth be known, missy, the dry goods business isn't what it might be these days."

In other words, thought Tess wryly, to turn down the clothing would impose financial hardship upon a woman alone in the world, a woman who must make her living in the dry goods business. Mrs. McQuade, for example.

Tess sighed. Soon enough she would be in business herself, probably struggling to make ends meet. She had no wish to cost Mrs. McQuade her profits out of pride. She also had no clothes except those she had worn that morning. Keith still had her valise—heaven knew where he was by now—and the contents of that were pitiful enough.

"If you could bring in some underthings," she finally said.

Mrs. McQuade chortled once and then swept out of the room, returning, moments later, with an armload of drawers and camisoles and chemises, all of them soft and fancy. Some were trimmed with lace, others were emboidered. And, unlike the muslin she'd worn for so long, they were made of silk and satin. Not since St. Louis had she had such lovely things.

When Mrs. McQuade had obligingly turned her broad back, Tess bounded out of bed and slipped on a pair of blue satin drawers edged in snow-white lace. Through the lace, a narrow cerulean ribbon had been woven. Barely able to resist crowing with delight she put on a matching camisole and whirled, reveling in the sensuous smoothness of the fabric against her skin. Oh, how she had missed having pretty clothes.

The trying-on began then. Tess chose cambric and gingham dresses, practical skirts and shirtwaists to wear in her shop, shoes, and sturdy, ribbed stockings. For parties, should she be invited to any, she selected a gown of pretty, sunshine-yellow lawn. This would serve, too, for the wedding of her mother and Asa Thatcher.

All the while, Mrs. McQuade chattered on and on about how she loved a wedding, yes, indeed, and how beautiful were the clothes the future Mrs. Thatcher had chosen. At the end of all this, she handed Tess an ivory-backed comb, brush, and mirror set, along with a packet of hairpins.

"Your mama wants you to put up your hair for the ceremony," she said importantly, looking at Tess's free-falling, still-damp mane with good-natured disapproval. "Shall I help you?"

Tess bit back a smile. "I think I can manage, Mrs. McQuade, but thank you all the same. And thank you, too, for bringing all these lovely clothes."

Mrs. McQuade gathered up the items that had not been chosen and, after a few polite words of corresponding gratitude and farewell, left the room.

Alone, Tess put on the beautiful yellow lawn gown and set about wrestling her sleep-snarled hair into a coiffure fit for a wedding that was at least twenty years overdue.

The ceremony, small and dignified, took place an hour later, with a justice of the peace reciting the special words and Tess and Rod looking on as witnesses.

Olivia was particularly lovely in her dress of ivory

silk. She wore shiny slippers on her feet, golden and fit for a fairy tale, and her hair was swept up in a soft cloud of gray-streaked mahogany and held in place by a half-dozen tiny diamond-studded combs.

For her mother's sake, Tess tried to forget all the difficulties and indignities of the past five years and take joy in the fact that Olivia's association with Asa Thatcher would, at last, be one of honor and not shame. Still, looking at those diamond combs, she couldn't help recalling all the things they had done without.

When the wedding was over and kisses and tearful congratulations had been dispensed with, Asa suggested boyishly that it was a fine city, Portland was, full of good restaurants and entertainments that would surely appeal to Rod and Tess.

"He wants to get rid of us," Rod whispered, when Tess would have demurred, preferring to go back to her room and rest.

Tess blushed. Surely Asa and her mother didn't mean to—didn't mean to consummate their marriage? Why, they were past that, weren't they? And Olivia had been so ill. . . .

"Come on, you ninny," Rod insisted, grasping her arm and fairly thrusting her toward the suite's small entryway. As he did so, he was tucking the generous wad of currency Asa had given him into the pocket of his new black broadcloth suit coat. Apparently, he, too, had enhanced the financial situation of Mrs. McQuade.

Tess was warming to the idea of dinner in a restaurant and a play to watch, but when they reached the entryway, her bright mood fled. Leaning against the wall was her bicycle, her valise in the basket. Her camera sat on a small table.

She knew then that Keith Corbin was not coming back, not even to say goodbye. And though she gave no outward sign of it, her heart cracked from top to bottom and then tinkled down into her midsection in tiny, irreparable pieces.

Keith paced the sumptuous, seldom-used hotel suite impatiently. He'd bathed, he'd eaten, he'd shaved. His clothes were clean.

All ready to face my brothers, he thought, with wry, rueful amusement.

Tess. He knew that she was safe, that she would be taken care of from then on. Asa Thatcher had made his devotion to his daughter clear enough and, from the windows of his own plush sitting room, Keith had seen the proprietress of McQuade's Mercantile carrying stacks of brightly colored fluff across the street. He knew the things were for Tess, and he was buoyed by the delight he knew she would feel, but he was also a little sad. It would have been nice to buy pretty things for her himself.

He thrust his hands into the pockets of his trousers. The bank in Port Hastings had wired him the funds he'd requested; he could stock his wagon with supplies and leave again.

A slow smile spread across his face. Tess was going to be all right. She was going to be loved and provided for. Why shouldn't he go back to selling his medicines in the towns and the lumbercamps, camping in meadows and fields at night, thinking his own thoughts?

The fact that Jeff and Adam would be furious if they arrived and found him gone made his smile widen accordingly. It would serve them right.

Still grinning, Keith gathered the few things he'd brought to the suite, took the key from his pocket and flipped it high, caught it with a flourish. And even though something within him screamed for Tess Bishop, he went downstairs, checked out of the hotel, crossed the street, and haggled with Mrs. McQuade for half an hour.

When he left her store, Keith had crates of laudanum, castor oil, and liver tonic. He had food for himself and the mule. And he was miles outside of Portland before he could bring himself to look back.

Of all the scenarios Emma Hamilton could have imagined, there wasn't a one to equal her father's reaction to the news that she had been compromised by Joel Shiloh, the peddler. So wildly did her parent rant—his nose became red and small blue veins sprouted all over it—that she trembled with fear. He would see that miserable drummer hanged, he raged. He would see him shot. He would see him bludgeoned to death with a fence post.

Emma shivered. She had no doubt that her father would do all those things to Joel Shiloh and more, should he ever catch up with him, though not necessarily in that order, of course. What, for instance, was the good of hanging someone who had already been shot and then beaten to death? "Papa, I—"

Jessup Hamilton turned from red to purple. A spasmodic hand rose, shaking, to grasp his chest. And then he fell.

And it was too late to tell him the truth; Emma knew it before she knelt beside him. She'd killed him. She'd killed her own father, because she was wanton and she was a liar to boot.

Emma's mother was trying to shake her husband back to life, sobbing wildly. Her knuckles were white where she gripped his lifeless shoulders. "Get the doctor—oh, Emma—get the doctor—"

To please her mother, Emma stood up and took her shawl from the peg beside the door. There was no use in finding Doc Smithers, no use at all, but if it would help Cornelia, she would do it. She went blindly into the chilly April night, finding the physician's nearby home by rote.

"My papa is dead," she said to his wife, when that lady opened the surgery door to her. "Mama wants the doctor to come."

Doc Smithers was a young man, earnest about his profession, handsome in an innocuous, boyish sort of way. He grabbed his bag in one hand and Emma's elbow in the other and they were on their way back to the small, comfortably furnished apartment above the store.

Jessup Hamilton was indeed dead, and by the time Emma and the doctor reached the scene, Cornelia had accepted the fact. She looked at the daughter she had always cherished with cold hatred in her eyes, all the while that Doc Smithers fussed over the body, all the while that the Presbyterian minister was there, saying prayers. Even after Mr. Meidlebaum, the mortician, had come and taken away the remains, she stared at Emma like that.

"You," she said, when they were alone.

It was enough for Emma, just that one word. Her father wouldn't have died if she hadn't been a hussy, if she hadn't lied about Joel Shiloh. If she hadn't thrown herself at Roderick Waltam.

And Tess wasn't even here to talk to, to cry with, to explain, to lie and say, "Oh, Emma, you goose, it wasn't your fault."

While Emma was packing her carpetbag, she felt a cramping in her abdomen, a sticky warmth between her legs. She knew little enough about the workings of a woman's body—she'd been half expecting a baby to sprout somewhere in her solar plexis at any moment—but she did know that if her monthly curse came, there was no child growing inside her. She'd learned that several months before, when a certain Mrs. Drews, a beleaguered mother of nine children, had come into the store and confided to Cornelia that her prayers had been answered: there would be no new baby because there was bleeding.

Unsophisticated as she was, the cruel irony of the situation was not lost on Emma Hamilton. She was bleeding and therefore barren. She needn't have lied, she needn't have confessed at all. If she had waited, just for a few hours, everything would be different.

There were no steamers leaving at that hour, and no

trains, either. It was dark and cold, and, down the street at the Blue Hammer Saloon, somebody was playing a spritely tune on a piano. People were laughing.

Stop that, Emma thought, as she carried her carpetbag down the outside stairs and started walking toward the roominghouse. She had arrived there, and turned the bellknob in the bargain, before she remembered that Tess was gone.

Derora felt charitable. Why shouldn't she, when she was free of Tess, free of that boardinghouse, free of Simpkinsville. She drew the wan and distraught Emma into her parlor, questioned her, found out soon enough that Jessup was dead and Cornelia blamed her child for the loss.

No amount of gently phrased queries would induce Emma to say why Mrs. Hamilton had made such an accusation.

"I'm leaving Simpkinsville tonight, Emma," Derora said. "I've hired a carriage so that I could leave right away. I'm off to Portland, although I'll be doing some visiting along the way. Why don't you come with me? Tess is there, I'm sure—in Portland, I mean. Perhaps we could find Tess and the two of you could room together."

Emma brightened, poor creature, at the prospect. "I must see Tess," she said.

"Then you shall. Let me make you some tea, and then we'll leave."

Emma nodded and Derora went off to the kitchen, still limping a bit because of that twisted ankle. Juniper was there, happily taking inventory of the supplies on the pantry shelves.

Derora wrote a reassuring note to Cornelia Hamilton, expressing her sympathy and stating that Emma would be safe in her care. She dispatched Juniper with this missive and then made tea, thinking all the while what a kind person she was.

Of course, from Portland she intended to travel to San Francisco, and from there—well, who knew? Emma could become a millstone around her neck if they didn't happen to find Tess.

She shrugged. If Tess wasn't available, she would simply deliver Emma to her good friend, Mrs. Hollinghouse-Stone. Lavinia was a wealthy widow with a grand home and she could surely find a paying position for the dear child, or even offer one herself.

Tess's throat was thick with despair, and she could only stare at the costly plate of prime beef on the restaurant table before her.

"Eat," ordered Rod, impatiently.

He's gone, Tess thought miserably. He's gone. It was as though Keith had died, so deeply did she feel his loss.

"I'm not hungry," she said.

Rod devoured a biscuit dripping with butter and honey before drawling, "Pining for your peddler, my dear?"

Was he going to start that again, that cruel gibing? Tess couldn't bear it if he was. "Yes, if you must know," she answered, with dignity.

"I understand now why you were so upset about my seducing your friend, at least," Rod observed. He was going to do it. He was going to be mean again. "Our friend Joel Shiloh did the same thing to you, didn't he, Tess?"

"No!"

"You're not only beautiful, you're a liar. If you're not going to eat that beef, give it to me."

"Why are you treating me this way?" Tess whispered, praying that she wouldn't cry. She'd had enough of disdain and moral outrage as a child, when the other girls in her convent school had taken such delight in reminding her of her scandalous status in the world. "I can't help being a—being a—"

"A bastard," Rod aided her placidly.

Tess picked up her wineglass and flung its contents into her half-brother's smug face. It dripped from his eyebrows like burgundy rain, staining his face and his shirt and the Grand Hotel's pristine linen tablecloth.

"Does this mean we aren't going to the theater tonight?" he asked, with consummate calm, as he took up a napkin and elegantly dabbed at his face and shirtfront.

Tess couldn't help herself. She laughed. "You would spend time with me," she marveled, "after what I just did to you?"

He smiled, every inch the actor, the dashing gentleman reared in elegance and luxury. "Oh, yes. I haven't much choice. We can't very well go back upstairs and interrupt the honeymoon, now, can we?"

Tess hadn't thought of that. It was a good thing Rod

was being so rational about the whole matter. "You can't go to a public theater looking like that," she pointed out. "People will laugh at you."

"Misery loves company," observed Rod, and then he took up his own wineglass, enjoyed an expert sip, and drenched Tess with what remained.

Chapter Ten

THE WINE MADE AN ENORMOUS BURGUNDY SPLOTCH ON the bodice of Tess's cherished yellow lawn gown. "You ruined my dress!" she sputtered, wadding a napkin and dabbing furiously, hopelessly at the stain.

"In this world, my sweet, you get what you give. You know, of course, that now we'll have to go upstairs and disturb the dewy-eyed lovers?"

Tess was simmering, but her emotions fell short of a true rage. After all, she had flung the first glass of wine. As much as she might have liked to overlook that small point, she could not. "I'll never forgive you for spoiling this beautiful dress," she muttered, as they rose simultaneously from their chairs.

"Buy another," said Rod, ignoring the speculative stares of all the other diners and suavely offering his arm. And Tess was amazed to see that even with wine droplets glistening in his hair and his shirt stained purple he managed to seem debonair.

Outside Suite 17, Tess waited nervously while Rod ventured in to get the lay of the situation. Across the hall was another suite, and, mostly to distract herself, she went closer to peer at the shining brass plate affixed to the door. "Corbin," it said, and beneath it, in letters just as elegantly etched, if smaller, "Private."

Tess was unaccountably jarred. Though she had known that Keith's family was rich—why else would they offer such a fortune for the return of their lost member—she had not guessed that they were *this* rich. Given the wagon, the mule, and that disreputable hat, it was difficult to think of Keith as wealthy.

Something made her try the door, and the knob turned in her hand. She peeked inside, found the room shadowy and dark. Perhaps Keith hadn't left after all—the very possibility made her feel as though she'd just awakened from the dead. Perhaps he was still in Portland.

"Keith?" She said his name even though she knew that he wasn't in the suite. But he couldn't have gone far, she reasoned, or he would have locked the place.

Tess reluctantly slipped back into the hallway and closed the door. When Rod came out, she was standing at a good distance from the Corbin suite, looking as though she'd never stoop to peeking inside it. "Well?" she snapped, conscious of the stain on her very best dress and the trickle of wine between her breasts.

158

"It's safe," her half-brother responded, with an impish grin. "They're sitting by the parlor fire, playing whist."

Tess tried to hurry past the newlyweds without drawing attention to herself, but her mother called to her.

Blushing, Tess turned.

"What on earth—?" Olivia whispered, frowning at the hideous blotch on her daughter's dress.

"There was a slight accident," put in Rod, who was being awfully diplomatic and brotherly all of a sudden.

Asa laid his cards down on the table and assessed his son with dark, wise eyes. "Strange that this strange fate befell you, as well," he observed, taking in Rod's purple shirt with remarkable equanimity.

"Do change out of that dress, dear," Olivia clucked. "Perhaps it can be saved."

When Tess went obediently—indeed gratefully—on to her room, her mother followed. Her fingers were awkward as she helped with the buttons at the back of Tess's dress.

"I'll be going away in a few weeks, Tess," Olivia said softly, tentatively.

So that was it. This was their first opportunity to talk in private, and Olivia meant to grab it.

"Yes," Tess replied, slipping out of her dress. There was wine on her camisole, too, and she silently cursed Roderick Waltam-Thatcher, or whatever the devil his name was. It was better than facing the fact that once Olivia went off to St. Louis with Asa, she herself would be well and truly alone in a very big world.

"You could come with us," Olivia suggested, as she inspected the stain on the yellow lawn dress. "You could meet a fine young man or go to college or whatever you wanted to do."

"I can't go, Mother," Tess answered. "I feel—well, I feel that my life is here. I can't really explain it but—"

"It's a feeling of destiny," Olivia put in, with remarkable confidence, considering all that she'd been through. "You've already met a man, haven't you, Tess?"

The directness of that question, the suddenness of it, made it impossible for Tess to lie. "Yes," she said, in despair.

"Is he married?"

A spirited denial leaped to Tess's lips, but she held it back. Keith might not be married to a living woman, but he was bound to the lost Amelie, all the same. "H-He's a widower, Mother."

Olivia gave a sigh of obvious relief. Who would better know the heartache of sharing a man? Who would better know the shame, the waiting, the uncertainty? "Is there hope of a life with this man, Tess? Can he—will he—give you a home? Will you have his name and bear his children?"

Tess lowered her head. "I don't think so, Mother. But I won't—I won't be his mistress, either. I'm going to work and learn and maybe s-someday I'll meet someone else—"

Gently, Olivia touched her daughter's face. "You are wise, little one. I have loved Asa completely, from the depths of my heart, from the very moment I met him. And for all we've suffered, you and I, I can't honestly say that I wouldn't do it all over again, given the chance. It's selfish of me, isn't it? But where Asa is concerned, I have no pride. I was born to be with him."

Tess could not speak. The strength of the love this woman bore Asa Thatcher was thick in the room, its force buffeting away her breath.

"I did a few things right, though, Tess. I did a few things right. Look at you—you're strong, you're beautiful, you're independent. Partly, that's because Asa came first with me and I never tried to hide the fact."

Still, Tess said nothing. It hurt to have her mother voice that, even though she had always known it.

Olivia gripped Tess's shoulders in hands that were thin, hands that trembled just a little. "It's a difficult thing for a mother to admit that to her child, Tess. A very difficult thing. But we've always kept to what was true, you and I. And though hearing it may hurt just a little now, you'll understand one day."

Sometimes, Tess did understand, but this wasn't one of those times. "Why, Mother? Was I lacking in some way? Was I bad?"

"You were and are a blessing from God. I cherished you and I always will. But a woman should love her man more than she loves her children, Tess. It sounds harsh, I know, but when you love a man as I love Asa—and I pray that you will one day—you will understand."

"What I don't understand, Mother, is your loyalty to that man!" Tess blurted out, forgetting, for the moment, Olivia's fragile condition.

But Olivia looked anything but fragile. She stood very straight, and her dark gypsy eyes flashed. "I consider myself fortunate to know him, to love him. Furthermore, if I could not have been his wife, I would have been glad to go on being his mistress!"

"There's where we differ, Mother. I won't be any man's plaything. I won't be visited whenever he has nothing better to do! I won't be hidden away like some shameful toy and bought off with presents! I could never love any man that much!"

For a moment, it looked as though Olivia would slap Tess. When the blow came, it was verbal, not physical. "Then I pity you, my dear. I pity you with all my heart."

Tess turned away, ostensibly to select another dress from the armoire. Tears burned behind her eyes, but she did not shed them until she heard the bedroom door open and then softly close again.

The stage curtains were trimmed in gold braid, and they were just about to open when Tess and Rod took their seats along the gaslit aisle. A sidelong glance at her brother indicated that he was imagining himself on the other side of the footlights.

Tess, still in a glum mood because of the scene with her mother, scowled and tried to read her program. The play was called *Travails of an Innocent* and starred a famous brother-and-sister acting team billed as the Golden Twins.

All the way over, in the hired carriage, Rod had prattled on and on about their talent, their fame, their angelic looks. Tess had never heard of them, and she'd only half listened to Rod in any case, for she'd been looking out the window at the seedy waterfront neighborhood, full of saloons and boxhouses and spooky-looking warehouses. She would have traded that elegant carriage for the medicine man's wagon in a moment.

Now, sitting in the theater, watching as the heavy curtains were drawn back to reveal a painted set, she remembered how it had felt to have Keith's hands on her breasts, his mouth. She shivered, and a treacherous warmth spread through her. Maybe she wasn't so different from her mother, after all. . . .

She forced herself to concentrate on the play. It was a tired, overly sentimental piece and Tess hated it, but the performances of the much-admired Golden Twins were quite another matter. Never, in all her life, had Tess ever seen people so beautiful, so perfect. Both of them had abundant hair of silvery-gold and eyes so green that they were visible even from a considerable distance, and the man's skin was as sumptuous as the woman's.

"Do you want to meet them?" Rod asked, when the third act had ended and the theatergoers were applauding with deafening appreciation.

"Who?" puzzled Tess.

"The Golden Twins," came the forebearing response. "Good Lord, I knew Simpkinsville was a hole, but everybody has heard of them!"

"I haven't. And I think the 'Golden Twins' is a silly name." Tess replied with weary dignity. Much as it might befit them, she added to herself.

"Ninny," huffed Roderick. "Their names are Cynthia and Cedrick Golden. And they're twins. Ergo—"

"Oh."

"Oh? Is that all you can say? Just, oh?"

"What else is there to say, Rod? That I want to kiss their feet? That I want to be their slave forever? I'm tired and I want to go home."

"We're not leaving until I've spoken to my friends. Now, you can come along or you can sit here and be ogled by lingering lumberjacks. The choice is yours."

This having a brother was annoying business. Tess wasn't at all sure she could get used to it. But she didn't want to be "ogled," as Rod had so vulgarly put it, so she left her seat and allowed her companion to usher her back stage.

Here, there were crowds of people—the other members of the play's cast, stagehands and roustabouts, and the Goldens. Up close, the twins looked even more beautiful; they were breathtaking, like exquisite French porcelain figures, perfect in every way. Indeed, a radiance seemed to emanate from them.

They couldn't be mortal. Not with faces like that, teeth like that, hair like that. They had to be angels, gone astray. Wandering wide of celestial paths.

"Roderick!" chimed the sweet creature called Cynthia, flinging alabaster arms around Rod's neck and wriggling her lush little body just briefly against his.

"No angel after all," muttered Tess. Not that she cared what Miss Golden did to Rod, or where. They could fall down on the floor and copulate, for all it mattered to her. She only wanted to go home.

"And who, pray tell, is this?" drawled the male part of the matched set. His eyes, like Cynthia's, were a devastating shade of emerald and fringed by sooty lashes. And they were fixed on Tess's bosom.

She squirmed a little. Odd that after all the liberties she'd allowed Keith Corbin to take with her body, she should feel so uncomfortable under the gaze of this man who seemed a shade too pretty.

"This is my sister," Rod said, unwinding Cynthia Golden and stepping back. "Tess Bishop."

"Her name is Bishop. Yours is sometimes Thatcher, sometimes Waltam. How can she be your sister?" This came from Cedrick; Cynthia was busy staring up into Rod's flushed face, her plump pink lips forming a beguiling pout.

"Born on the wrong side of the proverbial blanket," answered Rod matter-of-factly.

Tess was abysmally embarrassed. Couldn't he have said she was born of another marriage or something? Why was he so kind some times and so cruel at others?

"Your brother is a very rude man," soothed Cedrick smoothly. "Tell me, dear. Have you ever thought of treading the boards?"

"Doing what?" frowned Tess.

Cedrick laughed in a studied, unsettling way. "Acting. Have you any interest in theater work?"

"No," replied Tess flatly.

"Tess tends to be blunt," Rod said, giving his sister a wry and somewhat patronizing look. "Her mother was an actress, in fact."

"Then you must be very familiar with our art!" crowed Cedrick.

"Not at all," said Tess, aware that, for some inexplicable and probably petty reason, she did not like Cedrick Golden or his sister. "I was never allowed near the theater. Besides, by the time I was old enough to

165

notice, Mother was only dabbling at acting. She was and is totally devoted to my—my father."

"I must persuade you at least to read for a role in our new production!" wailed Cedrick. It almost sounded like a life or death matter.

Tess shook her head. "Never."

"Never say never, my precious," said Cedrick, waggling one finger at her as though she were a simple-minded child.

"Don't call me precious," said Tess, and Rod, standing beside her now, gave her a subtle kick in the ankle.

"Delightful," muttered Cedrick, choosing, apparently, to ignore what she'd said entirely. "Delightful. Rod, you must bring this sister of yours to our house. Tomorrow."

"I'm busy tomorrow," said Tess.

"We'll be there," said Rod.

They argued all the way back to the brick-lined road, where they were, fortunately, able to hire another carriage.

"You'd better not ever do that again, Rod!" sputtered Tess, settling herself into the carriage seat and furiously smoothing her skirts. "I have no intention of going to the Goldens' house tomorrow or ever!"

"Cedrick was taken with you!" Rod reminded her, giving the statement all the import of a summons from God Himself.

"So? I wasn't taken with him. He's a fop and, unless I miss my guess, a lecher in the bargain!"

"He could also give me a steady job, in a real theater! I could do *Hamlet, Macbeth, Richard III!*"

"Hooray," sighed Tess. The night was dark, but there were millions of stars in the sky, gleaming silver, some being born and some dying, some looking almost close enough to touch.

"Cedrick Golden has the power to give me everything I want!" insisted Rod.

"You poor wretch," said Tess. But then her gaze was drawn back to her brother's face, barely visible in the shadowy coach. "Oh, Rod—you're not—you're not one of that kind—one of those—"

"Of course I'm not!" snapped Rod furiously. "Didn't you see Cynthia crawling up my ribcage?"

"I thought she was going to drag you behind a trunk and have her way with you," was the blithe response. "If you want parts in Mr. Golden's plays, it seems to me that you could get them through Cynthia and leave me out of the whole nasty thing."

Rod was sulking. "He's interested in you," he said sullenly, when they were nearing the hotel.

"You're not going to trade me for a tunic and a pasteboard dagger, Rod, so forget it."

Rod was so furious at this that, when the carriage stopped in front of the brightly lighted Grand Hotel, he got out and stormed inside, leaving Tess to fend for herself.

She was used to that. With dignity, she got out of the carriage unaided, paid the gawking driver, and swept into the lobby.

There was an elevator, but Tess chose not to use it. The one time she had, she'd been with Keith and had felt safe, but she hadn't liked the way the thing lurched and squeaked on its cables.

The hallway on the top floor was empty. Tess started to open the door of Suite 17 and then, still a little breathless from climbing all those stairs, she turned, without planning to at all, and knocked on the door of the Corbin suite instead.

When there was no answer, she brashly turned the knob and again it gave and the door opened. She stepped inside, felt for the dial that would ignite the gas lights.

The suite was not, as she had expected, an exact duplicate of Asa's. Oh, no, it was very different.

And Tess felt like a burglar. "K-Keith?" she called out, pleasantly.

No answer.

"Keith!"

Still no answer. Damn that man, where was he? In a saloon somewhere, drinking himself into a stupor? With a woman?

Tess preferred to believe that he was anywhere but with a woman, even in jail. She would wait here, that's what she would do, because after what had transpired in that wagon of Keith's, she had the right to a civilized goodbye, at least.

She explored the suite to occupy herself, feeling like a skulking snoop but enjoying every second of the adventure anyway. There were five large bedrooms in that elegant quarter, along with an enormous, fully equipped kitchen, two bathrooms, and a library that boasted its own billiard table.

Tess ran one hand over the green felt surface of that table, feeling lushly sinful just for touching it. Probably, no woman had ever dared play the game here; it was strictly reserved for men.

She yawned, covering her mouth with one hand. When Keith came back, she'd make him teach her how to play billiards. In the meantime, however, she'd just sit down on that Moroccan leather couch beneath the windows. . . .

Tess opened one eye, closed it again. Good Lord, there were two men in the billiard room, two enormous, formidable men, and neither of them was Keith. She lay perfectly still on the leather couch, hoping that they wouldn't notice her.

"Will you look at this?" one of them fairly shouted, and Tess knew that he was standing over her, for every sense she possessed swore to it.

"Good Lord," said the other one, from a distance—though not quite the distance Tess might have wished.

Her nose began to twitch, and she was sure that a deaf man could have heard the thundering, terror-stricken beat of her heart.

"Open your eyes, minx," ordered the nearest giant, though not unkindly.

Tess compromised by opening just one. The man was fair, like Keith, and his features were at once ruggedly masculine and patrician. His eyes were the keenest, fiercest shade of indigo-blue that she had ever seen, and they were snapping with annoyance.

If the Archangel Michael were to descend to earth, Tess reflected, this was how he would look.

"Who are you?" he demanded, bending slightly.

Tess did her best to melt into the sofa back. "I—I—who are you?"

"Leave her alone, Jeff," interceded the other man, and Tess looked past the archangel to see a dark-haired, devilishly handsome fellow with eyes of that same disconcerting blue. "You're scaring her to death."

Jeff stepped back, albeit reluctantly. He looked as though he might like to close his hands around Tess's neck and squeeze until her eyes popped. "Who are you?" he repeated, irritation ringing in every tone.

"M-My name is Tess. Tess Bishop."

"Where is my brother?"

Tess sat up, still terrified. He meant Keith, of course. He had to mean Keith. "I don't know. I really don't."

"That must be why we found you sleeping in his suite!" challenged Jeff.

"Calm down," ordered the other man, with a certain quiet firmness. "It's obvious that she hasn't been with Keith. If she had been, she wouldn't be sleeping on the library sofa, you idiot."

"I would tell you where he was if I knew," lied Tess sweetly, trying to enlist the further sympathies of the dark-haired man.

He came to the sofa and crouched before her. "My name is Adam Corbin," he said. "This maniac is my brother, Jeff. We don't plan to hurt you and we don't plan to hurt Keith, either. We just want to talk to him, to make sure he's all right."

Though Adam Corbin spoke kindly, quietly, Tess knew she hadn't fooled him by saying that she would betray Keith's whereabouts if she only knew them. "I haven't seen him since"—she saw the light of dawn coming, gray-pink, through the windows—"since yesterday."

"That little bastard," muttered Jeff, pacing back and forth on the other side of the billiard table.

Tess would not have described Keith Corbin as a "little" anything, but she supposed that, to that man,

170

who probably lived at the top of a beanstalk and could smell the blood of Englishmen, he was. "I'll thank you not to use language like that in my presence," she worked up the nerve to say.

Adam's dark blue eyes danced. He still crouched before Tess, but now he took her hands in his. Held them gently. "You still think we would hurt him, don't you?"

"You did offer a reward for his capture!"

"His capture?" Adam made a visible effort not to laugh. "Tell me honestly, Tess: can you imagine anyone capturing Keith?"

Tess bit her lower lip and thought. She smiled to remember that crazy man flinging dishpans and coffee-pots at a deity who could strike him dead if He so wished. "I guess not," she said.

"We had a wire from a woman in Simpkinsville, saying she'd seen Keith and that he was using the name Joel Shiloh. She also said that her niece, Tess, had run away with him."

Trust Derora. Tess lowered her head. "I didn't actually run off with him," she almost whispered. "I couldn't live with my aunt anymore, so he brought me here, to Portland."

"And?"

Tess met Adam Corbin's blue eyes. Behind them flashed a lethal, penetrating sort of intelligence. She lifted her chin, "And I guess he's gone. I waited here all night. I hoped he would come so that I could say goodbye—"

"Some preacher he is," muttered Jeff, still pacing.

"Preacher?" Tess nearly swallowed her tongue. Images of the sweet yet wicked things she and Keith had done together burned in her mind, hot as the coals of hell. "He's a preacher?"

Adam flung one scathing look at his blond brother and then rose to his full height. "Yes. Or, at least, he was."

"Until Amelie was killed," said Tess, and the mourning she did was not for the dead girl but for her own hopes.

"The day she was buried, he threw his clerical collar into the river," Adam said, and the tone of his voice was gruff with remembered horror and grief. "He rode out that night and none of us have seen him since."

Amelie's wedding ring glinted and gleamed in Tess's mind. No doubt it was hanging from its chain, as always. "He still grieves for her," she said softly, brokenly, betraying more than she realized. "He still loves her."

"He's a fool!" put in Jeff.

Tess decided that she disliked at least one of Keith's brothers. Specifically Jeff. But before she could make the tart retort that sprang into her mind, Adam spoke.

"Is he, Jeff?" The question was evenly modulated, but it sounded dangerous, too. Almost like a warning of some sort. "What if it had been Fancy who died that day?"

"It wasn't Fancy. Or your Banner. So what is the point—"

"The point is that Keith apparently isn't ready to deal with any part of his old life, and that includes us. I just suggested this before; now I'm ordering it. We leave him alone, Jeff. We call off the detectives. We pull the reward offers out of the newspapers."

"But—"

"But nothing. Keith is a grown man now; he's no longer the little boy we took whippings for. When and if he wants to come back, he will."

"Damn it, I love him!"

Tess looked at the archangel in wonder.

"So do I." The indigo eyes of Adam Corbin touched Tess briefly, perceptively. "So do we all. And that's why we're going to leave him alone from now on."

"What if he needs us?" fretted Jeff. What was that moistness in his eyes?

Tess heard the echo of Keith's voice; he'd wept when they made love that night, in the wagon. It's fashionable in my family, he'd said.

"I must go," she said. Neither man seemed to hear her, and when she left, neither tried to stop her.

Chapter Eleven

KEITH CORBIN FINGERED THE WEDDING BAND AS THOUGH it were a talisman, capable of dispelling all the lethal things he was feeling. Amelie, he chanted to himself. Amelie.

But her name worked no magic. He still missed Tess, still wanted her.

He grasped the small of his back and flexed all his muscles, like an old man calling attention to his rheumatism. In the polished morning sky, a bird passed over, swooping and swirling. The mule snuffled companionably, as though to greet it.

"I suppose you think this is funny," Keith said, to the sky. "Well, let me tell you something. I don't believe in you anymore. And nothing you can do will make me marry that woman!"

He stopped himself. Why was he standing here talking to someone he didn't believe existed? Furthermore, who had said anything about marriage?

The mule neighed.

"Who asked for your opinion?" barked the man, kicking dirt over his campfire. But, all the same, he permitted himself to imagine being married to Tess, imagined himself surrounded by a flock of wild-haired, blue-eyed children calling him "Papa." He imagined building a house, preaching sermons again—

"No!" he bellowed. "No!"

And then he broke camp, without even having coffee, let alone breakfast. He hitched the mule to the wagon. He would go to Simpkinsville again—thanks to Tess, he hadn't called on any customers there. He would concentrate on things that mattered. Selling laudanum, castor oil, and liver pills.

Having made this firm and fast decision, he climbed into the wagon seat, took up the reins, and headed straight for Portland.

Tess hovered in the hallway, wondering what to do. She couldn't very well just bounce into Suite 17, with her hair falling and rumpled and her dress all wrinkled, now could she? She paced a little, rubbing her upper arms with nervous hands. What was she going to say to Asa? To her mother? How was she going to explain being gone all night?

She was still in the clutches of this disturbing dilemma when the door of the rooms she didn't dare enter swung open and Rod's head popped out.

"Where the devil have you been?" he demanded, in a hoarse, furious whisper.

Tess prayed that Keith's brothers wouldn't come out of their suite and speak to her. If they did, all sorts of errant conclusions would be drawn. "I don't have to tell you!" she whispered back.

Rod looked back over his shoulder once and then came out into the hallway. His voice was still low. "You owe me a debt, little sister. I told Father and Olivia that you had already gone to bed. Fortunately for you, they didn't bother to confirm the premise."

Tess gave a sigh. "Rod, what am I going to do?"

"First you're going to get your bustle into your room—our newlyweds are still sleeping—and then you're going to repay me by calling on Cynthia and Cedrick Golden."

There was no point in arguing. And she couldn't stand there in the hallway all morning, in a dress she had obviously slept in, with her hair all atumble. Besides, she needed to wash her teeth, and her skin felt grubby and she was hungry.

"All right," she agreed.

She reached her room in moments, her heart hammering as she closed the door behind her and pulled off her dress and underthings in awkward haste. Having done this, Tess put on one of her new wrappers, one of soft, golden corduroy, and let down her hair. She walked sedately across the hallway, to the bathroom, and took care of her morning ablutions, then went back to her room.

Twenty minutes later, she entered the suite's small dining room, wearing a crisp black sateen skirt and a white shirtwaist, to join her family for breakfast. To please her mother, she had even swept her hair up into a loose knot at the top of her head.

"Our daughter is a vision," observed Asa fondly, squeezing Olivia's ready hand. There were already plates on the table, and steaming chafing dishes contained scrambled eggs, patties of sausage, riced potatoes.

"She radiates virtue, doesn't she?" observed Rod, lifting his coffee cup to his mouth and glaring at her over the rim.

Tess colored richly—let them all think that she was embarrassed by praise—and took her place at the table.

"Today we'll look for your shop," Asa announced, loading his plate with a small mountain range of scrambled eggs and potatoes. "Livie is looking forward to the fresh air. Always loved a carriage ride, didn't you, dear?"

"Tess and I have plans for today," Rod replied flatly, and his brown eyes, still fixed on her face, dared her to say otherwise.

Tess swallowed hard, suddenly not feeling hungry at all. But before she could speak, Olivia unwittingly interceded in her behalf.

"Oh, couldn't you change them? If we don't go to find a shop for Tess, Asa will make me rest all day!"

Asa looked at the small hand on his arm and then at Rod. "I think you could change your plans," he said evenly.

Tess tensed, sure that Rod would spitefully proclaim to all and sundry that he'd found her pacing the hallway at a disgraceful hour. And she knew that she had to appease him, somehow, in order to avert disaster.

"Couldn't we call on dear Cedrick and Cynthia tomorrow, Rod?" she asked sweetly.

He looked petulant and quite undecided. "Why not tonight?"

"They'll have a performance then, I suspect," Tess sang back. How docile she sounded, how submissive to the superior wishes of her brother. She could almost have thrown up. "Please, Rod? Tomorrow?"

He deliberated, scowling now, turning his coffee cup in its saucer. "All right," he finally conceded grudgingly. "Tomorrow."

Tess bent her head, to hide her relief, and picked delicately at her breakfast.

It was the best of luck and the worst of luck that they found just the perfect shop within an hour of leaving the hotel. It was a narrow little building, with three tiny rooms upstairs, a privy out back, and lots of potential. The photographer who owned the place sold it complete with a variety of cameras, developing supplies, and outstanding accounts.

"It's so grim," breathed Olivia, looking up at the cobwebs netting the low ceiling. "Oh, Tess, to think of you living and working in this place—"

Tess was in love with every dusty, shabby inch of the tiny shop. After all, it was, or would be, hers, and that one shining fact went a long way in making up for its shortcomings.

Asa and Mr. Lathrop, the previous proprietor, had gone across the street, to the bank, to make arrangements. Rod remained to "look after" the women, and he looked as disdainful as Olivia did. Touching the small, pot-bellied wood stove and then scowling at the dust that clung to his fingers, he said, "Doesn't look like such a prosperous enterprise to me. You'll be starving in six months."

Tess dared not annoy her brother, not yet. He might still decide to tell Asa and Olivia that she hadn't been in her room the night before. "Nonsense," she said cheerfully. "The place just needs a good cleaning and a little paint, that's all. If Mr. Lathrop hasn't done well, it's only because the shop wasn't kept up properly."

"If you say so," sighed Rod, philosophically, but his eyes were laughing at her. Lord, how he enjoyed having her at such a disadvantage.

Which accounted, of course, for the bad part of her good luck. Now that the shop had been found, and purchased, he could insist that she visit those disturbing Golden people with him. No doubt, he would even expect her to fawn over Cedrick.

Tess clamped her lips down tight. She would call on the Goldens—that was the bargain. But she would not cow to them, no matter what Rod threatened to do. Explaining that she had walked into someone else's suite and fallen asleep on a couch would be better, ever so much better, than having to make up to Cedrick Golden.

On the other hand, how bad could it be, just calling on the Goldens, on a bright spring afternoon? They would have tea, they would talk a bit, Rod would smoothly call attention to his abilities as an actor. And then they would go back to the hotel and Tess could start making plans for her shop, real plans. Asa knew about business—she would ask his advice on bookkeeping procedures, things like that.

By the time Asa returned, Olivia was looking alarmingly tired and very drawn. Solicitously, her husband saw her home and tucked her into bed.

Tess was in the suite's kitchen, brewing tea for her mother, when Rod joined her. How smug he was, smiling that way. Leaning against the doorjamb with his arms folded across his chest.

"Wear something pretty," he said.

Tess colored with annoyance, but she held her tongue until she could speak in civil tones. Which was almost a full minute. She looked down at her skirt and shirtwaist.

"What's the matter with—" she began.

"You look like a schoolmarm," Rod broke in.

Tess had privately fancied that she looked like a businesswoman. "What would you have me look like, Rod? A concubine?"

"That would be nice. However, it's too much to ask, even of you. We're leaving in ten minutes, sweetness, so fuss over your mother and change your clothes."

"You know something, Rod? You are a real bastard."

"Me?" he laid one hand to his breast, as if mortified, and made a face to match the gesture.

Tess fumed, but there was nothing she could do to retaliate, not at that point, anyway.

"Oh, don't look like that," he scolded. "You've been made legitimate, so to speak. It isn't your fault it took almost twenty years."

"Get out of here."

Rod assessed the steaming teapot in her hand, as well as the expression in her eyes, and subsided to the parlor to wait.

Olivia was alone in her room when Tess reached her, cosseted under a blue silk comforter, satin pillows plumped at her back. She seemed much revived, though her hands trembled just a bit as she took the cup of tea her daughter poured for her.

"Asa spoils me so," she said.

Tess bit back a reminder of the difficult years just past. "Yes," she managed to agree. And then she sat down on the edge of the wide bed and folded her hands in her lap. "I'm very grateful to him for buying the shop."

"I didn't hear you thank him," pouted Olivia. And for all the gray in her once-lush hair, for all the lines of pain and old despair around her eyes, she looked like an indignant little girl.

Tess was quick to mollify her. "I will, Mother. I promise I will, as soon as I leave this room."

Olivia sniffed. "I don't like that shop. It's dirty and dark and any kind of ruffian could wander in off the street and attack you."

Tess suppressed a sigh. Olivia hadn't been a mother in five years, hadn't been capable of it, of course. Apparently, she had decided to make up for lost time by being difficult now. She was really more of a child than a woman, though Tess had never before thought of her in quite that light. "Mama, it's in the best part of town—only a five-minute walk from this hotel!"

"I don't care. I want you to forget the whole silly idea and come back to St. Louis with your father and me."

Tess stiffened. "I absolutely will not. I will not be a child again, Mama. I couldn't even if I wanted to."

"It's that dratted peddler, isn't it? I know you weren't in your bed last night, Tess. I went in to bid you good night and you weren't there. I haven't said anything to Asa, but that doesn't mean I won't."

"I wasn't with Keith, Mother!" Tess whispered desperately. Oh, Lord, she could imagine what Asa would do if this theory were presented to him now! He might take back the shop. He might even insist that Tess return to St. Louis with him and Olivia. Under the law he could do either of those things, or both!

"Then where were you?"

"I went into his suite—his family keeps the one just across the hallway." Tess lowered her head and swallowed. "I know I shouldn't have done it, but I wanted to see Keith just once more. I wanted to say goodbye. Only he wasn't there. I sat down on a sofa to wait for him and—and the next thing I knew, it was morning."

"I see," said Olivia, who clearly did not. "He is gone? Out of your life?"

Tess's heart squeezed painfully down to the size of a walnut and then expanded again. "Yes," she said miserably. "He's gone."

"I still think you should come home with us. We're going to Europe next spring, and you could go, too. You could meet someone—"

"Mother, you could force me to go. I know you could, by persuading Asa that it would be best. But I beg you not to."

"Tess, I love you. I only want—"

Tess took the teacup from Olivia, set it aside, and grasped her mother's hands in her own. "I know you love me, Mama." She said softly, earnestly. "I love you, too."

Olivia started slightly and looked down at Tess's

hands. A frown narrowed her eyes as she inspected fingers that were still reddened from working in Derora's roominghouse.

"She used you like a servant," whispered the older woman.

Tess averted her eyes. Olivia touched her cheek and forced her to look at her again.

"You were a maid in my sister's house," she said, her dark eyes snapping with a new vigor that was heartening to see.

"S-She needed someone to help after her husband left her, Mama. And you were sick. There were expenses."

"Oh, Tess."

"Mama, don't. Don't feel badly, please. You would have done the same thing for me, wouldn't you, if I'd been sick?"

"I'm not sure I would have had either the strength or the wherewithal. You're even finer than I thought, Tess, even finer than I thought. It's clear that you can take care of yourself, even in a rough-and-tumble place like this."

"I can, Mama. I swear I can. And I'll write to you every single week. I'll send you photographs and tell you all about the people who come in to have their pictures made—"

"Oh, my darling," Olivia almost wept, "it is so hard, having children. They grow up and they want to leave you."

"You have Asa." Tenderly, Tess kissed her mother's cool, silken forehead. "You'll be happy. And you mustn't let those awful women torment you, either."

Olivia laughed now, though it was a sniffly, crying

sort of sound. "What 'awful women' do you mean, Tess? The very proper friends of Violetta Thatcher and her daughter, Millicent?"

"Yes," whispered Tess, her own eyes clouded with tears. "You're fragile, delicate. They could—"

"They can do nothing, besides gossip and indulge in the occasional snub. Do you think I care what those fusty crows think of me, Tess?"

"But, your collapse—"

"I collapsed, as you so politely put it, because I thought I'd lost Asa. Now, he's mine again, I am his wife. Everything else, my dear, is a trifle. Go now. Your brother is anxious to keep that engagement."

My brother, thought Tess, with anything but familial charity. "Yes. You'll rest, won't you?"

"I promise that I will."

"And you won't say anything to Asa, about my going to St. Louis?"

"No." The word was said firmly, if reluctantly, and Tess took her leave.

The Goldens lived in an impressive house, Tess had to say that for them. It had belonged to a sea captain at one time, Cynthia proclaimed proudly, as she led Tess and Rod out of the entry hall and into a sumptuously furnished room overlooking the ocean. From the windows, Tess could see—even hear—the waves crashing on the rocky shore.

For some reason, the experience made her uneasy.

Tea was served and Cedrick made an entrance, wearing sleek black trousers and a rather gaudy smoking jacket of burgundy velvet. Tess had mentally compared him to an angel the night before; now, remembering Keith's brother, Jeff, she lowered Cedrick to the rank of cherub.

They all chatted for a while, Tess trying not to glance at the small glass clock on the mantel too often, and then Cynthia playfully grasped Rod's hand and dragged him off to some other part of the house, giggling all the way.

Tess was furious, but there was nothing she could do without making an absolute fool of herself. She wasn't going to thank Rod for leaving her alone with Cedrick Golden, that was for sure.

"I was hoping for a few moments alone with you," crooned Cedrick.

I'll bet you were, you—you actor, thought Tess vehemently, but she sat up a little straighter in her chair, smiled over the silver-trimmed teacup in her hands, and tried to assume the aspect of a lady. "Why?" she asked, softly.

"I've written a play," Cedrick confided importantly.

Every actor has written a play, reflected Tess. "Oh? How interesting."

"The lead is Cynthia's, of course."

"Oh, of course."

"But there is a part for you. A good part."

"I am a photographer, Mr. Golden. Not an actress."

It was as though she hadn't spoken. Cedrick was beaming dreamily into space. Tess suspected he spent a lot of time there, like any good cherub. "And naturally there would be a part for your brother."

Ah. So Cedrick was not quite so vacuous as he seemed. "And if I read for the female role, Rod will be in the play, too," she guessed.

"You are not only beautiful, but perceptive."

"I am also completely uninterested. Mr. Golden, I have no talent, no desire—"

"I sense that you have more than your share of desire," interrupted Cedrick.

Tess blushed and lowered her eyes.

Cedrick bent forward in his Morris chair and patted her hand. "Now, now, my dear, I'm not going to pressure you. Not at all. All I ask is that you read my play. As a favor."

Tess swallowed. "All right. I'll be happy to read your play—"

"Good, good! That's all I ask of you. Let us just have our tea and chat like the good friends we are."

Tess felt a shivering uneasiness in the pit of her stomach. Perhaps it was the sound of waves beating on the nearby shore, perhaps it was this man. She didn't know and hadn't the wit, at the moment, to decide. "Where do you suppose Rod is?" she asked, after her teacup had been drained.

"At the portals of heaven, I would imagine," said Cedrick.

The implication was not lost on Tess. Crimson climbed up from beneath the bodice of her sprigged cambric dress and pounded in her cheekbones.

Cedrick laughed throatily at her discomfort. "My dear, my dear—don't look so scandalized. You must know how very—er—affectionate theater people are with each other."

Tess knew. She had been raised in a household where actors and actresses congregated on a regular basis, calling each other "darling" and exchanging embraces the way most people exchanged handshakes. "Not being an actress myself . . ." she began, somewhat lamely.

Cedrick laughed again. But then he took mercy on Tess and began telling her how he and Cynthia had been born of theater people, how they had tired of the road, and, having had some considerable success, decided to buy a theater of their own. They'd had good fortune with their productions and, just recently, given up their rented rooms and bought their current residence.

When Rod reappeared, fully an hour later, he did indeed look as though he'd spent the time in heaven. Tess wanted to slap the sappy expression right off his face.

"We'd best go home now," she boldly suggested, setting aside what must have been her ninth cup of tea and rising out of her chair.

"Ummm-hmmm," sighed Rod, smiling foolishly down into the glowing and upturned face of Cynthia Golden.

Tess was just wondering whether she would have to peel the woman out from under Rod's armpit when Cedrick graciously interceded.

"Heel," he said, looking pointedly at his sister.

Somewhat petulantly, she subsided, that accomplished lower lip jutting out again, just as it had the night before, backstage at the theater.

In the carriage—Rod must have been given money by his doting father, for the driver had waited all this time, and cheerfully—Tess fixed her brother with an icy glare.

"Don't look at me like that," he whined. "You didn't have such a bad time, did you? Cedrick didn't chase you around the parlor."

"Not physically," said Tess, looking down at the manuscript in her lap. It was a play, probably long and insufferably dull, and she had promised to read it. As if she didn't have enough to do, what with her shop in the state it was.

"I had a good time," insisted Rod.

"That was quite obvious," replied Tess.

"Don't play the prude, Tess," snapped her brother. "You're no angel yourself."

There was no denying that. "I'm just tired, that's all. I've got to make plans for my shop—"

"That shop is a joke and you know it. The peddler will come back, grunt a couple of times, whack you over the head with his club, and drag you off to the nearest cave."

"I hate you, Rod Thatcher."

Rod smiled fondly. "I'm crushed. Where were you last night, anyway?"

"That is none of your business."

"Oh, but it is. I'm your brother. When Father and Olivia railroad off into a blissful glow, I'll be charged with looking after you."

"I don't need looking after."

Rod ignored her words and sighed a long-suffering sigh. "I can see it now. I'll get nothing done for dragging you out of caves."

"Or dragging Cynthia into them."

Rod grinned, and this time his sigh was entirely different. The carriage came to a stop in front of the

Grand Hotel, and brother and sister gave every appearance of total devotion as they alighted.

"I despise you," beamed Tess, letting Rod take her hand and help her down.

Rod bent to kiss that very hand. "If I thought I could get away with it," he crooned, "I would wring your little ivory neck. Darling."

The peddler standing a little distance away took in only the last word of the conversation. The scene said enough, all by its self.

The actor. Damn it all to hell, he'd been brooding over her. He'd been drawn back to her when he should be anywhere but where he was. And she was letting that pompous actor fawn all over her!

Keith Corbin felt very sorry for himself.

The shock in Tess's face when she saw him comforted him just a little. What was that light in her eyes?

"Keith!" she cried, in seeming delight, and it was almost as though she was glad—even overjoyed—to see him.

Keith could not look at her. He turned his gaze to the actor, who seemed a little pale. "We meet again," he said, in a low voice.

"Unfortunately," replied Waltam.

Keith prided himself on his reason, his ability to overlook the flaws in others. He'd been trained to be calm, after all. Rational. Forgiving.

He clasped Roderick Waltam by his tweed lapels and flung him unceremoniously against the wall of the Grand Hotel. And this with Tess and half of Portland looking on.

Tess flung herself at him like a frightened, furious bird, clinging to his arm, saying his name over and over again.

And that made him madder still.

He landed a hard punch in the actor's middle and savored the whooshing grunt of pain and surprise that followed.

Tess stepped between him and his prey and her hazel eyes were full of tears. Tears that cooled his temper.

"You beast," she said.

And before he could answer, they were on either side of him, their arms folded, their indigo eyes bright with triumph. His brothers.

Keith swept off his bowler hat and smiled. He was conscious of Tess collecting her gasping swain and disappearing into the hotel, but, at the moment, he couldn't pursue the matter.

"Hello, Keith," said Adam, arms still folded, sending one look after the vanished Tess.

Keith's grin widened and he risked a glance at Jeff, who stood at his other side, glowering. He had definitely taken his big brother pills.

Shit, Keith thought. But what he said was, "I've been looking all over for you guys!"

Chapter Twelve

DURING THE NEXT TWO DAYS, TESS PAUSED SEVERAL
times at the door of the Corbin suite, trying on each
occasion to work up the nerve to knock. And on each
occasion she failed.

Sometimes she heard yelling from within, sometimes
laughter. Most often, it was the latter, accompanied by
the distant click of billiard balls.

In between, she worked, painting her shop, studying
the musty instruction books that Mr. Lathrop had left
behind. At night when, for all her exhaustion, sleep
proved elusive, she read Cedrick Golden's play.

It was surprisingly good, so good that she showed it

to her mother, who, having been a gifted actress, was something of an authority on such things.

Olivia, much recovered and busily preparing to depart for St. Louis with her new husband, read the manuscript with absorption. "The role of Marietta Blake is perfect for you," she observed pensively, late one afternoon when the two women were alone in the suite's trunk- and valise-cluttered sitting room. "And, yes, even though it is a minor part, I can certainly see Rod as Colonel Wilmington."

Olivia spoke fondly of Rod, always, as though he had sprung from her own loins, and why not? Though he was most often sardonic with Tess, delighting in reminding her that she had been born out of wedlock, he petted and fussed over his stepmother; one would never have dreamed that he bore her any ill will at all. And maybe he didn't. It did appear that Rod was not the sort to carry grudges. After all, he had never mentioned the attack Keith Corbin had made upon him in front of the hotel.

"I don't want to play Marietta Blake or anyone else," Tess said quietly. "I'm not an actress."

"I am most relieved to hear you say that. The theater, for all its excitement, offers a very difficult life."

Perched on the arm of her mother's chair, Tess gnawed slightly at her lower lip, a habit Olivia hated and frowned at now. "Rod wants the part of the colonel. He wants it very much."

"I know," smiled Olivia. "I've heard him rehearsing the lines."

"He's not going to get it unless I play Marietta. Cedrick Golden as much as said so."

"How unprofessional! If Rod is suited to the role, then he should have it—"

"Nevertheless—"

Olivia patted Tess's hand. "You mustn't allow yourself to be coerced, my dear. Not in any manner."

Odd advice, coming from Olivia, reflected Tess. But as her time with her mother was limited, she didn't mention it. "I won't. I plan to open my shop, on schedule."

"Good," said Olivia, and then Asa came into the room and Tess might have been a vase on the mantelpiece or a tassle on a rug for all of her mother's awareness of her.

She decided to wrestle her bicycle downstairs—even now, she would not use the elevator—and take a ride. Perhaps take a few pictures of her shop from the outside. The windows were clean now, as was the modest interior, and had been emblazoned with the magical words, "Tess Bishop, Prop.," in flowing, golden script.

Tess did not know whether it was good luck or ill that she encountered Keith Corbin on the landing between the second and third floors.

"Hello, shoebutton," he said idly. He wasn't wearing his plain peddler's clothes or his bowler hat, but a finely tailored suit of gray broadcloth, complete with a silken vest to match, and shiny black boots.

Tess felt a pang at seeing him again so unexpectedly, at realizing that he was not a peddler and never really had been.

She tossed her head, so that her hair swung back over her shoulders in a heavy curtain. She'd meant to put it up, but the decision to ride her bicycle had pushed the idea right out of her head. "I've got a shop of my own now," she said, for suddenly it was important for him to know that she had prospects, too.

"And a lover?"

The question gave Tess pause; an alert, wary feeling leaped within her. "I beg your pardon?"

"Roderick—Waltam, wasn't it? The actor?"

"Rod, a lover?" She had gasped the words, but, an instant later, she had recovered herself, squared her shoulders, lifted her chin to an imperious angle. "Hardly. Rod is my half-brother. And it was cruel of you, by the way, to attack him in that manner."

A smile curved his lips. "In what manner should I have attacked him, shoebutton?"

Tess was blushing. Why, oh why, did she have to blush now? "Why, you should not have attacked him at all!"

"I didn't know he was your brother," Keith replied quietly, as though that explained everything, made up for his barbaric behavior. He approached and, without so much as a by-your-leave, took the handles of the bicycle from her, wheeling it through a doorway and into a hall. "Speaking of brothers," he went on, as he reached the elevator doors and summoned the machine with a twist of a knob, "I understand that you met mine."

Tess wanted to wrench her property away from him, but she knew a futile undertaking when she saw one. Usually. Her pulse was beating on her cheekbones, and her heart seemed determined to rise into her throat. "Yes," she admitted, closing her eyes to remember how she had met them, and where.

"They're gone now," he said. The elevator, with its

grillwork doors of black iron, came to a stop before them with an alarming lurch.

Tess was a little relieved. In their way, Keith's brothers were as unsettling as that elevator. "Oh," she said, wondering why he would trouble to tell her something that was really none of her concern, all things considered.

The doors of the monster creaked and slammed as they opened, but since Keith rolled her bicycle between them, her camera riding in the wicker basket, she had no alternative but to pass through. There was an operator inside the contraption and, because of his presence, neither Tess nor Keith spoke or even looked at each other until they had been delivered safely to the hotel's busy lobby.

There, Keith assessed her with those azure eyes, those eyes that could uplift or wound, and said, "I'd like to see this shop of yours, shoebutton. May I?"

Tess knew that she should have said no, knew that it wasn't wise to let this man know where she would be working, but she couldn't have refused him for all the developing fluid in the world. It was no comfort at all that she recognized him for the one man who could overrule all her fine intentions and turn her into anything he wished to make of her. Be it harlot, mistress, or wife.

"It's just down the road and around the corner," she heard herself saying.

"Close enough to walk. Or ride your bicycle." He glanced down at that apparatus with mingled fondness and amazement, but did not surrender it to her keeping. On the sidewalk, he walked beside it, being careful not to bump into passers-by.

"I won't be staying here at the hotel," Tess babbled out, not thinking. "There are rooms above the shop and I'll live there."

He stopped. A middle-aged matron in a fusty sateen dress gave him a killing glare and then swept around him and the bicycle with a whish of skirts. "Alone?" he demanded.

"Yes," Tess replied loftily. "Alone."

Keith considered this for a moment, still stopped, like a log upended in a stream, forcing the foot traffic to flow around him. Tess had, of course, no choice but to stop, too. A slow smile lifted one corner of his mouth. "Alone," he repeated, and this time he did not sound appalled but intrigued.

"You needn't think for one second, Mr. Corbin, that that is going to make any difference to you!"

He laughed and began rolling the bicycle along again. Tess was annoyed to realize that she had no idea what he was thinking.

It was both a relief and a problem to reach the door of the little shop. Tess's hand trembled a bit as she grappled in her pocket for the outsized key and then worked the lock. While she was doing that, she was disturbingly conscious of Keith's every movement. He was resting the bicycle against the storefront, removing the camera from the basket. Waiting for admission to a place he could so easily become master of, even though he had no right. No right!

The inside of the small establishment smelled pleasantly of pine soap and new paint. The walls were white, the shelves were sturdy, the heavy wooden counter had been polished to a proud shine. Even the little heat-stove, so dusty that first day, gleamed like the armor of some great knight. When winter came, it would be ready to warm all who ventured in.

Keith set Tess's camera down on the counter and looked about him with a careful, pensive sort of interest. "It's nice, shoebutton," he said, after a very long time. "Really nice."

Those words, as simple as they were, set Tess's pride in the place alight. She glowed with excitement, and never mind if that excitement ached just a bit in the vicinity of her heart. "Come and see the cameras I've got!" she crowed, bursting through a curtained doorway and trusting Keith to follow.

Of course, he did.

"Can you operate all this stuff?" he frowned, taking in a virtual army of shadowy equipment.

The doubt in his voice hurt. "Of course I can. I've got books and more books to tell me how! Look—look at this camera! It takes stereoscopic pictures. You know, the kind that look so real—"

Keith smiled. "Yes. I'm familiar with the technique. My sister has a stereoscope and takes delight in boring us all with the three-dimensional ruins of Rome."

Tess felt an unaccountable heat in her cheeks; maybe it was the closeness of Keith, the smallness of the developing room, the shadowy ambiance. She didn't know.

Keith came closer, took her easily in his arms. "I've missed you more than I ever thought I could miss anyone," he said, in a low, gruff voice.

Tess struggled to keep her wits about her and promptly lost. His mouth was descending toward hers, to conquer, and she could make no move to resist. She couldn't even *think* of a move to resist.

He kissed her and the floor seemed to roll beneath her feet like the deck of a ship on stormy seas. Her heart was beating in every part of her body, instead of just her chest, and the hard pressure of his body against her own soft one made her yearn to be possessed by him again.

Their tongues did tender battle as the kiss deepened and became something that mastered them both. Tess felt his fingers at the bottom of her prim cotton shirtwaist and welcomed their brazen heat. Her breasts grew heavy as he bared them, their nipples reaching for him, craving his greed.

Keith bent, nipped at one sweet peak, groaned hoarsely in his hunger.

Oh, Lord, thought Tess, in sweeping, glorious despondency, he's going to take me, right here, right now . . .

Except that the little bell over the shop's front door tinkled suddenly and a familiar feminine voice cried out, "Tess! Are you here? Oh, Tess, tell me you're here!"

"Emma!" whispered Tess, flushing hotly, stepping back to right her camisole and button her shirtwaist.

"Damn," muttered Keith, turning away to brace himself against a worktable with his hands. His breathing was deep and very ragged.

"I'm here, Emma! I'll be right out!"

"I'm here, Emma!" mocked Keith in a sharp undertone. "I'll be right out!"

"Shut up," hissed Tess. And then she smoothed her

hair, her shirts, and her manner and swished out into the main part of her new shop.

Sure enough, Emma was standing there, looking forlorn and lost, her clothes rumpled from heaven knew how many wearings, her hair dank, her eyes hollow.

"Oh, Tess," she cried, dropping the single valise she carried to the rough wooden floor. "I've killed my own papa! Mama wants nothing to do with me—can you blame her—and Mrs. Hollinghouse-Stone wouldn't take me in so Derora just left me—just left me! It was only by the grace of God that I wandered past this shop and saw your name on the window—"

Tess was quick to enfold her friend in a comforting embrace. "Hush, now. Hush. Everything will be all right, I promise. We'll go back to my hotel and you can have something to eat and a bath and a rest, and then you can tell me the whole story."

Docile as a child, Emma nodded. "I'm so glad I found you. So glad."

"I'll take care of you, Emma," Tess promised. And it was no idle vow; she knew that she would follow through willingly if things came to that pass. "Everything is going to be all right."

It was then that Keith came through the curtain separating that part of the shop from the workroom. He looked grim and not a little annoyed, and Tess was in her turn annoyed with him. Couldn't he see how Emma needed her help? Like all men, he was just concerned with his own interests.

Emma took one look at him and her brown, thickly lashed eyes widened. She gave a little scream and swooned to the floor.

"What the—" rasped Keith.

Tess was already kneeling on the rough boards, chafing her friend's plump wrist. "You'd better go. Obviously you've upset her."

"What did I do?"

Emma was moaning, tossing her head back and forth.

"Just go!" hissed Tess.

Keith shrugged angrily and walked out, the little bell ringing extra hard as he slammed the shop's door behind him.

Getting Emma onto her feet and then to the Grand Hotel was no mean enterprise, but Tess managed it. Because she needed all her strength to usher her vaporous friend, she had to lock the bicycle inside the shop.

By the time they had reached and entered Suite 17—now, for the sake of Emma's comfort, Tess willingly braved the elevator—Emma had told her an incredible and somewhat incoherent story involving Rod, a lie told to her parents, her father's sudden death, her mother's anger and blame, a trip, in Derora's company, to Portland. It had taken forever, Emma babbled on, for Mrs. Beauchamp had wanted to stop in every town along the way, it seemed, and tell her scattered friends that she was rich.

Not even trying to make sense of the epic at this point, Tess simply took her friend to her own room, persuaded her to undress and put on a wrapper.

"You rest, Emma," she said, with gentle firmness. "I'll go and make you some tea. Are you hungry?"

"I want a bath!" wailed Emma, for all the world like a little girl.

"You won't swoon again, will you?" Tess fretted. "You could drown—"

Emma's eyes widened at the prospect, but some of her aplomb returned, too. "Of course I won't drown. I'm a grown woman, Tess Bishop!"

Tess didn't bother to argue to the contrary; she simply led Emma across the hallway to the bathroom and started water running into the huge, claw-footed tub.

Just sinking into that water seemed to restore Emma immeasurably. She asked for soap, and when that was produced she sighed with contentment and crooned, "My tea, please."

Shaking her head and biting back a smile, Tess closed the door on her friend and hurried down the hallway, through the sitting room, through the dining room, and into the kitchen.

Asa and Olivia were out, seeing to their railroad passage east, but Rod was very much in evidence. He was, in fact, opening the doors of cupboards, peering inside, and then slamming them closed again.

Tess felt a certain sweet triumph. For once, she was to have the upper hand where this troublesome new brother was concerned.

"Emma is here," she announced briskly, as she took the teapot from the gas-powered stove.

It was as though she had flung a spear into Rod's back. He stiffened and slowly turned to watch Tess as she filled the teapot at the sink and then set it on to boil.

"What?" Rod echoed, in a choked whisper. He had no color at all, and certainly that smug look was gone from his eyes.

"Your dear Emma. The girl you besmirched in Simpkinsville. She's in our bathroom—"

"In our—"

"Bathroom."

"What's she doing here?!"

"I imagine she's looking for you," Tess couldn't resist telling him. "Isn't that sweet, Rod? That she's so devoted, I mean?"

Rod's Adam's apple seemed to take on a life of its own, bobbing up and down along the usually flawless column of his manly throat. "You've—you've got to get rid of her!"

"I can't do that. She's my oldest and dearest friend and I'm afraid she's destitute. Thanks to you, to hear her tell it, her father has perished from the shame and her mother turned her out." Tess spoke these words flippantly, but as their full import struck her, she paused and turned as pale as Rod. "The least you can do is marry her," she finished hollowly.

"Marry her? You must be mad! Cynthia Golden—"

"Cynthia Golden has nothing whatsoever to do with this matter, Rod, and you know it. Your chickens have just come home to roost!"

"One night—it was one night—"

"Sometimes one night is enough, Rod."

In this case, as it happened, one night turned out to be more than enough. When Asa heard the whole of the story—and neither Tess nor Rod had to tell it because Emma assaulted the man with every detail the moment he entered what had been a relatively stable, if temporary home—he insisted that his son do the honorable thing.

Which was, to Asa's repentant and thus morally inclined mind, to marry Emma Hamilton.

The two men retired together to the sitting room to discuss the matter—their shouts could be heard if not understood even from the parlor—and then reappeared, Asa gazing fondly upon Emma, Rod looking as though he would like to murder her where she stood.

A justice of the peace was sent for and, in good time, Emma and Rod became husband and wife.

Rod's compliance was not hard to understand, once Tess had really thought about the situation. Born and raised in a wealthy family, he had grown used to comfort, to having plenty of money. And though he had forsworn those benefits for some years, probably coming near to starvation as an actor, he had had a renewed taste of them of late and become dependent again.

No doubt Asa, in his outrage, had given his son a choice between permanent penury and holy wedlock. Being nobody's fool, Rod had chosen the latter.

Emma was overjoyed and immediately dispatched a wire to her mother, informing her of the happy event. And the fact that Rod slammed out of the apartment instead of romancing her in their marriage bed did not seem to bother her in the least.

The next morning, Tess moved into the quarters over her shop. There was a room for her with a spacious bed, a bureau, and a small wardrobe, a tiny kitchen with a wood-burning cookstove, and a "spare room," hardly more than a closet, actually, that held one narrow cot.

To her, the place might as well have been a palace. It

was her own, after all, every nook and cranny and corner of it.

An account had been opened for Tess, across the street at the bank, so that she would have money to cover her living expenses until her business began to show a profit. It was with enormous pride that she withdrew a small sum to buy provisions at Mrs. McQuade's dry goods store—a teapot, a set of dishes, towels, and sheets, grocery items. She felt rich, and that made it easier to part with her mother.

Asa and Olivia were leaving, that very day, for St. Louis. They would travel by train, stopping off occasionally to "see the sights," as Asa put it. The real purpose, of course, would be to make the long journey as easy as possible for Olivia.

Asa's devotion to Tess's mother, belated as it was, was a tremendous comfort to Tess herself. She found, as she bid them both goodbye, at the railroad station, that she could put aside her own resentments and take joy in the fact that they had at last found each other.

All the same, as she rode back into the main part of the city with a sullen, pensive Rod and a chattering, incandescent Emma, Tess allowed herself a few tears and a modicum of self-pity. She was well and truly on her own now.

Well and truly on her own.

This came home to her with the force of a sledgehammer's blow when she was dropped off in front of her shop, Emma singing a cheery goodbye from the carriage window, Rod sulking in the corner.

The newlyweds were to remain at the hotel, in luxurious Suite 17, until more permanent quarters could be found.

Watching as the carriage rolled away, Tess dealt with her own fears and misgivings by pondering what would become of Emma. Surely a loveless marriage, indeed a forced marriage, would be fraught with dangers and pitfalls of every sort.

Tess was frowning as she unlocked the shop door and went inside. She would have to keep an eye on Emma, who now referred to herself as Mrs. Roderick Waltam-Thatcher and seemed to have forgotten all about her father's death and the further tragedy of her estrangement from her mother. But, then, that was Emma, the sunshine child, born to look on the bright side.

Humming, Tess climbed the stairs to her small quarters above and looked around with pride. She began uncrating the pretty dishes in the middle of her tiny kitchen table, checking each one for chips and cracks. When that was done, she stoked up her wood stove—Asa had even seen that there were chunks of pitchy pine for the purpose—and heated water in her new dishpan.

She bustled about happily, washing her dishes, putting them away on her shelves, washing her forks and knives and spoons and putting them in their drawer.

"Tess," said a familiar, longed-for voice behind her.

She stopped, her back rigid, her soapy hands in midair. Keith. Had she said his name aloud? She didn't think so, but she wasn't sure. And she didn't turn around. "You might knock or something," she choked out.

"On what?" he asked softly. Hoarsely.

It was a reasonable question. She had, after all, neglected to shut the door to her quarters. It was fortunate that it had been Keith who walked in, and not some—some ruffian.

Was there a difference?

She closed her eyes, willing her heart to beat at a pace that did not steal away her breath and close her throat.

He was behind her, his hands strong on her shoulders, but gentle, too, as they turned her.

"I love you," he said.

The words came as a shock to Tess, like being drenched in ice-cold water or startled on a very dark night. She could say nothing, see nothing—except for the golden wedding band that hung in the V of his open-necked shirt.

"Tess."

She broke free of him, turned away again. "The ring. Amelie." The words were broken, incoherent. But they were the best she could manage. "Please, go away."

Keith did not go away. She heard a chinking sound and turned to see the ring and its chain sitting on the table in a little, glimmering pyramid. "I love you," he repeated.

Tess stared at the small rise of gold and then shifted her gaze to his face. His beloved face. "If you want me for a mistress—"

He only waited, watching her. Was that smugness gleaming in his sky-blue eyes, or was it tender amusement?

"I won't be that." Brave words, she thought to herself. If he kissed her, she would respond like a hussy—she wouldn't be able to help herself.

He came nearer and then nearer still, and Tess trembled as he cupped her face in his hands, entangling his fingers in her hair. He bent his head and his lips were warm, tantalizing at her temple.

"Why didn't you tell me you were a preacher once?" she demanded, in desperation. Tingles of heated desire were already prickling through every part of her.

"You didn't ask," he muttered, and each word had the effect of a caress, going from the top of Tess's head to the tips of her toes.

"A person wouldn't think to—"

He undid the tiny buttons of her prim shirtwaist, easily displaced the frilly camisole hidden beneath.

"A person couldn't know—"

Keith chuckled and took the peak of one full and eager breast into his mouth. And, after that, Tess didn't even try to talk anymore.

Chapter Thirteen

CORNELIA HAMILTON STOOD BEFORE HER HUSBAND'S RAW grave, stricken and alone. Jessup was gone, Emma was gone. Both of them dead, though Emma did not rest here in the churchyard, like her father.

There had been a wire—from somewhere. Where? Oh, yes. Portland. Emma was in Portland, married. Happy.

That was a lie, of course. Emma was dead, just as Jessup was dead. And it was all the fault of one man, one evil, despoiling man.

Cornelia tilted back her head, searched the bright April sky for a sign from God. Seeing none, she wrapped her spring cloak tighter around her thin frame. Jessup, Jessup—such a generous, kind husband he had been. "Choose any cloak you like, my love," he'd said. "Choose any cloak in the catalogue."

She shivered, though it wasn't cold. She was not a strong woman, like Derora Beauchamp or her niece, Tess—no. Cornelia could not survive without her man, and she hadn't the spirit to find another.

Soon enough, she would rest here, beside Jessup, her own grave freshly mounded, like his. But first—first there was one thing to do.

She looked up at the sky again. "Just one thing to do," she whispered, and, in the distance, she heard the lonely whistle of the train. Quickly. She must prepare for the journey quickly.

Tess was powerless to stop the man taking suckle at her breast; indeed, she had no desire to stop him. She moaned as he made a sweet feast of her, her fingers knotted in his wheat-gold hair.

Gradually, Keith lowered her until she lay upon the table, beside the box that had contained her new dishes. He plied her other breast now, suckling and then kissing, nibbling, and then gently, gently biting. Tess was electrified and near blind with the need of him.

She felt her skirts edging upward; there was a cool rush of air upon her most heated part as his hand captured her, touched her, tormented her. Her legs dangled over the side of the table and parted willingly enough at his urging.

"Keith—"

"It's all right."

"T-This is a t-table!"

"And you are a feast."

His hand undid the ribbon ties of her drawers. He did not lower the garment, but instead reached inside. Heated moisture was there to greet him; Tess's hips began to lift and then fall again, repeatedly.

Keith left her breasts—they felt damp and good and fiercely peaked—and then suddenly he was nipping at the core of her, through the thin fabric of her drawers.

She gasped, knowing that she would be bared to him. Soon, she would be bared to him, to be savored and enjoyed at his leisure. The excitement quickened her already thunderous heartbeat and made her breath come in throbbing gulps.

"Keith, Keith—"

He brought her drawers down, slowly. Skillfully. She shivered and then cried out hoarsely because he parted her for claiming.

Keith kissed her softly, causing her to writhe now and wail to be taken, consumed. One of his hands rose to attend a pulsing breast, cupping, caressing, gently rolling a pleading nipple between thumb and forefinger. He chuckled—it was a rich, masculine sound—and then his mouth devoured her.

Tess cried out again and convulsed, so ferocious was the pleasure to which he subjected her, but he was not moved to mercy. No, he was avaricious, nipping her and then tonguing her and then taking full suckle.

Treacherous heat built within Tess, she moaned and tossed like a wild thing, exalting in the giving and in the taking, in the terror and the beauty. Finally, there was a sweet, tearing burst of light and warmth within her, and she stretched her hands high above her head, her breasts jutting proud and bare with the motion, in delicious, abandoned surrender. Her cry of release was a high, keening cry of some savage creature living within her.

His hand still working the imprisoned breast, Keith kissed her, softly, again and again, until she had reached another point of shuddering, incomprehensible need.

"Have me—" she choked out, "—oh, God, if you don't have me—"

She thought he would carry her to the bed; he did not. He drew her upright with his hands and then sat down in one of the three kitchen chairs, facing her. Casually, as though it were an everyday matter to make love in a kitchen, he undid the buttons of his trousers, revealing the proud shaft of his manhood.

"Come to me," he said, in a voice so low that Tess might have sensed it rather than heard it.

Obediently, Tess slid off the edge of the table to stand on her own tremulous feet. Keith's hands eased her drawers the rest of the way down; she stepped out of them. A delicious, tingling chill moved beneath her skirts.

Catching bunches of those skirts in both hands, Keith lifted them until she was again bared to him, still damp from the first pleasuring, aching now for more, for the final, wondrous, and wounding fulfillment.

He drew her down carefully, his powerful shaft moving further and further inside her as he lowered her onto it.

Keith was leisurely in his conquering, content to fill her to brimming with himself, delighting in the passion playing in her face. She gasped again as he smoothed her dress aside to reveal her breasts, to admire and caress, to trace the pointy pink nipples with an index finger.

Tess groaned and tried to move upon him, for therein, in the friction of their joining, she knew she would find what he had caused her to need so desperately.

His hands came to her hips, staying their motion with a strength that only made her desire sharper, a thing of madness now.

"Oh, please," she whispered.

Keith chuckled, bent forward slightly to take playful suckle at one vulnerable breast. "Soon," he promised.

Soon was not good enough for Tess. Her need was too savage; she had been driven far beyond the boundaries of civilized reason. She rose and fell, making a wild sound in the depths of her throat, and his hands could not stop her—did not try to stop her. Keith was moaning as she moaned, his head thrown back, his eyes closed, his hips thrusting without restraint.

He muttered wicked, incoherent things as they both struggled toward the pinnacle, things Tess would have slapped him for at any other time, things that were oddly fitting in those moments of glorious, straining passion.

They reached the heights at the same time, his body slamming upward as hers descended. Steel was sheathed in rippling velvet, the essence of one was blended with that of the other.

Tess sank, still quivering, to bury her face in the curve of his neck. "Ooooooh," she breathed, as the last sweet tremors shook her.

Keith stiffened violently, rasping her name, and then

he, too, shuddered into a gasping stillness. "Bed," he said, when he could speak.

Tess gestured vaguely toward the doorway beside the cookstove.

After a few more moments of recovery, Keith stood up, Tess still riding scandalously upon him, her legs wrapped around his hips.

"This is awkward, you know," he said, in a husky voice.

Tess sighed. Though he had been satisfied, his manhood was a firm sword within her. "But so nice."

Keith laughed and buried his face in her neck, nibbling at that moist column as he progressed carefully toward the bedroom. There, on Tess's neatly made bed, with its white iron headboard and ready-made quilt, they made love again. Their needs were not so urgent as before, at least not at first, so they took the time to undress each other fully, to wash each other with tepid water from the basin on Tess's bureau, to touch and learn each other.

For all this, their joining was a furious one, one of tender savagery.

They lay curled together, exhausted, for some considerable time, neither speaking. Tess, for her part, knew a sort of beautiful melancholy. It was humbling to be shown that she was no more modern than her mother, not when it came to this man. Others—such as Cedrick Golden—she could have refused all her life. This one, however, could take her when and where he wanted—hadn't he just proven that?

She sighed.

Keith's fingers were playing idly in her hair, his

shoulder was damp and strong beneath her cheek. "What is it?" he asked softly.

"You made love to me in a kitchen."

Keith laughed; the sound was low and husky and somehow comforting. "That could become a habit."

Tess balled her fist and slugged him, albeit half-heartedly, in the midsection. "It won't become anything of the sort, Keith Corbin. I told you I wouldn't be your mistress and I meant it."

"What do you want to be, if not my mistress?" he asked wryly, turning onto his side now, smiling down into her face.

Your wife, the mother of your children, thought Tess rashly, but she said nothing. She simply bit her lower lip and looked up at him.

Keith ran one hand from her shoulder to her breast—this he briefly cupped—and then down over her ribcage and her hip. Clasping her bottom, he pressed her closer to him. "Tess," he prompted.

Instead of answering, she closed her eyes and stretched, kittenlike, her arms above her head. This proved to be a strategical error, for Keith caught her wrists together and held them against the cool iron of the headboard.

Her breath caught as he surveyed the spoils of the tactic.

"Beautiful," he muttered, and Tess could feel her breasts growing heavy, feel their tips puckering to please his mouth. She tried to lower her hands, and he held her tighter, though painlessly, her arms stretched to their full length. "If you don't answer my question—"

Tess gasped as his other hand came boldly to the triangle of silk between her legs and daudled there, playing. Teasing. "Wh-what question?"

Keith bent his head, circled the taut pink point of her right breast with the tip of his tongue. At the same time, he was parting her legs with his free hand, stroking the inner thighs, venturing back to a place already preparing a musky welcome. "You know very well what question."

"I wo-won't say it!" she whined.

"If you're going to be my wife, you're going to have to learn to be more obedient, shoebutton."

He was mastering her with his fingers, making her writhe and then thrust her hips up to make deeper contact. He still held her hands, and he was tonguing her breasts thoroughly. "I'll—never—be"—she was tossing now, wildly, her breath heaving in and out of her lungs—"obedient!"

"You're being obedient—right now," he pointed out. His hand moved faster, setting a pace for her, and instinct forced her to keep up. Her naked knees fell wide and she groaned helplessly.

"No! No, I'm not—I—" A violent shudder shook her, sweet heat exploded in her depths and sent flaming bits of her pride in every direction. "Ooooooh!" she cried, as feminine muscles tensed convulsively around his fingers. "Keith! Keeeeith—"

He suckled at her breast until the crisis passed, all the while making it keener with his hand.

"You son-of-a-bitch!" she hissed, when she could breathe again.

"I beg to differ. My mother is a very nice woman."

Just for good measure, he tongued the nipple of her right breast into a shape he liked. "You'll be very fond of her."

"I will not." There were tears shimmering in Tess's eyes, blurring her vision. No matter how she hated that fact, it was the truth. "I'll never meet her and you know it."

"How can you get out of meeting her? You did ask me to marry you, didn't you?"

Tess swallowed hard, staring up at him. Confused. He had mentioned marriage, in the heat of their passion—or had he? She couldn't remember. "I—I most certainly did not," she said.

He laughed. "I'm devastated. I thought such an intimacy naturally implied—"

"Stop teasing me!"

Now, he kissed her. Briefly and tenderly. "All right. Since I can't seem to maneuver you into a proposal, I'll just have to take care of the matter myself. Marry me, Tess."

"Why should I?" What was she saying? What was she doing? Nothing, nothing in the world could be better than being married to him!

"Because I love you. And I think you love me." He kissed her again. "Can't have you on the loose," he added, after a long time. "You might take up with that free love bunch again."

Tess ached with joyous despair. "I love you," she confessed. "And I want very much to be your wife. But—"

"But, what?" Keith frowned, stroking her again, issuing no demands but making it very hard for her to think properly, all the same.

"My shop. I can't just give it up—just walk away—"

Keith rolled away from her, sat up, began to dress. There was no anger in the motions, just an easy grace. "We can talk about that another time. Right now, I want to buy a ring and corral a preacher." He turned to look back at her briefly, azure eyes impish.

What was it, this perverse thing inside Tess that bade her argue against what she wanted most? "Oh, sure. And then, when we're married, you can force me to give up the shop. What I want won't matter then, because the law will be on your side!"

He stood up, buttoning his trousers, his chest bare and glinting with a matting of dusky-gold down. "I will never force you to do anything, Tess," he said seriously.

"Are you willing to live here, with me? In my shop?"

"For now." Keith reached for his shirt, shrugged into it, began fastening the buttons.

"I won't have to obey you?"

"I didn't say that. There are certain areas where I expect total obedience, Tess."

"Such as?" she snapped, determined to find something wrong.

"If I send you to our bedroom, for example, I expect you to go without any arguments, tears, or attacks of the vapors. You will await me there and you will accommodate me."

Tess felt a delicious sort of rage at the very idea. "Suppose I send *you* to the bedroom?"

Keith threw back his head and laughed. "You may take your pleasure as you wish. But I expect the same kind of co-operation, Tess—don't forget that."

She sat up on the bed, scandal pulsing in her cheeks.

She would have to obey him in that area, but he would have to obey her, also. It was a fair enough bargain, as far as she could see. "Anything else?"

"Yes. You'll have to stay away from free lovers. And you'll have to be faithful to me, Tess."

"Will you be faithful to me?" she asked softly, and so much depended on his answer that she held her breath to hear it.

"Absolutely," he said, with conviction. "Now, do I accept your kind proposal or what?"

Tess laughed and flung a pillow at him. "You accept," she said. "In fact, you're honored!"

He hurled the pillow back. "Honored?!"

"Yes," said Tess. "You're lucky to get a wife like me, you know."

Keith spoke softly. Seriously. "Yes. I know." He came to the bedside, bent to kiss her. "I'm going out for a little while."

Tess felt daring and brash and totally happy. "Be back soon. I might want to send you to bed."

He chuckled and drew her to her feet, pulling her against him. As he had once before—it seemed so long ago and so far away—he swatted her firm bottom. "I certainly hope so," he said, and then he was turning away, disappearing through the bedroom doorway.

Cedrick Golden paused on the sidewalk, admiring himself in the window of Tess Bishop's laughable little shop. The minx. She belonged on a stage, not behind some tacky counter, selling photographs.

Satisfied that he looked as handsome as ever, Cedrick tried the door and found it open. A small bell tinkled over his head as he passed inside.

"Tess?"

She came down the stairs, a bounding, gazelle-like creature, her delightful hair tumbling about her shoulders and breasts, reaching well past her waist. There was a fetching pink glow in her cheeks and a sparkle in her eyes that bespoke of an interesting afternoon.

As he removed his fine beaver top hat, Cedrick wondered idly who had taken her. In the final analysis, he didn't care—having her himself would be no less of a pleasure for it. Virgins were so tiresome, while women who knew the possibilities of pleasure were generally pliable, responsive.

"Hello, Cedrick," she said, somewhat shyly, averting her eyes for a moment. He pondered the fact that the bodice of her pink calico dress was misbuttoned and, imagining the plump delights hidden beneath, felt himself harden.

He bowed slightly, his hat still in his hand, glad that he hadn't worn his cutaway coat, but one that hid his masculine appreciation. "Tess," he greeted her, in cordial return. "Have you read my play?"

All day long he'd been preparing himself for whatever polite excuses she would offer. He was quite taken aback when she said, "Yes, I've read it. And I liked it. Very much. I have it here, in fact—if you'll just wait a moment—"

Suavely, Cedrick nodded. Oh, to get that little wench into a closed carriage or a dressing room at the theater. . . .

She disappeared again, into the upper apartments, a place no doubt as dreary and common as the shop itself, returned in moments with the play. She offered the manuscript shyly, as she had offered her smile earlier.

"You will consider reading for a part?"

"I couldn't," came the soft response. God, whoever had tamed her had done a masterful job of it. Gone was the saucy hoyden of before, in her place was this angelic little confection, all pink and gold and pliant.

Cedrick had been of the opinion that Tess needed nothing so much as a thorough spanking; he was almost disappointed to find her so docile. "Please reconsider," he said. "And by the way, Cynthia and I were hoping that you might join us at dinner tonight. We don't have a performance this evening, and Rod and his lovely new wife have already agreed—"

"I'm busy tonight," she said. Sweetly, but firmly, too. So taken was he with her that it had taken Cedrick all this while to realize that she was saying no to the role in his play. Saying no to everything.

He was quietly furious. Oh, to toss up her skirts and doff her drawers and discipline her as she so richly deserved! But Cedrick didn't dare, not until after he'd bedded her. Once that sweet chore had been taken care of, he would bring Tess Bishop swiftly to heel. Oh, yes. After she'd brought him a slipper and bared her sweet, plump bottom to his manly punishment a few times, she would obey him without question. "I'll send our carriage by tonight, just in case you change your mind," he said, calling on all his acting abilities, keeping a rein on his temper.

Outside, his play under one arm and his pride under the other, Cedrick climbed back into his carriage, where a young actress awaited him. Eleanor was a

woman who understood obedience, understood masculine superiority.

The imaginary scenario with Tess was vivid in his
mind. He couldn't stop picturing the golden-ivory
bottom, upturned in his lap. It would flush a pretty pink
when he'd spanked her. . . .

Cedrick hardened to the point of pain. He snapped
his fingers and scowled at Eleanor, who promptly knelt
between his legs, unbuttoned his trousers, and attended
him. Because he imagined that it was Tess who pleasured him—a contrite and henceforth obedient Tess—
his release was explosive.

Still, when the carriage came to a stop, some minutes
later, in front of his stately house, he glowered at
Eleanor.

"You have displeased me," he said.

It was a game, they both knew that. And Eleanor
played for her own reasons. No flash of rebellion
sparked in her blue eyes, and the flush in her cheeks
was not one of anger. She climbed out of the carriage
without Cedrick's help and walked into the house.

Cedrick loved this game; it made him feel strong, and
in command. But today, as he took off his light suit coat
and hung it on the hall-tree, along with his best beaver
hat, he looked forward to the scene that would take
place in his room with something other than
anticipation—contempt. He felt contempt, for himself
as well as Eleanor.

Tess left the shop door open to the spring breeze
after Cedrick had gone, though she couldn't have said
why. It was as though he had left a bad smell behind.

She hummed as she dusted a counter she hoped would soon be lined with customers. And in addition to her business, she would have a husband, a man she truly, fiercely, shamelessly loved!

Was ever a woman so wealthy?

The bell over the door chimed in the soft wind, and Tess looked up automatically, smiling.

Emma stood before her, looking plump and disgruntled in one of her many new dresses. "Oh, Tess," she began, and then she positively blubbered with unhappiness.

Inwardly, Tess was annoyed, but a look of concern for her friend passed over her face and she asked, "Emma, what is it?"

"Rod is seeing another woman!" wailed Emma.

Tess gathered her friend under one arm, ushered her to one of the chairs underneath the windows, where clients would soon await their sittings. "But you've only been married—"

"I know how long we've been married!" cried Emma. "And he's smitten with that—that blonde actress! He told me so himself!"

Tess gritted her teeth. Rod certainly hadn't waited long; the moment Asa and Olivia had left town, he'd dropped all pretense of being a real husband. "Emma, you did force him to marry you—"

"I thought I c-could make him happy!" came the moistly nasal response. "But he didn't even give me a chance!"

"I'm sorry," said Tess, in a gentle voice. For she was sympathetic, if not surprised.

Emma was dabbing at her sodden cheeks with a handkerchief already bearing her monogram in silken thread. "There's more!" she sobbed dramatically. "We're being put out of our hotel, too!"

"But Rod had money—I know he did!"

Emma's curvaceous little body trembled with outrage and hopeless despondency. "He invested it all in that stupid play of Mr. Golden's! He says it's going to make us rich in our own right, so that we don't have to take so much as one more red cent from Mr. Thatcher—"

"That fool!" spat Tess. "Did he get a part in the play, at least?"

"W-We're supposed to find out tonight. Oh, Tess, where will we live in the meantime? What will we do?"

Tess would have liked to say that that was rightfully Rod's problem, but she couldn't bring herself to do it. Emma seemed so small and young and scared. "What did Rod say about it? About where you would live, I mean?"

"He said you would put us up. Right here." Emma sat up very straight and looked damply hopeful. "Oh, would you, Tess? Just until Roderick realizes that I'm the woman he needs—"

"Emma, I'm being married today! I can't have you and Rod here—"

Emma's brown eyes widened. "You're being married? And you weren't going to tell us? Your own family?"

Tess had never wanted to slap Emma before, but the desire was all but irresistible now. "We made the decision rather suddenly—"

"Who? Who is he?" Emma broke in, eager now. Even after her own devastating experience with marriage, the institution seemed to fascinate her.

"Keith Corbin. His name is Keith Corbin. Emma, you and Rod will just have to—"

"I won't make a sound, I promise!" Emma swore, tears welling in her eyes again. "And Roderick—Roderick probably won't even be here—"

"Probably? Rod 'probably' won't be here? Emma, you know how small my rooms are—"

"I'll be on the street if you turn me away."

Tess began to pace, wanting to scream. Wanting to throw things. Wanting to wring Emma Thatcher-Waltam's neck.

"I'd invite you in a moment," Emma bristled, sitting up very straight now, "if the situation were reversed. And you know it, Tess Bishop!"

Tess did know. She couldn't refuse her friend shelter, for heaven's sake. "You could leave Rod. I would buy you a train ticket back to Simpkinsville and—"

"Never," said Emma firmly.

Tess gave a heavy sigh. Some wedding night this was going to be, with Emma blubbering in the spare room and Rod throwing in his hat at who-knew-what hour, after a tryst with Cynthia Golden. Some wedding night indeed.

Chapter Fourteen

IT WAS SO EASY TO FIND HIM. SO EASY.

The Lord had His hand on Cornelia Hamilton's shoulder. How else could she have known that she would find the peddler here, in Portland? How could she have encountered him, in a city where there were thousands of people, within minutes of her arrival?

But there he was, walking out of a jewelry store. He was wearing finer clothes than he had in Simpkinsville, and smiling. Smiling.

Cornelia hated him. He was a demon from hell, surely—look what he had done to her family. She fell into step behind him, her cloak pulled tight around her.

He walked rapidly, as though eager to complete his business. Cornelia had to hurry to keep up with him.

Once, he looked back, as though he had sensed that someone was following him. Seeing Cornelia, he dismissed her.

A mistake.

Oh, but he was handsome. She could almost see why Emma had succumbed to him. He had the face one might expect of a warrior angel.

She had lost Jessup, lost Emma. Because of him. She reminded herself of that as she hurried along.

The city was so noisy, and full of strange smells. Cornelia didn't like the city, wanted to get away.

He stepped into an alleyway, whistling. Never dreaming, probably, that justice was upon him. Or almost.

Cornelia followed him into the alley; he was striding through the shadows, probably taking a short cut somewhere. He seemed so busy.

"Mr. Shiloh?" Cornelia called after him.

He stopped, turned. Cornelia read polite impatience in his manner.

"Mr. Joel Shiloh?"

He looked as though he might deny the name, then sighed and inclined his head. "What is it?"

Cornelia drew the small, two-shot derringer out from beneath her cloak. She leveled it, he lunged toward her.

He was too late. One bullet struck him in the head, the other in the area of his heart, as far as Cornelia could discern. He collapsed, face down, and blood stained the dirt around him.

Cornelia heard the shouts, the running feet. There were people all around her, one of them wearing a badge, all of them chattering at each other. Talking so fast that she couldn't understand them.

She smiled, even as she was arrested. It didn't matter what happened to her; she was the woman who had killed the devil.

After settling the distraught Emma in the spare room, where she was now snoring like a lumberjack, Tess retired to her own small chambers to prepare for her wedding. Olivia had been able to save the yellow lawn gown that Rod had stained with wine that night at dinner; she would wear that.

She brushed her hair until it shimmered with coppery brown highlights and then pinned it into a soft knot on top of her head.

And then she paced.

Twilight came and Emma still slept noisily in the spare room, but Keith did not return. Tess went to her window, time and time again, but none of the faces passing by on the street below were his.

Where could he be? He'd said he would be back in a little while. But he had been gone for hours.

He had changed his mind, that was it. Maybe he had never intended to buy a ring, never intended to marry her.

Tess bounded out into the kitchen, blushed to remember what had happened on that table. Amelie's ring, still affixed to its chain, was there, mute and heartening proof—

Proof of what?

Tess paced here as she had paced in the bedroom. Perhaps Keith was in a saloon somewhere, fortifying himself for the ceremony to come. Perhaps—

But he didn't seem to drink much; she'd only seen him intoxicated the one time, back in Simpkinsville, after Mrs. Hollinghouse-Stone's free love lecture. Besides, he'd seemed eager to marry, not reluctant.

Tess bit her lower lip. Where could he be? Where?

The bell downstairs tinkled and she rushed to investigate, only to find a liquor-flushed, defensive Rod standing just over the threshold. "Is Emma here?" he demanded.

Tess's hand tightened on the stairway's rickety banister. "Yes. She was very upset when she arrived, Rod."

He bristled, closed the shop door behind him. "Emma is too easily upset."

"Yes," retorted Tess, with dry annoyance. "And over little things like having no money, no place to live, and a husband who openly admits to philandering."

"I invested that money!"

"You might as well have tossed it down the privy, and we both know it, Rod. You were trying to buy a part in Cedrick's stupid play."

"It isn't a 'stupid play,' Tess—it's a work of art. A part in it could make me—"

"You are a total idiot."

Rod absorbed this accusation with a grimace, swaying slightly on his feet. His eyes swept over Tess's salvaged yellow gown with brotherly appreciation. "At least you're going to dinner with us. That might help."

"I'm not doing anything of the sort. I'm supposed to get married."

"Married?! When? To whom—that peddler?"

"Yes, married. Tonight. To 'that peddler.'"

"Where is he, then?" asked Rod, reasonable in a testy sort of way.

I wish I knew, despaired Tess, blanching just a bit and losing all her aplomb.

Rod brightened. "Then you can help me. You can sell this shop and perhaps give me a loan from your account—"

No longer did Tess sag; she went rigid. "There will be no loan, Rod, and I'm not about to sell my shop. I'll look after Emma, and that's the extent of it."

"What about me?"

"You'll have to fend for yourself. This place is too small for four people."

"So he's going to live here, this husband you've snared. Can't he even provide for his own wife?"

"A remarkable question, coming from you, Rod—dear."

Rod had the decency to look somewhat chagrined. He thrust his hands into his no doubt empty trouser pockets and dipped his head. "It's not that I don't care for Emma—"

"Flinging your fascination with Cynthia Golden in her face hardly constitutes devotion, Rod."

Rod flinched. "I was forced into this marriage, Tess. You know that."

"And for what? Money to give to Cedrick—who probably has plenty of his own?"

"You've got to help me, Tess. Please. Be in the play—that's all I ask. Then I can be in it, too, and prove to Cedrick that I—"

"Cedrick, Cedrick. Rod, wake up. You've been had,

229

don't you see that? Fleeced. I have a shop to run and absolutely no desire to be an actress—"

"If you won't do it for me, do it for Emma."

Tess averted her eyes. Shadows were netting the streets, people were hurrying homeward for supper. Where, oh, where, was Keith? "There are some things I will not do, Rod—not even for Emma."

"At least go to dinner with us."

"I told you—"

"I know. That you were getting married. You look a little frazzled to me, Tess. It's almost as if you think—"

"Think what?" snapped Tess.

"That you've been had. Fleeced, as you put it before."

Tess paled again, her grasp on the banister tightened. Damn it, Rod had reached inside her, somehow, and touched her rawest fear.

"He isn't going to come back, Tess." Again, Rod's eyes swept over her, this time with something very much like contempt. "My guess would be that your peddler has already gotten what he wanted. No doubt, he's moved on by now."

"No," Tess said weakly. "No."

Rod only shrugged. "I want to see my wife," he said, and as he passed his sister on the stairs, he was careful not to look at her.

Tess went to the shop's front window and peered out. Keith, she thought, in despair. Keith.

He did not answer her summons; only strangers passed the shop.

Full darkness came, and, with it, Cedrick Golden's carriage.

Emma and Rod came down the stairs arm in arm, as though this were their home and not Tess's, ready to go and hobnob with the Goldens.

"Come with us, Tess," Rod urged softly. "It's obvious, after all, that you've been stood up."

It was. Tess lowered her head as Cedrick came into the shop, filling it with that sweet-spicy scent that made her want to fling open windows.

Cedrick caught her hand in his and suavely kissed it. "You've changed your mind. Oh, Tess, how lovely you look—"

This is supposed to be my wedding night, Tess wanted to scream.

"My sister is looking forward to joining us," Rod put in archly. "Aren't you, dear?"

Tess glared at him, flushed. She was trapped. She had a choice between pacing that shop like a forlorn ghost or getting through the evening by visiting the Goldens. In her heart, she knew that Keith was not going to come, that there would be no marriage.

"Yes," she said lamely, not meeting Rod's eyes or Cedrick's or even Emma's. "Yes."

"Wonderful!" crowed Cedrick, offering his arm, which Tess took with the greatest reluctance.

He was spinning, end over end, through a wide tunnel. As he drew nearer to the dazzling light at the end, the warming, pulling light, his pace slowed and he floated.

He did not seem to have a body, though he was conscious of being himself.

The tunnel faded, and Keith was in a place he could

not define or describe; a place that was not a place but more of an entity.

And she was there. Amelie. Walking toward him, smiling. Whole and alive.

It was impossible.

She spoke to him in a voice heard with the heart, rather than the ear. "Keith."

He did not try to touch her. He had an unsettling feeling that he was not seeing her as she was, but as he remembered her. Thunderation, what was the matter with him? He wasn't seeing her at all, she was dead. He'd been there when she died, he'd seen it happen. . . .

"Go back," she said.

The light was a healing, holding thing. Keith was not eager to leave it. But there was Tess—Tess wasn't here—

"She's waiting," said Amelie. And then she smiled. "In December, she will bear you a child."

Tess, he thought, fiercely. Desperately. Tess, Tess—

And then he was spinning backward, through the tunnel, away from the healing light, away from Amelie. He opened his eyes and found that the ugliest nun he'd ever seen was peering down into his face. She smelled of cloves and old age and maybe just a touch of medicinal brandy.

"Ah," she observed. "You are awake."

Her tones were heavily accented—German, he thought. "I just had the damnedest dream—"

"What is your name?"

Keith had a feeling that she knew his name already and was testing to see if he shared this knowledge.

"Keith. Keith Corbin. I've got to go now. I'm supposed to get married."

"You go novhere!" barked the nun.

Keith subsided into the pillows. "But—"

"You vill not get married this night, my fiend," she said, more moderately.

His head ached. His shoulder throbbed. And he felt sick to his stomach. It was true that he was in no condition to get married, he guessed, but Tess would be waiting. Worrying. Thinking she'd been left at the altar, so to speak. "What happened to me?"

"You ver shot," said the nun, frowning at the bandages on his head. "Dere vas much bleeding. You sleep now and get married another time, no?"

Keith sighed. He didn't remember getting shot. But he did remember a woman calling out to him, calling him "Joel Shiloh." She'd seemed familiar—who was she? Oh, yes. That Simpkinsville storekeeper's wife—

Wife. He ached to think what Tess must be going through now, what she must be imagining.

"I want you to send a message to a Miss Bishop, on Herald Street. Twelve Herald Street."

"Tomorrow, message. Tonight, sleep."

"Please—"

"Sleep," said the nun fiercely.

Keith swore and closed his eyes, hoping he wouldn't have that dream again.

Dinner conversation was a torment for Tess, and trying to eat was worse. She smiled whenever Rod nudged her.

The Goldens' dining room was as elegant as the rest

of their seaside house. The table was set with real silver, not plated tin, and the dishes were of the finest bone china. The glasses were crystal, the food was served by a pretty maid in a prim uniform, the conversation sparkled with wit and theatrical urbanity.

Tess was miserable.

It was Emma who distracted her from her own despair. She was glaring at Cynthia Golden as though she'd like to crown her with a casserole dish. Cynthia, who was beautiful but somewhat lacking, upon closer observation, in intelligence, ignored Emma and bestowed her glowing countenance upon Rod like a smothering light.

Cedrick, in the meantime, was vying for Tess's attention.

". . . simply awful, wasn't it? A shooting, in broad daylight . . ."

The remark, only half heard, brought Tess's gaze instantly to Cedrick's face. "What did you say?"

Cedrick smiled and patted her hand, for she had been seated at his immediate right. A choice she would not have made for herself. "There was a shooting late this afternoon. Didn't you hear about it?"

"Wh-who was shot?"

Cedrick fluttered one perfectly manicured hand, while the fingers of the other lingered over Tess's. "Some peddler," he said.

What little dinner Tess had managed to eat rose to her throat and burned there. She fought it down even as she wavered to her feet. "Did he die?"

Cedrick only looked at her, stupidly. Tess wanted to slap him.

"Did he die?!" she screamed.

Cedrick paled, just a little, and then shrugged. "Sit down, dear. What does it matter?"

Tess did slap him then. With all the strength she could muster. And then she dashed out of the Goldens' opulent dining room in a blind, frantic daze. Shot, shot, the peddler shot—the images flashed through her mind, bright with blood.

The door. Where the devil was the damned door?

Rod caught up to her, restrained her. Or tried to. She struggled and kicked and hissed until he was forced to release her.

"Where would they take him, Rod?" she demanded, as Cynthia and Cedrick and Emma all gathered around to glare at her. "Take me there! Now!"

"Tess—" her brother was trying to soothe her, dissuade her from leaving.

"I swear to God I'll walk there if you don't help me—"

It was Cedrick who stepped forward, out of the pounding haze, and despite the blow Tess had struck him, he spoke gently. "I'll take you wherever you want to go, Tess."

"The hospital—how many hospitals are there in Portland—"

Rod looked at Cedrick, and, in her frantic, distracted state, it almost seemed to Tess that she saw an unspoken warning pass from her brother to the other man. "I'll go along," he said.

"And leave me here with her?!" shrieked Emma, indicating the still smiling Cynthia with a wave of her hand.

Rod became, in that confused instant, a firm husband. "You will do as I tell you, Emma. Is that understood?"

Emma flushed prettily. "Yes, Roderick," she said sweetly.

Tess was wild to leave. Furthermore, she didn't care if Emma had to wait with Sitting Bull. "Please—let's go!"

They rode in Cedrick's fine carriage, the three of them, Rod thoughtful and distracted, Cedrick repeatedly patting Tess's hand. Only by great effort did she keep from screaming at him to leave her alone.

The police station was the first stop they made and there, while Cedrick waited in the carriage, Rod and Tess went in. A sergeant told them that a man named Keith Corbin had been shot that afternoon, by a woman now in custody. He'd been taken to City Hospital.

"But his name—" Rod began.

Tess was already racing back to the carriage, her hair falling from its elegant wedding do in glistening tendrils, her eyes stinging with tears. "Oh, Rod, shut up!" she cried as she ran.

They reached the hospital a mere five minutes later, though it seemed like five hours to Tess. Before Rod and Cedrick could so much as rise from their seats, she was out of the carriage and halfway up the walk.

"No visitors," said a nun roughly the size of Mt. Baker, when Tess came to a stop before the admissions desk.

"I'll find him if I have to look in every single room!" insisted Tess.

"You are the bride, no?"

"No. I mean, yes!" Tess knew that Cedrick and Rod were standing on either side of her now, but she did not spare so much as a glance for either of them. "Where is Keith Corbin?"

"Bride?" echoed Cedrick, in wounded tones.

"I'll explain later," answered Rod.

"What room?!" shouted Tess.

The nun was not intimidated; Tess suspected that nothing could have frightened that woman, not even a demon chorus singing hell's anthem. But she did relent.

"Room 14," she said, gesturing toward one of four hallways. "You must be quiet and not avaken him."

"Thank you," Tess whispered, hurrying into the shadowy, quiet hallway the nun had indicated and searching frantically for Room 14.

Behind her, at the desk, she could hear Cedrick rasp, "Married?"

Rod said something, she was in too much haste to care what it was.

Room 14 was at the end of the hall, and although it had four beds, all but one were empty. Keith lay in that one bed, his head and one shoulder neatly bandaged, his flesh pale as parchment.

Tess touched his face. "Keith?"

He opened one eye. And then the other. "Hello, shoebutton," he said. "What are you doing here?"

Tess wanted to laugh and cry, but she did neither. Or was it both? "What do you think I'm doing here?" she whispered. "I'm looking for the man who left me standing at the altar."

He laughed hoarsely. "I bought a ring—I was going to the livery stable—this woman—"

Tess touched his mouth; it felt too dry and too warm,

and she cast about for a water pitcher and glass, found them. She held both the cup and his injured head while he drank. "You don't need to explain, Keith. Not now."

His wonderful, pale blue eyes were full of pain, some of it physical and some of it, Tess thought, emotional. "I'm sorry. You were waiting. You didn't know—you must have thought—"

She silenced him with a tender kiss. "Hush. You need to sleep now."

"You sound like Attila the Nun," he said obliquely.

At that moment, Cedrick and Rod came in. Rod was quiet, watchful, but Cedrick was in a grand rage. "Now," he boomed, glaring at Tess. "I assume you're satisfied and we can go back to our dinner?"

"Dinner?" Keith whispered, looking at Tess's dress again, at the coiffure that had been so special. The pain in his eyes was more than she could bear to see, but bear it she did. "You were at dinner?"

Tess ached. "You don't understand, Keith—I thought—"

"I know what you thought," he hissed. "It didn't take you long to mend your broken heart, though, did it, shoebutton?"

"Keith!"

He rolled away, facing the wall. And it was then that Tess Bishop's heart broke. Exactly then. "Please, Keith, listen to me."

Silence. He was not going to look at her, not going to listen.

Rod took her arm gently. "Come on, Tess," he said, sounding for all the world like a devoted brother. "You can explain tomorrow. I'll help you. But you need to rest now, and so does he."

"Rest?!" thundered Cedrick. "What about my play? What about Tess's part in—"

At this, Keith stiffened beneath his thin hospital blankets. She reached out to touch his bandaged shoulder and then drew back, thinking better of it.

"Take your goddamned play and—" Rod began angrily, but before he could finish—and perhaps that was fortunate—the German nun swept in and ordered them all out.

Cedrick pouted all the way back to his house, but Rod was gentle, even solicitous. "Tess," he kept saying, "everything will be all right. I promise that it will."

Tess clung desperately to those words, but they made a scant handhold, and she felt herself slipping away from them, into hopelessness. Keith was a stubborn man, so stubborn. He was never going to believe that she had only gone to dinner at the Goldens' because she couldn't bear to wait and worry all by herself. Never.

Further drama awaited them at the Golden house. It seemed that Emma and Cynthia had gotten into a spirited row; there was food all over the dining room floor—it even dripped from the wainscotting—and Cynthia was standing in the middle of the table, shrieking.

Emma stood like a small boxer, her fists in position for round two. "Come down here, you hussy, and I'll—"

Rod turned bright red and then pure white. "Emma!" he gasped in horror.

"Oh, help me!" wailed Cynthia, with added drama. After all, she had an audience now. "Save me! Someone save me!"

"What in the name of Zeus is going on here?!" bellowed Cedrick.

"That woman is trying to kill me!" whined Cynthia, pulling one dainty foot out of a pound cake. "Oh, Cedrick, it was horrible—"

"Horrible?" leered Emma, her arms folded now, her hands still making pudgy little fists. "I'll show you 'horrible,' you brazen—"

"Emma!" shouted Rod. His acting career was over, as far as Cedrick Golden was concerned, and the knowledge flared bright red in his face. "Apologize immediately!"

"I will not!" screamed Emma.

Good for you, thought a weary and, despite everything, wryly amused Tess.

Cedrick was making a visible effort to control himself. His somewhat narrow chest moved rapidly as he drew deep breaths and his eyes were tightly closed. "Our driver," he said, with consummate politeness, "will take you home."

Rod collected his wife and fairly thrust her out of the Golden house, down the walk, and into the waiting carriage. Tess followed numbly along behind, wishing that this dreadful day would be over. Or better yet, that it had never dawned at all.

What if she'd lost Keith? What if he wouldn't listen, wouldn't understand? It was just a simple misunderstanding, really. Surely, he would be able to see that.

Rod instructed the driver to stop at Tess's shop and climbed into the vehicle to sit beside Emma. To his sister, he said, "We'll be in Father's suite at the Grand Hotel, should you need us."

Tess was too tired and too soul-sick to say more than, "I thought you'd been turned out."

Rod glared down at his unrepentant, tight-lipped wife. "We have another week," he said, in tones that promised that it would be a dire week indeed.

When they reached the shop, Rod got out and waited conscientiously while his sister unlocked the door. When she had, he accompanied her inside, found a lamp for her and lit it.

"I'm sorry, Tess," he said. "About Cedrick and the play and everything else."

"You won't—you wouldn't beat Emma or anything, would you? She was only jealous—"

Incredibly, Rod smiled. "She was wonderful, wasn't she?"

Tess found a smile somewhere inside herself and held it for a fleeting moment. "She was magnificent. Good night, Rod."

"Good night," he replied, brushing her forehead just briefly with his lips. He waited on the sidewalk until Tess had again locked the door, and, as she went up the stairs, carrying her lantern, she heard the rattle of carriage wheels on the rutted street.

What might have been the happiest night of her life was to be, after all, the loneliest.

Chapter Fifteen

KEITH STARED BLANKLY UP AT THE CEILING OF HIS HOSPI-
tal room. The pain was unrelenting.

The ache in his shoulder was a constant, fiery
throb, and the place just above his right temple,
where the other bullet had grazed him, stung like
the venom of a thousand bees. Both injuries were
trifles, though, compared to what Tess had done to
him.

He swallowed hard. When he'd lost Amelie, he'd
thought that there could be no greater pain. Apparently, Tess Bishop had been sent into his life to prove how
wrong he'd been.

The German nun stood at his bedside, and he

focused his attention on her, desperate to distract himself from thoughts of Tess.

"I suppose you've contacted my family," he said, in hollow tones.

Attila nodded, sympathy written in every line of her starched and bulky being. How much did she know? Had he been raving in his sleep, calling, God forbid, for Tess?

Tess, Tess. Her name pounded beneath his injuries like a steel hammer.

It was as though just thinking her name had worked the magic necessary to conjure her. She came bursting into the room then, her heavy hair already rebelling against its pins, her eyes enormous, her fine cheekbones flushed.

Keith gazed at her steadily, fiercely, because he could not look away. He was absorbing the sight of her, storing every detail within himself. In the days and months and years ahead, he knew, he would need the memory to sustain him.

"He is resting!" protested Attila sharply.

"I don't care," replied Tess, in an even voice, her small shoulders squared, her eyes never leaving Keith's face. "He can rest another time. Right now, he's going to be married."

Married. Keith used all his considerable will to tear his gaze from her, to focus again on the ceiling. There were rusty blotches in the plaster, where the rain and snow had leaked through, and he methodically counted them. Again.

He felt Tess drawing nearer to his bed; all his senses leaped in response, and the pain, suddenly, was much keener than before.

She touched his face, her hand cool and light and still slightly rough from years of hard work. "Why are you so angry with me?" she whispered brokenly. "I only went to dinner—"

"With an actor," Keith said, still not daring to look at her. He knew he was behaving like a spoiled child, knew it but couldn't seem to stop.

Tess persisted. "I thought you had abandoned me, you know," she said.

"So you found yourself someone else." His voice was gruff, rattling in the sore depths of his throat. "You're resourceful, I'll say that for you."

Her voice rose a little. "You are being deliberately difficult, Keith Corbin, and we both know it. I didn't know that you had been shot. I thought you had—you had just gotten wh-what you wanted and left."

"You must have been devastated. For five minutes at least."

Her hand tensed against his face; she tried to turn his head, make him look at her, and he resisted stubbornly.

Tess drew a deep, quivering breath. He heard it, felt it in his own lungs. "Rod—my brother—had been pressuring me to go to dinner at the Goldens'. You see, Mr. Golden is producing this play and Rod is an actor and he wants a role very badly—"

"What does that have to do with you?" Keith was thawing, gentling toward her, against his will, against his every effort.

Tess sighed. "Mr. Golden wanted me to be in the play, too. I've told him that it's out of the question, but he just keeps asking."

Tess's fingers were moving on the unbandaged side of his face, their touch almost imperceptible and yet devastating. "Then it would make sense, it seems to me, to avoid him—not to go galavanting off to his house on what was supposed to be your wedding night!"

"You're jealous!" Her laughter pealed, soft and musical, in the dreary room. "You're actually jealous of that presumptuous, effeminate fop!"

Keith could no longer keep his eyes averted; they darted to her face, caressing, memorizing, searching. "You don't like him?"

She laughed again, but there were tears shining in her bright, hazel eyes. "Would I call him such names if I liked him, you goose?"

"You call *me* names," he pointed out, somewhat petulantly, looking at the ceiling again. The same eleven rusty blotches looked back at him.

"That's different," she said softly. "There is no reason for you to be jealous, Keith—not of any man in the whole world."

Man? He felt more like a child. His throat drew closed, tight as the top of a tobacco sack, and he fought back the tears throbbing behind his eyes.

She bent, kissed him softly. "I love you," she said. "And I mean to marry you. Right now."

"Right now?" he croaked, staring up at her.

Tess nodded, crystal tears blooming in her eyes. "I brought a justice of the peace. The same man who married Asa and Mother and Rod and Emma. That's all right, isn't it? Our being married by a justice of the peace, I mean?"

It was more than all right; it was his salvation. "Yes," he managed to say. "Wh-where is he?"

"Waiting in the hallway." She was frowning pensively at his bandages. "Now that I really look at you, I'm not sure you're up to a wedding at all. How serious are your wounds, Keith? Did they operate on you?"

It was a long time before he could answer, for his throat was drawn taut again, this time with joy. "I've got a few stitches, but I'll be fine."

"Do the police know who shot you?"

"They have a woman in custody, I'm told."

Tess swallowed visibly, and Keith wished that he could reach up, touch her slender, alabaster throat, but both his shoulders were too sore to permit that. "A woman?" she echoed, her eyes wide.

He laughed. "It isn't what you think, Tess. I don't know why she wanted to kill me, but I guarantee you that she wasn't a jealous lover. In fact, she was the wife of that storekeeper in Simpkinsville—"

Tess's face drained of all color. "Cornelia Hamilton?" she whispered. "Emma's mother?"

"I guess. I only remembered her because I used to do business with Jessup sometimes, when I went through Simpkinsville. Tess, what's the matter? You look—"

"Oh, my God," breathed Tess. "My God!"

"Tess?" He was frightened by the look on her face, the expression in her eyes. "Tess, what—"

"Would the police let me see Mrs. Hamilton, talk to her? Keith, do you think they would let me see her?"

He didn't want her going off to a jailhouse, trying to see a woman who was probably dangerous. "Why would you want to?" he stalled.

Tess seemed to have difficulty meeting his eyes; it was a long moment before she did. "S-She was my friend. I want to know why—why she would do something like this."

"What does that matter?"

Tess stood very straight. Her color returned, in shades of pink and gold, and her eyes snapped. "It matters very much to me. I love you. I mean to marry you. Suppose she had k-killed you?"

"She didn't, Tess. That's the important thing. Leave it alone."

Tess bent, kissed his forehead in a businesslike way that said she had other things on her quicksilver mind. "I'll be back later, Mr. Corbin. Right now, I'm going to pay a call on your would-be murderer."

He was desperate to stop her. Pain be damned, he reached out, caught her arm in one hand. "No, Tess. She might hurt you—"

"I'm sure she won't."

Keith wished that he could be so certain. He held onto Tess in a grip he knew must be painful to her but could not relax. "You promised to marry me, remember?" he persisted. "You said you brought a justice of the peace."

A light seemed to go on in her face, glowing behind the weariness. "So I did."

They were married minutes later, by a harried little man wearing a mail-order suit and a nervous smile, with Sister Attila and a consort for witnesses. Keith couldn't help recalling another wedding, beneath the wind-rustled leaves of a churchyard tree, and his mood was somber. He knew that he had not really dissuaded

Tess from her intention of visiting Cornelia Hamilton; he had only forestalled the inevitable. After all, he was tied to that bed as surely as if he'd been manacled; there would be nothing he could do to stop his wife from plunging headlong into a potentially dangerous situation.

And God help him, he couldn't bear to lose a second wife. Inwardly, he raged at his helplessness, repeating the wedding vows through clenched teeth.

Tess, for her part, looked distracted, almost as if she couldn't wait for the wedding to be over and done with.

When it was, she paid the justice of the peace, dismissed him, and announced, "I'll be back this afternoon, during visiting hours. I do hope that nun will be elsewhere."

Keith was annoyed. Scared. "Thank you, dear," he muttered furiously, "I'm overjoyed that we're married, too."

Tess kissed him again, briefly, as though anxious to be on with more pressing matters, now that the troublesome task of marrying him had been taken care of. "I'll be perfectly safe with Cornelia, so stop your fretting."

"Damn it, I'm ordering you not to go!"

She laughed, damn her. She actually laughed. "You're in no position to stop me, are you? Goodbye, darling. And I love you."

"Tess!"

She was already at the doorway of that great, dreary room, her back straight, her steps sure. She didn't pause, she didn't even answer.

So much for Tess's promise to love, honor, and obey, thought Keith furiously, reaching out at great expense to his injured shoulder and sending the metal urinal flying across the room to bounce off the wall with a bell-like clang.

It was only as she swept imperiously past the German nun, who sat, glaring, at her polished wooden desk, that Tess remembered the incredible story Emma had told her, about her father dying and her mother turning her out. And a lie. Emma had mentioned a lie.

Suddenly, it was no longer important to see Cornelia; it was important to see Emma.

The breeze, scented of seawater and sawdust and horse dung from the road, met Tess Corbin as she came out of the hospital and grasped the handlebars of her bicycle, which rested against the trunk of a sturdy elm tree. Knowing Emma as she did, she could almost have told the tale without confronting her friend at all.

Tess got onto her bicycle, arranged her skirts as best she could. Mixed with her rising anger and her sense of purpose was something precious, something joyous, something to be cherished no matter what might happen in the future. She was Keith Corbin's wife, and he was her husband. Nothing and no one would ever separate them again, she vowed, as she pedaled toward town, not Emma's lies, not Cedrick Golden, not even her shop.

As she rode, she reviewed the events that had probably preceded Keith's shooting. Emma had thrown herself at Rod, that night of the show aboard the *Columbia Queen,* determined to win him in any way she could. And, of course, Rod had availed himself of a night's diversion, never planning to stay and fulfill

Emma's childish fantasies. When he had gone away, Emma had panicked, felt a need to confess to her parents, lest there be a baby. For reasons of her own—probably to protect Rod from her father's inevitable moral outrage—Emma had laid the seduction at the feet of the man she knew as Joel Shiloh.

Keith.

Tess pedaled toward the Grand Hotel with furious motions of her strong, slender legs, her mind moving much more rapidly, much more furiously. Emma had been stunned and guilt-stricken, of course, over her father's death, and it had probably never occurred to her that Cornelia might suffer mental collapse, having lost him, that she might avenge the loss. Against the wrong man.

Reaching the hotel, Tess abandoned her bicycle out front without a backward glance, leaving it to lean against a streetlamp. She stormed through the lobby, turned the elevator knob, barked a command at the operator when the mechanical horror arrived, lurching and creaking on its cables.

Within seconds, she was pounding at the door of the suite that had, until so recently, belonged to Asa and Olivia. When Emma answered, she looked so wan and distraught that some of Tess's anger seeped away.

"Tess. How nice of you to—"

Tess was instantly furious again. Jessup Hamilton was dead, after all, and Cornelia was probably hopelessly insane. Her own husband was confined to a hospital bed, perhaps permanently disabled. And all because Emma had been so thoughtless, so self-serving, so ignorant!

"I want to know," she began, in a harsh rush, as she strode past Rod's wife and into the suite, "about that lie you said you told."

Emma grew paler still. "Lie? What lie?"

"The night your father died and your mother turned you out," Tess insisted ruthlessly. Her hands were clenched at her sides, her heart was beating against her ribcage as though to break through. She knew she was flushed by the almost intolerable heat in her face. "You told them that you'd been with Joel Shiloh, didn't you, Emma? That's why you fainted that day, when you first came to the shop and saw him there."

Emma fluttered one hand in front of her face and wavered her way into the sitting room, where she sank into a chair. "Yes."

"Your mother shot him."

Emma's mouth dropped open for a second, and she swayed in her chair. "Mama?! Mama did that?"

"Yes. She thought she was avenging your honor, Emma. God in heaven, how could you? How could you tell such a lie?"

"Tess, I was desperate! I didn't know what would happen—it seemed safe to name Mr. Shiloh, because he was gone—"

"Safe?! He was nearly killed because of you, Emma! My husband was nearly killed because of you!"

"Wh-where is Mama? Is she in jail? Oh, Tess, what will they do to her?"

The rush of frantic questions weakened Tess, made her feel sick with despair for Cornelia, for Emma. For Jessup. She fell into a chair herself and covered her face with both hands just briefly, until she could look at her friend again. "Where is Rod?" she asked, in a soft, defeated voice.

"He went out this morning, with Cedrick Golden and that hussy Cynthia. Something about the play." Emma shot out of her chair and then sagged back into it again, wringing her hands. "I can't think about him now—I don't care about him—I've got to go to Mama!"

Tess drew a deep breath, steadied herself. "Emma, wait, please," she said gently. "Wait for Rod. It would be better if he went with you."

"I can't wait! I won't! I did this, it's all my fault!" Her voice wavered, tears welled in her wide brown eyes and trickled down her cheeks. "Mama must be so frightened, all alone in that dreadful place—"

"Emma, listen to me. You can't—"

"No!" screamed Emma, suddenly, shrilly. "No, don't try to talk me out of going, Tess! You're always talking me out of things—and into things. I want to see Mama!"

Just then, the suite's door opened in the near distance and Rod called out his wife's name. There was no trace of the anger he'd borne Emma the night before in his tone; he might have been a bookkeeper coming home to have midday tea.

With him, looking cherubic and dapper, was Cedrick Golden. When Cedrick's eyes touched Tess, a guarded sort of fury sparked in their depths and was instantly quelled.

Rod was staring at Emma, and it almost seemed that he had come to love her, so obvious was his concern for her. "Emma, what is it?"

"My mama—oh, Rod, it was my mama that shot Mr. Shiloh—"

"Keith," Tess corrected her quietly. "His name isn't Joel Shiloh, it's Keith Corbin."

No one, with the exception of Cedrick, seemed to hear her. Rod was embracing his trembling, tearful Emma, crooning words of comfort into her hair. Tess wondered, with an odd idleness, where Cynthia had gotten off to. Hadn't Emma said that she was with Rod and Cedrick?

"She's in jail, Rod!" Emma prattled, in hysterical horror. The full import of what she had done was penetrating then, and Tess was sorry for her. "My poor mama, in jail, with all those dreadful criminals!"

"We'll go there, right now," Rod promised rashly, eager to comfort. Very eager, for a man who had resisted the constraints of marriage even after the fact. "Everything will be all right, Emma. I promise you that."

Tess felt Cedrick's gaze upon her and shifted her eyes to his face. What she saw, in that unguarded moment, startled her. The actor looked as though he could cheerfully murder her where she sat.

Of course, being the consummate performer that he was, Cedrick suppressed the emotion so swiftly, so skillfully, that Tess could almost believe she had imagined it.

"Cedrick," she said, in polite, belated greeting.

He inclined his too-handsome head. "My dear," he replied.

Tess felt queasy and very uncomfortable. Given the circumstances, that wasn't surprising, she supposed, but she did wish that Cedrick hadn't come in with Rod. He never failed to disturb her, to make her feel off balance, like a person groping in the dark.

"Do you want to come along, Tess?"

Rod's question, gently put as it was, startled Tess, made her jump reflexively in her chair.

"I don't think that would be appropriate, under the circumstances. You see, I just married the man Cornelia shot."

There was a charge in the room, almost a tangible thing, thick and threatening, and it wasn't coming from Rod, who was, despite his invitation, completely absorbed in an equally oblivious Emma. No, it was coming from Cedrick Golden, that oppressive feeling of hatred, and Tess was stunned by the strength and scope of it.

Cedrick addressed Rod, though his eyes, unreadable and veiled, were fixed on Tess. "I'll see you there in my carriage, of course," he offered, ever the polite, accommodating friend.

And if he was a friend, why did he dangle the part in his play before Rod like a carrot before a dray horse?

"Won't you let me drop you off at your shop on the way, Miss—Mrs. Corbin?"

Tess rose out of her chair, shook her head. Never, at any time in her life, had she felt so threatened, so unsafe. "No," she blurted, too quickly. After a moment, she regained her composure and spoke more moderately. "No, thank you. I have my bicycle."

"Did you tell her about the money you borrowed, Rod?" Emma chattered feverishly, into the heavy silence that followed. "Did you tell her about the money?"

The floor shifted and rolled beneath Tess's feet. "What money, Rod?" she demanded, glaring at her half-brother, trying to withstand the new and sudden horror that was thundering against her like an incoming tide. "What money?!"

"I'll explain later," said Rod, avoiding her eyes, his tone brusque, clipped, his face flushed. "Can't you see what a state Emma's in?"

"You got into my bank account somehow, didn't you?" insisted Tess frantically. "You—you loaned my money to this—this confidence man!"

"Confidence man?!" snarled Cedrick.

Tess wanted to pursue the matter, but Rod was having none of that. He gathered Emma and bustled her out, Cedrick storming along behind them, red to his elfin ears, fury moving in every lithe line of his body.

"Rod Thatcher-Waltam!" Tess yelled. "You come back here, you thief! You—"

The suite's door slammed and she was alone. Without even going to the bank, Tess knew that she was, thanks to Rod, stone broke. She trembled with the worst kind of rage, the helpless kind. She would never have been able to withdraw money had that account been Rod's, but, because he was a man and her brother, the laws of the land apparently allowed him such a travesty!

Tess stood up shakily and left the suite in a stumbling state of blind, impotent rage. It hardly seemed possible that this was her wedding day; her husband was lying in a hospital bed, her best friend's mother had attempted to murder him, and now her money was gone.

Tess's bicycle still rested against the streetlamp. Glumly, she pedaled her way homeward.

Reaching her shop, she wheeled her bicycle inside, pulled down the shades on the windows facing the busy street outside, and locked the door. After a cup of tea and a long interval of staring off into space, she went across the road to speak with the banker Asa had placed in charge of her account.

He was amazingly offhand, considering that she had been robbed. Clerks made mistakes, after all, he maintained, and if Tess wanted to recover her money, it seemed to him that she would be better off to approach her brother.

"My father didn't arrange the account so that Rod had access to it, then?" Tess wanted to know, and mingled with her anger and her shock was a certain relief that Asa had trusted her.

"Oh, no. Though I did advise him to do so, of course," replied the banker blithely. The implication was that a mere, mindless little fluff of a creature such as herself could not be entrusted with such a sum. Might squander it on hat pins and French cologne and other gee-gaws.

"This bank was responsible for my money!" Tess insisted hotly. "I've been robbed and it's your fault! What do you intend to do about it, sir?"

"Do?" The banker shrugged. "I suppose you could press charges against your brother. Have him jailed."

Tess might well have done exactly that, had it not been for the hardship such an action would cause Emma. "I may press charges against your bank instead," she answered. There was a long silence, during which the banker didn't even have the decency to look apologetic. Tess had to puncture his pomposity, she simply had to, and the only needle at hand was her new name.

"Won't you please change the name on my account, if it's not too much trouble?" she asked, with acid sweetness and deliberately widened eyes. "I'm no longer Tess Bishop, you see. As of this afternoon, I am Tess Corbin."

She waited for the statement to sink in and was buoyed when it did. The banker jumped as though she had prodded his well-cushioned backside with a sharp stick.

"Corbin?" he choked out. "I don't believe you!"

Cooperatively, Tess took the wedding license, signed that very day by herself, Keith, and the justice of the peace, from the pocket of her skirt. She presented it with dignity.

The banker's fat hand trembled as he took the paper, read it. His jiggling cheeks, rosy with well-being only moments before, turned parchment-white. "You're married to Keith Corbin. Con-congratulations."

"Thank you," trilled Tess, taking back the license, folding it carefully, returning it to her pocket. "Of course, I don't think my husband will be very pleased when I tell him how casually this bank views its responsibilities to depositors—"

"We'll be happy to make amends, of course!" boomed the official, with sudden good will. "And you can be sure that such a mistake won't be made again, Mrs. Corbin!"

Both triumph and quiet rage mingled within Tess as she signed papers changing her name in the bank's records and was given a new passbook with the full amount Rod had taken from her written prominently inside. Triumph because she had made this pompous, impossible man restore her money and rage because a name could be so much more important than personal integrity.

"I'll be moving my money at the first opportunity," she said loftily, as she was leaving the bank again, her passbook firmly in hand.

"But we did everything we could to straighten the matter out!" protested the banker, frantic. Tess would have staked both her bicycle and her camera that he wasn't worried about her modest account but about funds that the Corbin family probably had on deposit.

"You did," Tess agreed, her chin high. "After I had proved to you that I am now a member of one of the most prominent families in the Pacific Northwest. You should have done it because it was right"—she paused and consulted the painted script on the bank's front window—"Mr. Filbertson. Who I was should not have mattered in the least. The important thing was that I had been grievously wronged and the fault was partly yours."

"Mrs. Corbin!" wailed the banker, spreading his hands, a thin film of sweat beading on his upper lip.

"Good day, Mr. Filbertson," said Tess, leaving the bank in a sweep of sateen skirts and righteous disdain.

Mr. Filbertson followed her over the wooden sidewalk, across the busy, rutted, dung-dappled road. "Won't you please reconsider?" he pleaded.

Tess smiled as she unlocked the door of her shop, shrugged prettily. "I may, Mr. Filbertson. Then again, I may not. Would you like your photograph taken?"

Chapter Sixteen

MR. FILBERTSON BECAME TESS'S FIRST CUSTOMER, SITTING nervously for his portrait, his barrel chest plumped, his muttonchop sideburns bristling just a little. He harrumphed loudly when Tess told him that his photograph would be ready by the next day. She knew that he was burning to ask whether or not her account would be transferred to another bank, and she did nothing to ease his discomfort.

To Tess's mind, he deserved it.

He paused in the shop's doorway, letting in the sounds and smells of the afternoon traffic bustling by in the road. "I hope we'll see you again soon, Mrs. Corbin," he said gruffly.

The lie was so obvious that Tess nearly laughed aloud. Had it not been for her marriage into the powerful Corbin family, he would be hoping for something entirely different.

Giving no answer, she politely inclined her head. Mr. Filbertson reddened and took his leave. Watching as he weaved his way between the wagons, buggies, and carriages clogging the street outside, Tess smiled to herself.

The worry gnawed at him like the teeth of a frenzied beast. Where was Tess? Why hadn't she returned? Had that mad woman, Cornelia Hamilton, hurt her in some way?

Keith sat upright, the muscles in his wounded shoulder screaming in protest. One thing was for certain: he was through lying around in this bleak hospital, passively allowing the events of his life to flow over him like a stream.

"Vhat do you think you are doing?!" boomed Sister Attila, when she swept into the room, her crisp black habit rustling. "Get back into that bed, Mr. Corbin!"

Keith was sitting on the edge of the bed. Cautiously, he eased himself over the side, to stand on his own two feet. The ward, empty except for himself and the German nun, seemed to sway and undulate around him. "I've got to—leave," he managed to say, even as the enormous woman maneuvered him back onto the mattress and underneath the covers.

"Sleep," ordered the nun, her mouth a tight line that barely moved as the word passed it.

"I can't—my wife—"

"Your wife is right here." The voice was like cool,

clean spring water flowing into a parched creek bed. Tess. Opposite the nun, her face moving in a shimmering fog of discomfort and incomprehensible fatigue, stood Tess.

"You're all right," he muttered wearily. The pain was deep-seated, overwhelming.

"Of course I'm all right. You, on the other hand—" She paused, smoothed his forehead with tender fingers.

He groped for her hand, held it desperately in his own. "Don't go."

"I won't," she promised softly, and he heard the nun leave the room.

And she didn't. Each time Keith surfaced from the depths of weariness and hurt that kept pulling him under, Tess was there, her hand gripping his own, her scent fresh and comforting in his nostrils.

Yawning, Tess fumbled in her handbag for the key to the shop. It was so early that dawn was just climbing over the eastern mountains, all golden and pink, and the only traffic in the road was a milk wagon.

"Tess!"

She started at Emma's cry of her name, turned to see her friend rushing up the sidewalk, looking disgruntled and afraid.

What now? Tess thought uncharitably. She was weary to the very fiber of her bones, having been up all night long with Keith. And she still had Mr. Filbertson's photograph to develop, a task she wasn't looking forward to. She had never done it before, and would have to depend on the instructions in the books stored in the back of her shop.

"Good morning, Emma," she said, as she opened

the door and went inside, her friend following virtually on her heels.

"Good morning yourself, Tess Bishop!" retorted Emma furiously. "Where have you been all night? I've been frantic, just frantic—"

"I was with my husband," Tess said evenly.

This announcement gave Emma pause—as Tess had guessed, she hadn't been listening the day before, at the hotel, when Tess had briefly mentioned her marriage to Keith. Her brown eyes widened and her mouth pursed into an O, and then she bristled, like a little hen that has just been dashed with the dishwater.

"Would that I could say the same," Emma said petulantly. "Tess, they have arrested Rod! Thanks to you, the bank had him arrested! And he's not going to be released until he gives them back the money he borrowed from your account!"

Emma's attitude nettled Tess. She flung her handbag down onto the shop's carefully dusted countertop and shrugged out of her cloak. "Borrowed? Emma, he stole that money from me."

"He did not! He only borrowed it!"

"Taking funds from someone's bank account without their knowledge, let alone their permission, is theft, Emma, not borrowing."

"How could you, Tess? How could you let this come about, when you know what's happened to Mama? Haven't I got enough problems without having my husband thrown into the hoosegow?"

"I happen to have a few problems of my own, Emma—not the least of which is my injured husband."

Emma subsided a little at the mention of Keith; indirectly, his shooting was her fault, and her recognition of the fact appeased Tess to some degree. "What am I going to do?"

Tess sighed. Lord, she was tired, and she still had to ferret through those dratted, musty tomes in the back and figure out how to develop a photograph. "If I were you, Emma, I would go to Cedrick Golden and ask him to return some of the money Rod invested in his play. I'm sure the bank would drop the charges against Rod if they had their funds back."

"Why should I go to Cedrick Golden?" blustered Emma. "You're the one who started this by demanding that the bank make good on the money that Rod borrowed from you in good faith!"

Tess shook her head in quiet, furious amazement. "You're not actually suggesting that I turn my money over so that Rod can be free, are you?"

Once again, Emma subsided, though her chin jutted out defiantly and her eyes were narrow. "I thought you were my friend!"

"I am your friend, Emma," Tess sighed. "But I'm not your guardian angel. This is one problem that you and Rod are going to have to solve yourselves."

Tears blossomed in Emma's eyes, Tess was determined not to be moved by them. Perhaps, by smoothing things over for Emma whenever she could, she had done her friend a disservice. How could a person possibly become strong if they never had to work things out for themselves?

"I'll show you, Tess Bishop. I'll go to Cedrick Golden. I'll straighten this whole matter out, without" —she paused to snap her fingers—"this much help from you!"

With that, Emma swept Tess up in a quelling glare,

lifted her chin, and left the shop. Smiling to herself, Tess went to the back room, found the book she needed, and set about learning how to develop the photographic plate she had taken the day before, of Banker Filbertson.

She was so engrossed in the looking up of formulas and the mixing of chemicals that she barely heard the tinkle of the bell over the shop's door. "I'll be right there," she called out distractedly, frowning at the dusty book and the shallow pan of chemicals she had already prepared.

"I can wait," answered an annoyed masculine voice, and Tess stiffened. Cedrick Golden. Her caller was Cedrick Golden.

After drawing a deep breath and smoothing her hair and skirts—she had not taken time to change her clothes or give her hair proper attention, she had been in such a hurry to develop Mr. Filbertson's photograph —Tess reluctantly left her work.

"Cedrick," she said, in greeting, stepping through the curtained workroom doorway, her smile polite but by no means welcoming. "May I help you?"

Cedrick looked distracted and more than a bit nettled. "Emma tells me that I must return Rod's investment in my play."

Why tell me? Tess wondered, but she said nothing. Something within her urged her to wait.

"I am not pleased by this," Cedrick complained, his eyes wandering about the shop in a quick yet aimless sort of way. "I am not pleased at all. An investment is an investment, after all. A deal is a deal."

"I agree completely," said Tess, still keeping her

distance. "In this case, however, Rod invested my money, not his own."

Now, the emerald eyes found her face, and Tess was jolted by the stark desperation she read in their depths. There was something feverish about Cedrick, something almost obsessive. "Never fear," he said, with carefully moderated annoyance. "I have made the necessary arrangements. No doubt, your brother is already free."

For some reason, Tess couldn't say thank you, though she was, for Emma's sake and Emma's alone, grateful. "That was fast," she observed, remaining in her doorway, arching one eyebrow as if to say, "but what has any of this to do with me?"

"What could I do?" Cedrick's narrow shoulders, cloaked by a pristine linen shirt and a bottle-green jacket of the finest quality, moved in a fitful shrug. "Emma would have it no other way. She ranted and raved until I had no choice."

Tess was secretly proud of Emma, though she hid that. She also suppressed the sigh of impatience inspired by an encounter to which she could see no point. "I really am quite busy," she said.

Cedrick was instantly flushed, and his eyes, as green as his jacket, snapped. "I see. What a provider that husband of yours must be. Imagine asking such a wife to work in a common shop!"

Now it was Tess who flushed. Anger surged through her in a heated wave, bracing her, causing her to thrust out her chin. "I did not marry my husband to secure myself a provider, Mr. Golden. I married him because I love him."

"Love! It isn't his 'love' that you want!"

At last, Tess understood why Mr. Cedrick Golden had put in his appearance on this otherwise pleasant day. He was angry about her marriage to Keith. As if it were any of his business! "Perhaps your interest in most people hinges on what they can give you, Mr. Golden," she said, with cool dignity, the cloth that covered the workroom doorway bunched in one hand, "but my outlook is somewhat different."

Cedrick's voice was a low, sardonic drawl. "You know as well as I do that you've married into one of the richest families in the country. Your wounded swain may be fooled by your appearance of fresh-faced independence, Tess, but I am not. I am an actor myself, and I know a theatrical production when I see one, whether or not it is played out on a stage."

Nothing he could have said would have insulted Tess more. When she'd fallen in love with Keith Corbin, she'd known nothing of his family or their money. And she sincerely didn't care whether she ever saw a dime of it or not. She wanted only to be near her husband, whether that involved traveling in his wagon, from town to town, or remaining here, in her shop, while he worked at some other profession.

But Cedrick Golden had no right to any explanations or denials. Who did he think he was?

"I have work to do, Mr. Golden," Tess said stiffly. "If you'll just excuse me, please."

She turned to go back into the shadowy workroom, back to her task of developing Mr. Filbertson's portrait, considering the conversation to be over. Angry as she was, it was a moment before she realized that she'd made a mistake.

Cedrick Golden had followed her.

Until that time, Tess had, for the most part, regarded this man as a pest, persistent at times, but relatively innocuous. Now, her every instinct told her that, under certain circumstances, he could be very dangerous indeed.

She stepped around the worktable, with its clutter of books and chemicals, to put some barrier between herself and him. "Please leave," she managed to say.

He ran one index finger down a page in one of the books. "It's dark in here," he observed lightly. "No windows."

A chill crept up Tess's back. "Darkness is required for the development of photographs," she replied evenly. "Please leave now, Mr. Golden. As I said, I have work to do."

"Photographs," he repeated idly, tracing the outer edge of a pan of developing fluid with one slender index finger. "Yes. The profession you prefer over the theater."

Tess was edging toward the door leading back into the shop. "Please, don't touch that. Th-the chemicals contain acid—they can be dangerous."

Cedrick looked up, assessed Tess with shadow-veiled eyes, and gave a chortle of smug amusement at her obvious attempt to escape him. "Are you afraid of me, my dear?" he asked, in a soft, disdainful voice.

"No," lied Tess, gaining the doorway and backing through it. Just as she did so, the bell above the front door chimed briskly.

Tess doubted that, however bad business might become, she would never be more grateful for the appearance of a customer than she was at that moment. She turned, smiling nervously.

The visitor was a woman, and she was, with her lush, cinnamon-colored hair and shamrock-green eyes, stunningly beautiful. "Tess?" she said, with an inquiring smile.

Forgetting all about Cedrick Golden and his quietly threatening manner, Tess nodded. Some instinct told her that this glorious, self-assured creature had not come to have her likeness taken.

The woman smiled again. "My name is Banner Corbin, and I believe I am your sister-in-law."

Tess went to take the extended hand, which was gloved in elegant kid. "Mrs. Corbin, I'm so glad to meet you."

Bright laughter rang in the little shop. "And I'm happy to meet you, too. Happier than you could possibly know. But, please—call me Banner."

Cedrick came out of the back room just then, and his presence embarrassed Tess. What would Banner think?

Wise green eyes assessed Cedrick and then Tess herself, revealing nothing of whatever impression might have been made. Cedrick muttered a few words of farewell and, looking exasperated, took his leave.

"I didn't mean to interrupt your work," said Banner, peeling off one glove and then the other. "I can come back tomorrow if that would be better."

"Oh, no!" Tess protested quickly. "Don't go, please. I—I want to get to know you."

Banner smiled. "As we all want to get to know you, Tess. The family, I mean."

"I've met Keith's brothers," Tess flushed at the

memory of their finding her asleep on the couch in the elegant suite at the Grand Hotel.

Banner had obviously heard the story from the men, one of whom must be her husband, and she looked amused. "I'm sorry that they frightened you that way," she said, after a short silence. "They can be overwhelming, to say the least. Adam, the dour one with the dark hair, is my husband."

Tess remembered Adam. For all his seriousness, he'd seemed the kinder of the two men and she had liked him. "He was very nice to me," she said, mostly to make conversation.

Banner laughed. "And Jeff was obnoxious. I hope you won't hate our mutual brother-in-law, Tess—he's really a very good man. It's just that he has never mastered subtlety."

Now, Tess laughed, too. "He certainly hasn't. My Lord, he scared me to death!"

"Jeff often has that affect on people." Banner sighed and reached up to unpin her hat. "Might I sit down for a few minutes? When we received the wire saying that Keith had been shot—well, we all panicked. I was elected to come and investigate, and the steamer trip seemed to take forever. Following that, of course, I hurried to the hospital as quickly as I could, and now I'm simply exhausted."

Banner Corbin was clearly a vital, energetic woman, but she did look tired. "Do sit down," Tess invited quickly. "I'll go upstairs and make you a cup of tea."

"Certainly not," said Banner, settling herself into one of the row of wooden chairs set out for Tess's customers. "I know you were working when I came in.

Just go back and finish that, and then perhaps we could talk more and visit Keith again, together."

"How is he?" Tess asked softly, chagrined that she had not done so before. What with the incident with Cedrick and then the unexpected visit from Banner, she had not thought to inquire.

"Irascible," was the instant reply. "Keith makes a dreadful patient. All he can talk about is getting out of 'that place.'"

Through the shop windows, the bank across the street was clearly visible. Tess was reminded of her responsibility to deliver Mr. Filbertson's portrait that day. "I should be finished very soon," she said, turning back to her work even though there were a thousand questions she wanted to ask about Keith.

The portrait of Banker Filbertson, the first Tess had ever developed, came out well, and on the first try, too. After hanging it to dry, on the small line stretched across the back of her workroom, she washed her hands and stepped into the shop again.

Banner was still sitting in her chair near the windows, her hands folded in her lap, her eyes closed. At Tess's return, she opened them and smiled brightly. "Finished already? You must be very good at what you do."

Tess shrugged. She had a lot to learn about photography, but she did possess a natural talent and she was proud of that. "I'm an apprentice, of a sort, I guess. I don't have anyone to teach me, so I have to study on my own."

"It's difficult for a woman to engage in a profession, I know," Banner observed thoughtfully.

Tess was surprised. Banner had spoken as though she

270

had a profession herself, and that seemed unlikely, considering the status of her husband's family. "You do?"

"I'm a doctor," Banner replied succinctly. "I share Adam's practice in Port Hastings."

Tess's mouth dropped open. Owning a shop was daring enough, for a woman, but being a doctor was almost unheard of. "Keith didn't tell me that," she said, after a few moments of amazed silence.

Banner laughed. "The Corbins take such things in stride. My mother-in-law is a suffrage crusader and a journalist, and Jeff's wife, Fancy, was an entertainer until her marriage."

"And Jeff made her stop working?"

"Fancy's heart was never in her work, if you know what I mean. She's happy to be a wife and mother." Banner did not speak with derision, but with quiet affection. "You'll like Fancy. She's very special to all of us."

Suddenly, Tess was hungry to hear more about Keith's family; it was as though, by knowing them, she might know him better, too. "Isn't there a daughter, too?"

Banner's smile was fond. "Yes. Melissa. She's just finishing college."

Tess listened eagerly as her sister-in-law told her about every member of the family, including her own three children and Jeff and Fancy's young son, Patrick. She was startled when Mr. Filbertson came into the shop, looking harried.

"My photograph is ready, I presume?" he asked, without sparing so much as a glance at Banner. His manner said that he hoped the portrait had not been finished, so that he would have some reason to believe Tess incompetent.

"It is," Tess replied coolly, turning to go back into the workroom, take the photograph from its line, and carry it to the front counter. "That will be fifty cents, please."

Mr. Filbertson harrumphed and wheezed as he rummaged through his pockets for the money. Presently, he laid two quarters on the scarred if immaculate countertop. "There," he said.

"I understand you had my brother arrested," she replied companionably.

Mr. Filbertson shifted and shuffled a bit, his hands resting on the counter. "Er—yes—well—the depositor's money had to be recovered, you know. In any case, restitution was made by Mr. Cedrick Golden, and, to my knowledge, your brother is no longer being detained."

Tess was enjoying the banker's discomfort, but she decided to take pity on him all the same. "I certainly don't blame you for recovering what was rightfully yours, Mr. Filbertson," she said, in businesslike tones. "We all must do that, don't you agree?"

Filbertson reddened; obviously, he knew that Tess was referring to the pressure she had brought to bear the day before, in order to get her own money back. "Yes," he grumbled, as though it pained him to have to capitulate in even this small way. "Yes, Mrs. Corbin, sometimes we must." With that, he snatched up his photograph and stomped out of the shop again.

"Are all your customers so warm and friendly?" chimed Banner, watching Mr. Filbertson as he thundered across the busy road, nearly getting himself run down by an ice wagon.

"He was my first," admitted Tess. "I hope the others will be more personable."

Banner laughed and agreed and then went on to say, "Your first client! This is an occasion. Let's celebrate with a nice dinner. Following that, we can go to the hospital and visit our surly patient."

Tess was hungry, and she was tired, too. After all, she hadn't slept the night before—she'd been too intent on her vigil at Keith's bedside—and now there were shadows stretching their way across the road outside. But there was one thing she needed more than a rest and a good, nourishing meal, and that was to see her husband, to touch him, to talk to him.

"Couldn't we go to the hospital first?" she asked shyly.

Banner shook her head in a firm manner that said she was used to giving directions and, more often than not, having them obeyed. "I'm positively ravenous, and I suspect that you are, too. Besides, you can't cater to these Corbin men, Tess. If you do, they'll walk all over you."

Tess couldn't bring herself to argue. "I'll just change and lock up the shop, then," she said, making her way toward the stairs leading up to her private rooms. There, she undressed, washed quickly, put on a clean skirt and shirtwaist, and hastily redid her hair.

When she came downstairs again, Banner was surveying the shop's bare walls, a pensive look in her beautiful, clover-green eyes. "I think you should display your work, Tess. Put some photographs in the windows and along these walls."

The idea was a good one, and Tess smiled as she pulled the window shades. "First I'll have to take some photographs to display," she pointed out as they stepped out onto the sidewalk, and she locked the door behind them.

"You can take mine," said Banner affably. "And Keith will be out of the hospital soon, so you could take his. . . ."

Keith was, as Banner had said, in a surly mood. When Tess came to his bedside and kissed his forehead in greeting, he scowled at her.

"I hope you didn't drop everything and rush over here on my account," he grumbled sardonically, casting one eloquent glance at the dark window nearest his bed.

Banner, standing on the opposite side, rolled her eyes and then gave Tess a reassuring wink before bending to kiss Keith herself. Having done that, she turned and walked out of the room without a word in parting.

Watching his brother's wife disappear from the ward, Keith struggled not to smile and failed. A corner of his mouth quivered and then lifted in a reluctant grin.

Relieved, Tess tried to swallow a yawn and smoothed the dark-honey hair back from Keith's forehead. "How are you feeling?" she asked.

The azure eyes darted to her face, reading the weariness there. "You've been working today, haven't you?" he accused.

It didn't occur to Tess to lie. "I did develop one picture. It was amazing, how fast this day went by—"

"For you, maybe," Keith retorted, grumpy again. "If I don't get out of this place, I'm going to go mad!"

"You will not go mad," Tess answered briskly. "You need to be here, to rest."

"You're a fine one to talk. You were up all night. And then you went to your shop and—"

Tess laid an index finger to his lips. "Shhh. Stop fussing. Losing one night's sleep won't hurt me, and I didn't do any hard work. I didn't even have to fix my supper—Banner bought that."

He caught her hand in his, removed it to a little distance, inspected the bare ring finger. "I forgot to give you your wedding band," he observed distractedly.

Tess felt suddenly, inexplicably sad. Or perhaps it was just her weariness that made tears spring into her eyes.

"Shoebutton," Keith said softly, and the word had the tone of a gentle reprimand. He wrapped his uninjured arm around her, drew her close, and held her.

Chapter Seventeen

Satisfied that Keith would indeed recover, Banner returned to Port Hastings the next morning. Tess, never having had a sister of any sort, was sorry to see her go. Sorry to be alone again.

Fortunately, there was work to be done. Tess went upstairs, made up her own bed and the one in the tiny spare room, where Banner had slept, cleared away the dishes left from their light breakfast.

As the morning passed, customers arrived, one and then another, keeping Tess gloriously busy. At one point, she thought to herself that, like a four-leaf clover, Banner had brought her good luck.

It was nearly noon when Rod and Emma arrived—

Rod looking subdued and slightly embarrassed, Emma patently miffed.

"We've come to have our portrait taken," she announced stiffly. "Sort of a belated wedding picture."

Tess recognized an olive branch when it was extended to her, however reluctantly, and she promptly led the couple into the tiny alcove that served as a sitting room.

Rod took the high-backed chair, looking solemn, while Emma stood behind him, equally somber, one plump hand on her husband's shoulder.

Tess made sure her camera lens was focused properly, measured out the correct amount of flash powder, and draped a heavy black cloth over her head and the camera itself. When the view she saw through the lens suited her, she squeezed the rubber bulb. The powder exploded and Rod flinched a little, though Emma stood, stalwart, through it all.

"I'll take one more, just in case," Tess said busily, mostly to herself, as she again fussed with the powder tray and the cloth. Banner's suggestion, that she put samples of her work in the shop windows, was uppermost in her mind, and Rod and Emma would make good subjects, for they were a handsome couple.

Rod shifted in his chair and muttered; the tightening of Emma's fingers upon his shoulders settled him. Tess found herself smiling beneath the heavy drape.

"Aren't you going to ask how poor Rod got out of jail?" Emma demanded, when, at last, the session was over.

Tess bit her lower lip and averted her eyes, amused by her friend's huffy indignation. "I don't have to ask," she admitted evenly. "Cedrick was here yesterday, and he told me."

"Aren't you even going to apologize?" prattled Emma, as Tess led the way back into the main part of the shop. "This was all your fault—"

Before Tess could spring to her own defense, Rod, to her amazement, did that for her.

"Blast it, Emma, it wasn't Tess's fault and we all know that. I shouldn't have done what I did!"

There was a short, thunderous silence. Emma absorbed her husband's statement, squared her shoulders, and turned a blinding, forgiving smile on Tess.

"Well, then, there's no reason we can't all be friends again, is there?" she sang out.

Tess chuckled and shook her head. "No, I guess there isn't. How is your mother, Emma?"

Emma deflated a little. "She's not at all well, Tess. Rod and I are thinking of taking her back to St. Louis. She could have the best of care there, and, well—"

"Why don't you just come right out and say it, Emma?" Rod broke in, in exasperation directed more toward himself than his wife. "I'm not accomplishing anything here, and it's clear enough that I can't stay out of trouble without my father around, holding my hand!"

Tess sighed, feeling sympathy for her brother, despite all the trouble he had caused during the short course of their acquaintance. "Rod, you're being too hard on yourself. You got along without Asa's help for years."

"This is different." He paused, gave Emma a pensive, wistful look. "I have a wife now."

"What about the money you gave Cedrick? What about the play?" To her own surprise, Tess found the thought of Emma and Rod going so far away very disturbing, even though she knew it might be the best thing for them to do.

Rod's shoulders moved in a despondent shrug. "He'll never give back my initial investment—the money Papa gave me. And he's not going to give me that part unless you join the company, too. Which, of course, is out of the question."

"I'm afraid it is," Tess said softly. "When do you plan to leave for St. Louis?"

"As soon as Papa sends the fare," sighed Rod, and he looked so defeated that Tess wanted to weep for him. Maybe he had been misguided in his efforts to become a great actor, but a dream was a dream, and Tess understood that as well as anyone. "A week or so, I guess," he finished sadly.

Tess looked from Rod's face to Emma's. "Won't you come and stay with me, here, until you go? There is no sense in your paying for a hotel room, after all."

No one said that there was no money for a hotel room, and probably none for food, either, though Emma's relief was visible.

"I could help you in the shop while Rod makes the arrangements for Mama!" she suggested brightly.

Tess knew that she could run the shop on her own, but, for the sake of her friend, she pretended enthusiasm. It would only be for a week or so, after all. "I would appreciate that, Emma," she said quietly. "And, of course, the portrait is my wedding gift to you both."

Having many errands to perform, including fetching their belongings from the hotel—Tess suspected that they had already been turned out—Rod left.

More customers came—a fancy gambling man wearing a diamond ring with a stone the size of a banty's egg, a somber woman with a row of stair-step children and a shy husband, a sailor on leave from one of the steamships constantly coming into the harbor.

Emma proved to be very good at greeting clients and keeping them occupied until their turn to sit for a portrait came, probably because she had grown up in a general store. Rushing about, seating people for their portraits, Tess was glad to have her friend keeping order out front.

Everything went along smoothly, during all of the morning and much of the afternoon. Tess was looking forward to closing up, changing her clothes, and going off to the hospital to visit Keith.

And then Cynthia Golden came in. The dislike Emma felt for this woman, and with justification, Tess had to admit, was palpable.

"I would like to make an appointment to have my portrait taken," Cynthia announced, ignoring Emma's quiet, stony ire. Or was she ignoring it? Tess couldn't tell. Cynthia, for all her striking beauty, was not a quick-witted woman, and the possibility that she hadn't even noticed Emma's rancor had to be considered.

"Certainly," interceded Tess, in a welcoming way, edging Emma out from behind the counter before she could drive off a paying customer. "Do you need them done today?"

"Oh, no," said Cynthia obliquely, giving Emma one curious glance, as though she thought she should know this person but could not quite place her. "I'll come tomorrow. With Cedrick."

Tess had no desire to see Cedrick, tomorrow or any other day, but this was, after all, a business, and she was determined to handle things in a professional manner. "Ten o'clock?" she inquired, pen in hand over the ruled—and so far, empty—appointment book on the counter.

"That's much too early." As if to add gravity to her point, Cynthia yawned prettily. "I don't even stir before eleven-thirty, my dear. Might I come at two?"

"Might I come at two?" mimicked Emma, in a tart undertone.

Tess nudged her friend hard in the ribs, smiling broadly at Cynthia, who, it seemed, had not heard Emma's mockery. "Two would be fine, Miss Golden," she said firmly.

"Thank you," said Cynthia, whose mind was clearly already grappling with some other monumental thought. Distractedly, she left the shop.

"Why did you have to be so friendly to her?" demanded Emma, a study in petulance, the moment Cynthia was gone.

"She's a customer," Tess said flatly. And the subject was closed.

Cynthia did return the next day, promptly at two, but, to Tess's vast, if secret, relief, Cedrick did not accompany her. In any case, she had little time to worry about Mr. Golden during the coming days, for she was literally swamped with customers, taking portraits all day long and staying up half the night to develop them. And despite all this, Tess invariably spent several happy evening hours with Keith.

He was getting stronger every day and more anxious to leave the hospital. Tess developed a new liking for the nun he privately called Sister Attila—actually, her name was Sister Margaret—who put up with his drastic changes of mood in a patient, stoic way.

Finally, after several more days, he was released. He would still be required to remain in bed for most of each day—a prospect he made more than one lewd joke about—but Tess was overjoyed, all the same. Having Keith near her, throughout the long workdays and the heretofore even longer nights, would give reality to a marriage that she had sometimes thought was only a product of her imagination.

Tess brought her husband home to the shop—they had already agreed that it would be impractical to live in the hotel suite when her work was here—in a hired carriage. With Rod's help, she managed to get him up the stairs, through the small kitchen, and into the bedroom. This had been carefully aired; the curtains danced in the afternoon breeze, and the covers on the bed were turned back. From the street came the encouraging sounds of everyday life.

Once Keith had been settled on the bed and Rod had left the room, Tess was oddly off balance. This was the man she loved, the man she had been scandalously intimate with, but now, for some inexplicable reason, she felt shy.

She bent to remove his boots and smiled to remember the first day she had met him, in his camp near Simpkinsville. And then she remembered what they had done, inside his peddler's wagon, and blushed crimson.

"What are you thinking about?" he asked, watching her. Though he was pale with the stress of just traveling to the shop and getting up the stairs, there was a mischievous light in his blue eyes.

"Nothing," lied Tess.

He was looking directly, shamelessly, at her breasts. "I want to make love to you," he said.

Tess flushed again. It wasn't as though she hadn't lain in that bed, alone and miserable, and wished that Keith were there to touch her, to kiss her, to drive her to that sweet madness that was so much like dying and coming to life again, but now she felt as nervous as a virgin.

"You are in no condition for that," she pointed out primly. "Besides, it's still daylight and Rod and Emma are here and there are customers—"

"Excuses."

Tess resisted a childish urge to stamp one foot and picked up a small bell she had set on the bedside table. "If you need anything, just ring this. I have to get back to work."

Azure eyes gleaming, Keith idly picked up the bell and rang it. A pulsing silence filled the room, and heat surged through Tess's body as he swept his eyes over her in blatant, masculine appreciation.

Tess swallowed and turned to leave, he caught her arm in his good hand and brought her back, toppling her down onto the bed beside him.

"Stay," he breathed.

The weight of him, the lean, hard pressure—Tess's head spun and her breath came in quick gasps. "I can't—customers—work to do—"

Keith was unbuttoning the bodice of her gingham dress. His eyes never left Tess's face, and the motions of his fingers were so practiced that she was sure he had been rehearsing them in his mind for a long time. "Umm—customers," he agreed, in a throaty whisper, as his mouth came down, hard and demanding and completely welcome, upon her own.

Involuntarily, Tess moaned as he kissed her, his tongue sparring with hers, his hand displacing her muslin camisole and closing possessively over the warm, plump breast beneath.

"Keith . . ." she protested weakly, aware of the bell downstairs, over the shop door, tinkling repeatedly. Customers were coming and going. Was Emma taking proper care of them?

His lips moved, heated and smooth, over her neck, down over her shoulder and collarbone, reaching her breast with unerring boldness.

As Keith's mouth closed over her pulsing, distended nipple, all thoughts of the shop fled her mind. In a convulsion of pleasure, she arched her back and knotted her hand in his hair, pressing him closer and then closer still.

He drank of her at his leisure, savoring her, driving her wild. Each playful nip of his teeth or foray of his tongue brought a small, fevered cry of need from her.

"We can't," she whined, in desperation. "Your injuries—"

"Oh, ye of little faith," he retorted. "We're going to die if we don't."

Tess couldn't say whether he would die if they didn't make love, but she knew for certain that she would. "H-How—?"

Keith took his time answering, attending the other breast with his tongue first, taking sweet suckle at a fount that swelled in his hand and blossomed in the warm moisture of his mouth.

"Lock the door," he said finally.

Dazed, Tess swung off the bed and stumbled across the little, breeze-freshened room to obey. The process of latching that door seemed entirely too difficult for such a simple task.

She managed it, however, and then stood with her back to her reclining husband, her forehead resting against the wood of the door, her breathing requiring too much effort. "You can't," she whispered fitfully. "You're hurt."

"Come here."

Tess turned, made her way to the side of the bed, for despite all good sense, it was not in her to resist him.

"Undress," he said.

Like a woman moving in her sleep, Tess removed her shirtwaist, the camisole beneath, her skirt and shoes and stockings and finally her drawers. The touch of the fresh air coming through the window was almost as sensuous a thing as Keith's calm, hungry perusal.

Tess quivered with anticipation and the special vulnerability that is womanhood as he studied every curve and line of her. The breeze moved over her like an invisible caress and, reveling, she reached up and unpinned her hair, allowing it to fall around her shoulders and breasts, down her back.

The motion undid Keith's resolve to prolong the experience; he groaned and caught her hand in his own, pressing it to the hard ridge of his manhood, straining beneath the cloth of his trousers.

Instinctively, tenderly, she caressed him. And then,

knowing now what to do, she undid the buttons of his trousers and laid the fabric aside, baring him. He was magnificent and, for a timeless moment, she stroked him, delighting in his groaning surrender.

When neither of them could bear another second of separation, he positioned her so that she sat astraddle of him and gently, slowly sheathed his sword within her.

The sensation was so wondrous that Tess gasped and flung back her head, baring her teeth in a soft, primitive cry of welcome. He stroked her breasts, first one and then the other, as they both climbed toward fulfillment, moving in fiercely metered unison.

Release came in a fiery burst that seared them both, causing them to cry out simultaneously and then sink, shuddering, into a deep stillness. Keith flung his head backward, as though to drive it through the pillow and even the mattress, while Tess sagged forward, sated into sweet exhaustion.

It was a long time before she came back to herself, but when she did her eyes widened with alarm and she drew in a sharp breath. What kind of hussy was she? Keith had just gotten out of the hospital, for heaven's sake, and his right arm and shoulder were still in a sling!

"Did I hurt you?" she whispered, on the verge of tears.

His laughter was a low, husky sound, joyous and vital. "Hurt me? If that was hurting me, I love pain."

Tess was swept up in a wave of happiness, of relief, of love. "I've missed you so much. Visiting the hospital just wasn't the same."

"Do you love me, Tess Corbin?"

She laughed now, and touched his wonderful face with the fingertips of her right hand, in wonder. To reassure herself, perhaps, that he was really there. "Oh, yes."

"Say it."

It came so easily. "I love you."

He smiled and tangled his good hand in her hair, stroking her, soothing. "And I love you."

Tess moved to leave him, he held her in place. When she was settled, he smoothed the moist flesh on her back.

"Keith—" she ventured, as the heretofore friendly breeze brought in a shiver of uneasiness.

He waited patiently for her to speak, giving no prompt, his hand still warm and strong on her back, his masculinity firm within her.

"When you're well, will we leave here? Will you go back to preaching?"

The hand fell away from her, instantly, and it was as though a veil had been drawn across the mischievous azure eyes, the strong chin, the arrogant mouth. "I'm not going back to preaching."

Tess had no desire to leave her shop, but she was stricken by his response, all the same. His face was closed against her, and the closeness between them had evaporated.

She shifted away from him, standing up on shaky legs, and he made no move to stop her. Indeed, he didn't look at her at all, and he didn't speak.

Tess could be as stubborn as anyone. If Keith was going to ignore her, refuse to speak or even meet her eyes, she wasn't about to let him know that she was hurt. Briskly, she dressed herself again, brushed her hair, wound and pinned it into a bulky coil, and left the room.

She and Emma worked until it was time to close the shop, and then they locked up and pulled the shades and went upstairs to prepare supper. Rod had gone to buy railroad tickets with the money Asa had sent for the purpose and would not be back until later.

Tess tossed one look in the direction of the closed bedroom door and sighed. Too late, she realized that Emma had been watching.

"You've had a fight already?" she asked, with typical bluntness.

Again, Tess sighed. "Not exactly. I asked Keith if he intended to start preaching again, and it was as though I'd slapped him or something. He was so cold, Emma—like he didn't even know me, let alone love me."

"Give him a chance to adjust, Tess," Emma said quietly. "He's just out of the hospital, after all. Did you know he isn't going to press charges against Mama? Rod spoke to him about it yesterday."

Tess only nodded. She and Keith had never really talked about what they would do after he recovered, whether they would travel in his medicine wagon or stay here, in her shop. That didn't really concern her, but something else did—the quiet, wounding certainty that he had not resolved his conflict with God. He was still angry, and he could be angry for only one reason: he still cared for Amelie.

Keith was awake when Tess took his dinner to him, but he refused to speak to her, and his eyes were fixed stonily on the ceiling. She set the tray down within his reach and went out.

After she and Emma had eaten and cleared away

their dishes, she checked on Keith again. He was sleeping, or at least he appeared to be, so she left him again.

Feeling restless, she went downstairs to develop some of the portraits taken that day while Emma sat at the kitchen table, paging through a fashion magazine and doubtless planning her assault on St. Louis society.

Tess worked for some time, until her muscles ached as keenly as her heart. Only one more portrait and she would be caught up. Lifting her eyes to the ceiling, above which Keith slept or mourned for Amelie, she sighed.

Staunchly, she set about developing a portrait of Mrs. McQuade, the storekeeper. She smiled, remembering how the woman had confided that she meant to send the finished product to a lonely hearts club and "get herself a husband."

The shop bell tinkled once, but Tess was so absorbed in her task that she hardly noticed, except to wonder why Emma had neglected to lock the door. She kept working, eager now to finish and talk with Keith. By heaven, she'd wake him up if she had to, and she'd demand to know what was the matter. . . .

"Such devotion," purred a slightly contemptuous masculine voice.

Tess looked up, frowning, and was startled to see Cedrick Golden standing in the doorway of the workroom. The expression on his face was an avid one, disconcerting and odd.

"The shop is closed," she said formally, retreating a step.

Though he hadn't moved from the curtained doorway, it was almost as though he were stalking her. "I didn't come to have my likeness taken," he said, in a toneless voice.

Tess considered screaming for Emma's help and then dismissed the thought as foolish. Cedrick wasn't going to hurt her. She wasn't going to let him hurt her. "Why did you come, then?" she asked, straightening her shoulders and lifting her head.

Cedrick came inside the workroom now, his arms folded across the braid-trimmed velvet of his elegant evening jacket. "You delight in driving me mad, don't you?" The words, so sanely spoken, were like a dash of icy water for Tess.

"I want you to leave now, Cedrick," she ventured cautiously. "I have work to do and I have to attend my husband."

"The invalid," he responded, making no move to leave.

Cedrick's madness was a subtle thing, quicksilver, there one moment and gone the next, but very much in evidence now. Why hadn't she seen it before, sensed it?

She swallowed hard and calculated the distance to the door leading out of the workroom and down a path to the privy. And all the while she knew that the latch was in place; opening it was difficult even when one had all the time in the world. Opening it now, when she needed to escape, would be impossible.

"Emma!" she called out, and the sound was a flimsy squeak that would never be heard from the second floor. Fear had drawn her throat into a knot.

Cedrick smiled. "Don't be frightened, darling, please." His green eyes were shimmering with some mental fever now, consuming Tess.

Don't be frightened. She might have laughed if her every instinct hadn't been coaching her to terror. "I-I'm not alone here," she managed to say, after a very long time.

"Of course you're not alone. You've got your crippled husband and your flighty little sister-in-law. Your brother isn't here, though, is he?"

Tess shivered, though she kept her chin high. Keith could not help her, that was true, and Emma would probably be too frightened to be of any use. Rod, most likely her only hope, was indeed away, and it terrified her that Cedrick had taken the trouble to find that out.

"Please, Cedrick. Leave. Right now."

"Without showing you that I am the man you need? Why, that would be foolhardy—"

"I don't need you, Cedrick," Tess retorted bravely. "I need my husband. Only my husband."

"You're so wrong, sweetling," he breathed, drawing nearer now.

Tess edged along the worktable, hoping to evade him. She tried once again to scream and failed. Her heart was pounding in her throat, dense with terror.

And Cedrick laughed at her fear. Indeed, it seemed to entice him. "Oh, those delicious breasts of yours. How I've longed to bare them, taste them—"

Tess felt the flat pan of developing fluid she had been using behind her. Cedrick came at her, closed his hands over her breasts, squeezing, hurting. Tess shoved him, hard, in a reflexive desperation that sent him stumbling backward.

The expression on his face as he righted himself was one of absolute hatred. "How dare you refuse me, you chit?" he whispered, in a rasp, running one hand across his mouth as though he had just taken a drink. *"How dare you?"*

He came at Tess again and she acted without thinking, sheerly on instinct. She clasped the pan of acid fluid in her hands and flung it at Cedrick.

Cedrick froze, lumbering slightly, and then screamed. The acid made a sickening, sizzling sound, and he sank to his knees, his shrieks fading to frantic, animallike whimpers.

Emma burst past the curtain, staring at Cedrick in horror. He was still kneeling, his hands over his face, his cries of pain terrible to hear.

"Get a doctor, Emma," Tess said calmly. "And then a constable."

Chapter Eighteen

THE HOSPITAL WAS QUIET, SEEMINGLY EMPTY. CYNTHIA Golden stood beside her brother's bed, watching him sleep. Poor, dear Cedrick—he was so much thinner than before, and he had to be strapped in, lest he do himself harm.

Cynthia winced to remember the maniacal scene he'd made, that day when the bandages had been removed from his face. Nothing had settled him, not the fact that he had not lost his eyesight, as the doctors first feared he would, not the assurance that the scars would fade a little with the passing of time. Cedrick had wanted—still wanted—very much to die.

And Cynthia didn't blame him. He was a wretched sight, a monster. The flesh on his face was blistered and stretched out of place, distorting his features. Yes, he resembled a monster more than a man.

His career as an actor, of course, was over. And with his livelihood would go Cynthia's, for she was not strong enough, not smart enough, not talented enough, to prosper without him.

Oh, she might marry, she supposed, but though she loved a dalliance with an attractive man, the idea of being bound to just one, for a lifetime, was inconceivable to her.

Resentment stiffened Cynthia's spine, hatred pounded beneath her temples. It was all the fault of that hoyden, Tess. She had done this dreadful thing to Cedrick and she hadn't even been arrested! Oh, no. The tramp had told the police that Cedrick had intended her some harm—ridiculous thought—and that she had only been defending herself when she'd flung that chemical into his face.

Incredibly, they had believed her. Cedrick had lain in this dreary place, helpless and despairing, longing to die, for nearly a month. And in that time, justice had certainly not been served. Tess Corbin was still free. Tess Corbin was busy with her shop, happy with that handsome husband of hers.

Cynthia was suddenly filled with the first true resolve she had known in all her sheltered life. She took a pillow from another bed, placed it over her brother's spoiled face, and held it there.

Cedrick had been sleeping, of course, and he was probably sedated in the bargain. Wide leather restraints made it impossible for him to do more than writhe slightly in a natural attempt to breathe. Cynthia knew what was good for him, though, and she held the pillow firmly in place until he was still.

Keith was almost completely recovered. He should have been happy, he guessed—he was alive, he was married to a woman he would have died for. All the same, he felt restless.

Tess slept beside him, exhausted, her beautiful face bathed in the moonlight streaming in through the bedroom window. He smiled and traced the outline of her jaw, so gently, not wanting to awaken her. She'd had a hard day, working in her shop, and the incident with Cedrick Golden, now several weeks in the past, still upset her when she permitted herself to remember it.

As if those things weren't enough, Keith suspected that she was pregnant in the bargain.

He lay back on his pillows and soberly studied the shadowed ceiling. Ever since the day he'd met Tess, he'd been healing, getting stronger, in a way that even the shooting couldn't have interfered with. It had been a painful, wrenching process at times, a gradual one at others, but it had never stopped. Not for one minute had it stopped.

He sighed, cupped his hands behind his head. Tess had been sent to him, he knew that now, and not as a replacement for Amelie, either. No. The boyish infatuation he'd felt toward Amelie paled in comparison to this. He belonged to Tess, had been born to love her. It was Tess who'd been meant for him all along, not

Amelie. And, just as surely, he had been meant for her.

It had been good to be with Tess again, so very good. They'd made love every night and sometimes during the day, and each time, though it seemed impossible, had been better than the last.

Now that he was strong again, Keith could face what he was, what he believed, what he needed. He wanted to preach again.

He shifted onto one side, watching Tess as she slept. She had made a success of her shop. A smashing success. Would she be willing to leave it, to follow him to Port Hastings? A verse from the book of Ruth rose in his mind. *"Intreat me not to leave thee, or to return from following after thee: for whither thou goest, I will go; and where thou lodgest, I will lodge: thy people shall be my people, and thy God my God."*

"Tess?"

She muttered something and pulled a tangle of sheets and blankets up to her nose, her eyelashes fluttering as if to ward off wakefulness.

He didn't have the heart to awaken her. Instead, he let himself imagine her as a pastor's wife. What a sensation she'd cause, with her wild, beautiful hair, her cameras, and her bicycle.

The thought brought an involuntary chuckle from the depths of his throat.

Tess yawned and opened one eye and then the other. "Keith? Are you all right? Wh-what's the matter?"

He pulled her head down to rest on his shoulder, the love of her a tight and twisting thing in his throat. "I'm fine. I was just thinking, that's all."

She yawned again and cuddled close to him, soft and

fragrant. "Thinking? In—the middle of the"—yet again, she yawned—"night?"

He had begun to want her, and that wanting made his voice gruff. "This is something I've had on my mind for a long time. Since I met you, in fact."

"What?"

"I'm not supposed to be a peddler or the indolent, unemployed husband of an up-and-coming photographer, Tess."

She shot bolt upright, her hair a moon-kissed curtain falling over one shoulder and tickling against Keith's chest. "You don't want to be my husband?" she whispered.

Keith drew her back, smoothing her tangled hair with one hand. "Of course I want to be your husband." He paused, searching within himself for the courage to go on. "But I also want to preach again, Tess."

There was a silence, during which Keith knew an agony of doubt. Suppose he lost her?

When she spoke, her voice was soft, almost inaudible. "You don't want to stay in Portland, do you, Keith? You want to go back to—what was that place? Wenatchee."

Her hair was like a spray of silken ribbons in his fingers. "No. Not Wenatchee. Port Hastings."

"Your family is there."

Another silence, this time, broken by Keith. "Yes. Will you give up this shop, Tess? If I promise to buy you another, that is?"

She laughed, actually laughed. "Of course. But it can't be an idle promise, Keith Corbin. I want that shop."

He laughed, now, more with relief, with joy, than

with humor. "You shall have your shop, Mrs. Corbin. I swear it."

Tess cuddled closer still, her fingers making swirls in the hairs on his chest. He was aware of her, and in need of her, in every part of his body. "I don't suppose your congregation will approve of me," she ventured softly, shyly, after a very long time.

"My congregation had better approve," he answered flatly. "They don't have a choice."

She was crying; he could feel the tears, cool and wet, on the flesh of his bare shoulder. "We'll see," she said.

He turned, so that she was beneath him, was careful not to rest his full weight upon her. "Tess. Don't cry. Please. If this makes you unhappy—"

"Unhappy?" She laughed, through her tears, and stroked the side of his face with one tender hand. "I've known since the day I saw you throwing dishpans and coffeepots at God that this would happen, you idiot. Even that was a form of faith few people ever have. God was so real to you that you would challenge Him to a fisticuff!"

"I suppose that is unusual," he conceded, embarrassed to remember.

"Unusual is hardly the word, mister. You should have seen yourself, ranting and raving, stomping around. I thought you were mad."

"But you stayed." He circled her lips with one index finger and let that finger stray down the length of her neck, over her collarbone, to her breast.

"It was raining and my bicycle wheel was bent—" She made an involuntary, crooning sound as he caressed her, her back arching.

"Excuses, excuses," he muttered, letting his lips follow the path blazed by his finger. "You were crazy about me."

He circled her nipple with the tip of his tongue and she gasped, her body groping for his.

"If anyone was crazy, Keith C-Corbin"—she quivered, her hands in his hair now, fingers splayed and strong as they pressed him closer—"it was you."

He could offer no argument. They made love, slowly, sweetly at first, and then with a fierce savagery that hurled their strong young bodies one against the other in a frenzied attempt to become bonded together forever.

The morning sunshine was bright. Smiling, Tess Corbin turned the golden wedding band on her finger, so that the small emeralds embedded in it caught the light and flung it, in shimmering patches, all over the tiny kitchen. Ever since Keith had given her that ring, while he was still in the hospital, she had felt that, to him, it was merely a formality, lacking the meaning that Amelie's had had. Now, after their talking and loving in the night, she knew better.

Tess drew a deep breath, to sober herself. She found an apron and put it on. Breakfast. The wifely thing to do was to cook breakfast.

She inspected the woodbox. Since Emma and Rod's departure for St. Louis, with Emma's subdued but recovering mother in tow, Keith had kept it full. Today, however, it was empty.

She could hear him stirring in the bedroom, grumbling and clunking his boots around. Those were such ordinary sounds, but they brought a bursting lump of joy to Tess's throat; if she loved that man another smidgeon, she marveled to herself, she just wouldn't be able to bear it, that's all.

Eager to please him, she dashed down the stairs. It wasn't as though she would cook breakfast every morning, Tess reflected, as she unlocked the shop door, for any early customers who might venture in, and put up the window shades. There was no law that said the Reverend Keith Corbin couldn't prepare a meal once in a while.

She made her way through the workroom, having her usual difficulty with the latch on the back door. She left it open, so that she would not have to walk all the way around to the front of the building to get in again, as had happened on several occasions.

The woodshed was filled with the pungent smell of aging wood, the dusty, half-imagined scent of cobwebs and mice. Unaccountably, as she bent to gather an armload of kindling, Tess shivered.

Woodsheds were shadowy, eerie places, she decided, but she brightened as she planned the meal she would cook for Keith before starting her own day in the shop. She would fix his favorites—bacon, flapjacks, and eggs hard enough to shape a horseshoe.

Tess was grinning as she straightened up, her arms full of scratchy wood. She was going to be the best wife any man, preacher or otherwise, had ever had.

Cynthia Golden was framed by the woodshed doorway, standing perfectly still. Barring her way.

Tess hadn't heard Cynthia's approach, and she was startled. Even frightened, though that didn't make sense. It was broad daylight, for one thing, and for another, when it came to protecting herself, she was a match for this woman any day.

She had not seen Cynthia since before her tragic encounter with Cedrick. Tess was damned if she was going to grovel, for Cedrick had attacked her and she had only used the first means at hand to protect herself. Still, she was sorry that it had come to that, that Cedrick had been scarred so badly. "I hope your brother is recovering," she said.

"As if you cared," replied Cynthia, and she did not move out of the woodshed doorway but, instead, clasped the framework on both sides of her with gloved hands. Tess could not see her face, and that, along with the sensation of being cornered, bothered her.

"I do care, Cynthia. And I'm very sorry that things turned out the way they did. Now, if you'll excuse me—"

Cynthia didn't move out of the doorway, but a dusty shaft of sunlight, coming in through one of the wide cracks in the woodshed roof, found her face. As beautiful as ever, she was also calmly, coldly rancorous. "You've ruined Cedrick, you know. Ruined us all, really. I had to save him."

Something in the tone of Cynthia's voice and the stance of her flawless body caused a chill to spin up Tess's backbone. "What do you mean, you had to save him?" she whispered.

Perfect shoulders moved in a shrug. "I couldn't let him live. He would have been an object of ridicule. Scorn. Cedrick could never have borne that."

Tess's stomach roiled, and a trembling seized her,

though she brought it under swift control. "Dear God," she breathed. "You don't mean that you—that you killed him?"

"I saved him," corrected Cynthia, in the sing-song, hide-and-seek voice of a little girl.

Tess was stunned, but her instincts kept her alert, wary. This was no time to let her wits go wandering hither and yon. "And what do you want with me?" she asked, slowly. Quietly.

"Oh, I mean to kill you, of course," replied the woman-child.

The wood Tess had held went clattering to the shed's dirt floor. She lunged forward, meaning to push past Cynthia, into the sunlight and sanity—and safety—of the world outside. That world was so close, yet so far away.

Small as she was, Cynthia stood like a bastion in Tess's way. Metal glinted silver in the patchy light, and something slashed at Tess's upper arm, stinging. She gasped and retreated a few steps, amazed. So amazed that the screams her instincts urged on her would not pass her throat.

She looked down, saw a long but not particularly deep cut on her arm. She was bleeding, and the slash stung fiercely. That was fortunate, for it brought Tess out of her shock and made her think with the cool clarity of those that are hunted. She edged into the deepest shadows, to hide herself.

Cobwebs draped themselves over her face and her hair, and something scurried down her arm.

Cynthia, still in the doorway, bent forward slightly, peering. Tess could see her clearly now, see the ordinary kitchen knife she carried in one hand. "Come out," she said, in that same schoolyard voice. "I can't see you."

Tess reached down, groped in the darkness for a chunk of cut wood, found one. Then, forcing herself to breathe normally, she clasped it in both hands and rose slowly to her feet. With it, she could get past Cynthia. She could get away.

Cynthia came further inside the shed, annoyed now, like a child who has been left to search too long for the hiders in some game. "Come out," she wailed.

Tess might have made her escape then, gotten clear of Cynthia and the shed without incident. But for the fact that Keith suddenly filled the doorway. She knew by his stance that he was momentarily blinded, his eyes adjusting from the bright light outside to the dimness of the shed.

"Tess? Are you—"

Cynthia, startled, whirled around. The knife was clasped high above her head, in both hands, ready to plunge into Keith's chest. Before he could react in any way, the weapon was descending.

Tess screamed. Wood splinters bit into her hands. She sprang from her hiding place, making an animal sound low in her throat, and struck the woman who would hurt Keith with all the strength she possessed.

And when Cynthia crumpled to the floor in a little heap of vengeance and cambric, Tess couldn't stop screaming.

Keith grasped her by the shoulders and shook her. "Tess!"

Still she screamed, and he slapped her. The force of

the blow silenced her, made her draw in her breath in a sobbing gasp.

"What in the name of God happened here?" Keith demanded, looking back at Cynthia and then going to crouch beside her on the woodshed floor. She was stirring now, making a whimpering sound.

Tess, hugging herself with both arms, swayed on her feet. "She—she was going to kill me—because of Cedrick—"

Outside, she could hear excited voices. Running feet. Her screams, apparently, had been heard from the street. Tess remembered how Cynthia had held that knife, how near she had come to killing Keith instead of herself, and folded to the floor in a deep faint.

When she awakened, she was inside the shop, lying on their bed. Her right forearm was neatly bandaged, and Keith was putting some kind of salve on the palms of her hands.

"It's over," he said, when he saw that she was awake and afraid. "You're going to be all right."

Tess didn't care about a few silly scratches and a cut. "What about you? Keith, did she hurt you?"

His wonderful mouth quirked into a teasing grin. "Do I look like I've been hurt, shoebutton?"

There were a lot of people in the kitchen. Suddenly, Tess was aware of them, hearing their muffled voices, their shuffling feet.

"The police are here," Keith explained calmly. "They want to talk to talk to you ."

Tess sank deeper into the pillows, gnawing at her own lip. "I must have killed Cynthia. I must have killed her."

Keith finished salving her hands, wiped his own on a damask towel, and shook his head. "No, shoebutton, you didn't kill anybody. At most, Miss Golden will have a few bruises and a headache."

Tess's eyes went to the closed door. "She isn't here, is she? She isn't out there—"

"She confessed to murdering her brother, Tess, though she didn't seem to see it as that. She's been taken away."

Tess was nauseated, and she had a headache of her own. "Why—why do the police want to talk to me?"

He bent forward, kissed her cheek. It made a reassuring, smacking sound. "They just want to hear your version. If you don't want to talk to them now, you don't have to. I'll send them away."

Tess considered, sighed. There was nothing to be gained by putting the ordeal off, she supposed. "I'll talk to them now."

Keith admitted one constable to the room and ordered the others out. Her husband's presence—he stood very near, leaning back against the bureau, his arms folded across his chest—made it easier for Tess to answer the grueling, endless questions that were put to her.

When the policeman was gone, she turned her head into the pillow. "I want to leave here, Keith. I want to forget this place, forget everything."

He sat down on the bed beside her, drew her into his arms. "Not everything, I hope," he teased gruffly, holding her tight. "For instance, I wouldn't want you to forget that day we made love in the suite, on the pool table—"

305

It was his genius, his magic, that he could make Tess laugh under almost any sort of circumstance. And she laughed then, though there were tears mixed with the sound, and her face was hot with a blush. "That was scandalous."

"I liked it," Keith insisted, his lips in her hair.

"So did I," Tess admitted, after a very long time.

February 1891
Port Hastings, Washington

Another Corbin wife.

Mrs. Jeremy T. Terwillagher sighed as she settled into the second pew from the front, where she could get a good view of the wife in question, once services were over.

If her friends could be believed, this one had a bicycle and meant to open some sort of shop in the spring. It was rumored that she had a past, too. There was madness in her family, for one thing, and, for another, she had been directly involved in that scandal concerning the Golden Twins a few months ago, down in Portland.

Mrs. Terwillagher harrumphed. Anyone who associated with theater people might *expect* to be involved in scandal, to her mind.

A longtime resident of Port Hastings, Mrs. Terwillagher was an avid follower of the doings of that outrageous Corbin family. Had been for years. Daniel and Katherine Corbin, the parents of this brood, had kept the waters stirred up, mind you, all by themselves. Still, once those three boys had grown up and started taking wives, well, things had just been fascinating.

First, Adam, the eldest son, had married that lady doctor, the red-headed one with the saucy tongue. Why, just last week, Mrs. Terwillagher had spoken to her in the general store, asked her if the infant she was carrying was her new baby.

"No," that outrageous hoyden had replied instantly, "this is my grandfather."

She'd apologized, of course—that was only right—but Mrs. Terwillagher was still very much miffed. For a woman who had reportedly once had two husbands, that Banner Corbin had her nerve.

As if Banner hadn't been enough of an insult to the good people of Port Hastings, the second son, Jeff, had gone right out and found himself a saloon singer or some such. She was a blonde, not so tart-tongued as her sister-in-law, but Mrs. Terwillagher didn't approve all the same. After all, how could a good, Christian woman be expected to approve of someone with a name like Fancy, for mercy sakes?

And now there was this new one. Even from the back, she looked wild to Myrtle Terwillagher. She had too much hair, for one thing—rich, brown stuff that threatened to tumble from its pins. She had been right there, it was said, while the new church and the parsonage were being built—taking pictures!

Inwardly, Mrs. Terwillagher winced. There was every chance that this Tess was even worse than the other two. After all, she'd been in the family way when this church was being built. Imagine prancing around a building site in that condition.

Mrs. Terwillagher reached for her hymnal, deliberately thumping it against the back of the next pew, in hopes that Tess Corbin would turn around and greet her, so that she could get a good look. Alas, she was disappointed. The pastor's wife was intent on the infant in her arms. A boy, according to the newspaper, named Ethan.

Mrs. Terwillagher sat back in her pew as Pastor Corbin came in to preach his first sermon in this brand-new church. Every eye in the place was fixed on him, and a commanding figure he was, too, speaking with his gentle authority instead of pounding on his pulpit and raging about hellfire and brimstone.

A little disappointed, Mrs. Terwillagher sniffed, her eyes wandering again. There was to be a potluck dinner, after church, at the new parsonage, and she planned to attend. She wanted to see if the Reverend and Mrs. Corbin really had a pool table in their parlor, like Ethel Claridge said. Ethel was a fine woman, but she did tend to embellish a story now and then.

Midway through the sermon, which seemed to hold everyone but Mrs. Terwillagher herself quite rapt, the pastor's eyes met those of his wife and lingered a moment. Some silent communication was exchanged. Myrtle Terwillagher doubted if anyone else in the congregation had even noticed. Merciful heavens, she despised people who didn't pay attention.

There was, indeed, a glow about the Reverend Keith Corbin, especially when he chanced to glance down at his brand-new wife. And Mrs. Jeremy T. Terwillagher would have bet the beef-and-mushroom casserole tucked away under her buggy seat outside that the glow wasn't spiritual, either.